TEMPTING
THE *Marshal*

JULIANNE
MACLEAN

Tempting the Marshal
Copyright © 2020 Julianne MacLean Publishing Inc.

Print edition ISBN: 978-1-927675-84-7
Ebook edition ISBN: 978-1-927675-42-7

First edition published by Harlequin under the title
The Marshal and Mrs. O'Malley
Copyright © 2001 Julianne MacLean

Cover and Interior Design: The Killion Group, Inc.

Chapter

1

Dodge City, Kansas, 1876

JOSEPHINE O'MALLEY'S STOMACH CLENCHED TIGHT with panic as she peered through the night along the dusty street, watching for potential witnesses. She couldn't let anyone recognize her in these clothes that had once belonged to her husband, God rest his soul. Especially after she pulled the trigger.

Fighting to keep calm, she opened her long slicker and palmed the walnut handle of her Colt .45— the handle her husband had worn smooth over the years. Her boots tapped lightly over the aging planks along the boardwalk, while her spurs chinked a slow rhythm. Music from a tinny saloon piano across the street seemed muffled beneath the erratic pulse that drummed in her ears, but she continued on, soberly watching the mannish lines of her shadow as she passed under a hanging lantern.

When she finally stopped outside Zeb Stone's Dry Goods Store, she took a deep breath and tried to relax. Over the past six months, raw fear had compelled her to learn how to handle her late husband's guns, preparing for this day, should it come. Hadn't she pictured this moment over and over in her mind, wanted it, known it was necessary? Wasn't it supposed to be filled with righteous determination?

Instead, she looked up at the huge painted sign bearing Zeb's name and felt only a sickening knot of intimidation and a horrible surge of dread. She'd never killed a man, never thought she could. It went against everything she ever believed in.

But she had to do it now. *Didn't she?* She couldn't stand by and watch her son, Leo, choke to death in a noose like her husband. Leo had been poking around the finer details of his father's murder lately, and Zeb, with his cold, black heart, was beginning to take notice.

No, the time had come for Jo to face Zeb once and for all. The law had done nothing to help her. If she was going to protect Leo now, she had to help herself.

Jo raised the red bandanna over her nose. As she reached for the brass doorknob, her hand trembled. She pulled it back and paused to fight the pulsing knot in her stomach, then pushed the door open. Bells clanged as she made her way quietly across the threshold.

Zeb Stone stood behind the counter wearing a black waistcoat and starched white shirt. His black bowler hat rested on the counter. His head was down as he scrawled in a notebook.

"We're closed," he said, his voice flat with disinterest. "Come back tomorrow."

Jo shakily drew one of her weapons and held it with both hands in front of her. Anxiety spurted through her, but this was not the time for doubt or hesitation. It would take a cool head to carry this through.

She crossed the room in three swift strides, stopping at the glass counter and breathing fast with panic. She shoved the barrel of her gun against her enemy's shiny forehead.

Zeb's fearless gaze rose to meet hers. The familiarity of those black eyes sent a hideous chill through her. "You're out of luck," he said, not recognizing her face behind the bandanna. "The money's already gone to the bank."

"I didn't come here for money," Jo replied in a calm, low-pitched voice, but inside, her heart was beating a breakneck rhythm.

"What do you want, then? Supplies? I'd best warn you, mister, nobody steals from me and gets away with it."

Jo stood motionless. So much of this did not seem real. It was as nightmarish as tossing that handful of earth on poor Edwyn's casket.

She swallowed hard as a wave of desperation washed through her. She had to see this through no matter how terrible it seemed. Finish it once and for all.

She touched her thumb to the hammer of the gun and felt her insides lurch with dread. "Are you ready to die, Zeb Stone? Because I'm here to send you to hell, where you belong."

Marshal Fletcher Collins led his horse to the Dodge House Hotel and flipped the soft leather reins around the hitching rail. He reached into his shirt pocket for half a carrot and stroked Prince's warm muzzle. "Here you go, boy. I might be a while. I gotta make the right impression my first night on the job, if you know what I mean."

Fletcher stepped onto the boardwalk, nodding to the cowboys sitting on the hotel steps. "Howdy, boys. Mighty fine evening."

One man tipped his hat. "Welcome to Dodge, Marshal Collins. Headin' down to the Long Branch for a drink?"

"Not tonight. I'm on duty."

One of them called after him. "That never stopped Marshal Peavy from filling his holster!" The other two exploded with rowdy laughter.

Fletcher stopped and turned around. The laughter quickly died. Straightening his black Stetson, he continued on his way.

A buckboard wagon rumbled by, lifting a cloud of dust. When the clatter of hooves faded into the night, Fletcher listened with a keen ear to the hoots and hollers from the dance halls across the street, the boisterous banjo music, the laughter and foot stomping.

He passed in front of Meuller's Boot Shop and glanced through the dark window. Looked quiet. In fact, he probably shouldn't be wasting his time over here in the business district. He should be enforcing the gun ordinance over in the Comique, where there was bound to be some fool packing iron.

Fletcher paused on the boardwalk for a moment, then decided to finish this block. He walked by Zeb's store and glanced through the window, but tensed when he saw Zeb—backed up against the wall with his hands in the air, facing an armed robber.

Fletcher hugged the brick wall just outside the door and drew his Peacemaker. He checked the cylinder for bullets, then clicked it shut and peered inside again. The thief looked like he was just itchin' to shoot.

Fletcher took a deep breath. No *do-si-do* for him tonight. Dodge City was a trial by fire for the new marshal, and he sure didn't aim to get burned.

With growing panic, Jo stared into Zeb's dark eyes and rubbed the clammy pad of her index finger over the trigger. She clenched her teeth together. She *had* to do this.

He paled visibly, perhaps realizing she meant business. "You won't get away with this. I have friends who—"

"I know what kind of friends you have. They're gutter swine." Jo pressed the barrel of the gun harder against his forehead. He squeezed his eyes shut, not so fearless now. It was a moment of terror he greatly deserved after all the pain he'd caused others.

A film of perspiration appeared around his dark mustache, but his voice remained calm. "I'll give you anything you want. Just don't shoot."

Good Lord! She couldn't do this! But what choice did she have?

Zeb cautiously opened his eyes.

Just then, the door flew open and slammed against

the inside wall. The doorbells clanged and clattered
to the floor.

Without thinking, Jo drew her second weapon. She
aimed it at the flash of movement in her peripheral
vision, hearing the man's commanding voice before
she could focus on him. "Drop the gun! *Now!*"

With a heavy weapon in each hand, Jo glanced
back and forth from one opponent to the other. The
stranger moved closer. She saw his black Stetson and
his long brown coat open in front, but it was the barrel of his gun that held her attention—a small black
hole pointing directly at her.

"I said drop it!" he yelled.

"You drop it, or I'll kill him," Jo replied, deepening
her voice as best she could without it breaking.

"Do that, kid, and you'll be waiting in line for a
coffin."

Perspiration dampened Jo's forehead. Her bandanna
began to slide down her nose. If it fell, she'd be done
for. "This ain't your fight, stranger."

"I own every fight in this town." He opened his
coat to reveal the steel badge pinned to his brown
leather vest.

Jo's stomach did a sickening flip. Who in tarnation
was this man? She'd been counting on Marshal Peavy
taking his early evening nap in the jailhouse. She'd
assumed this stranger was one of Zeb's men.

Feeling her fate grow more precarious by the minute, she gave the marshal a more mindful once-over,
concentrating on his face this time to see what she
was up against, what manner of man could aim a gun
at an opponent who held *two* of them—one in each

hand—and still be as heartily confident as the day was long.

To her dismay, he was calm—too calm—and his bold self-assurance made her teeter alarmingly on her already unstable courage.

He must have been watching her carefully, because he seemed to know that she was faltering. He took another slow step closer and spoke in a subtle Texas drawl that crumbled her grit to dust. "I'm the new marshal, kid, and my patience is dyin' fast. Either drop both guns now, or prepare to meet your maker."

She glanced back at Zeb and saw a bead of sweat trickling down his cheek.

The lawman took a few steps sideways toward the counter, his movements smooth and fluid. "I can see you don't want to kill anyone. Now do the right thing and lower your weapons."

Jo's mouth went completely dry at his gentle command. Her palms were wet and slipping on the handles of the guns. She didn't want to die and she certainly couldn't go to jail, not with Zeb alive to kill her son. But this man was right. Somehow he knew she wasn't a killer, and his calm presence was stirring something inside her—something she didn't want stirred.

Was it shame? Or was it compassion for a cold-blooded killer who did not deserve it?

Strangely, she found herself backing away, lowering her arms to her sides. She could not fight this man, this unexpected intruder. It was time to surrender.

The lawman moved forward, his gun still fixed on her, his green eyes flickering with reassurance. Something in his expression spoke to her. *You're not a killer,*

he seemed to say, without uttering a word. The odd-
ness of it all made her feel weak and dizzy.

She had done the right thing, she told herself. She
had to stay alive for Leo. He was only eleven years
old. He needed her.

All of a sudden, Zeb bent forward. Jo froze. She
watched transfixed as he drew a pistol from under the
counter, the steel barrel rising up as if in slow motion
to confront her.

A surge of clarity sliced through her mind. She had
come here tonight to kill Zeb Stone. If she was going
to plunge into hell in the attempt, she would take him
with her.

Jo cocked both her guns. She raised her arm in a
flash and aimed at her enemy, then shut her eyes and
pulled the trigger. The gun blasted, kicked back in
her hand, and she heard a body drop to the floor with
a dull thud. Feeling almost sick, she opened her eyes.

Oh, dear God. Jo stared numbly at the man lying
in front of the counter. She felt as if her heart had
stopped beating.

She'd shot the lawman!

A thunderous boom sounded and a bullet from
Zeb's gun ripped painfully through her shoulder.
The impact knocked her off balance and she stumbled
back.

Nausea weaved through her stomach. She clenched
her pistols as she staggered about in disbelief, fighting the reality of what was happening. Dazed, she felt
warm blood stream down to the top of the corset she
wore beneath the disguise. Jo heard a *click* and recognized the sound—the hammer of Zeb's gun. Her eyes

darted up to that dark barrel again, and she knew he wanted her dead. No mistakes this time.

Determined to save herself, Jo leaped through the air just as Zeb fired. The gun boomed like a thunderclap, and behind her, a bag of flour exploded in a cloud of white dust. Jo hit the floor and rolled, pain stabbing her in the shoulder with each frantic breath.

Rising to her feet, she saw a window, her only escape. She heard Zeb cocking his gun again. There was no time to think. Fighting panic, Jo yanked her hat down over her face, took off in a run and threw herself into the glass.

Panes smashed and shattered all around her. She flew through the air and landed hard on the dry dirt in the alley, scrambled to her feet and ran around the back of the buildings, brushing the glass off herself as she went.

Panting uncontrollably, Jo fought the pain where the bullet was lodged. Her stomach burned with fear. She heard Zeb yelling after her, heard his pistol fire two more times, but she was out of range.

She hugged her arm to her side to steady her aching shoulder and ran through the darkness like a hunted animal. Her boots pounded over the hard ground. Her frenzied breaths matched the rhythm. She had to reach the privy before anyone saw her.

She skidded to a halt, swung the door open and spun inside. A turn and a *click*...the door was latched. The thick stench of stale excrement assaulted her senses. A grunt escaped her. Thank God, the lantern she'd left there was still burning.

Jo dropped to her knees and felt around for the loose

board, raised it and pulled out her bag. She ripped off her coat and pain sliced like daggers down her arm.

Within seconds, she was fastening the tiny buttons on her bodice with shaking fingers. "Faster, faster," she whispered, trying in a panic to hurry, trying to ignore the blood that had soaked her chemise and was now staining her bodice, the blood that would drain the life from her if she did not somehow get out of there.

Voices echoed in the street, ricocheting off buildings like bullets. Jo tied her muslin bonnet ribbons under her chin, but pushed the bonnet back from her face to rest on her back. She swiftly stuffed the disguise into her bag, set it back into the compartment beneath the floor and lowered the boards.

She took a quick glance around the privy, then blew out the lantern. Blackness enveloped the fetid, makeshift haven, which would have been as silent as the grave, if not for Jo's small, frantic breaths.

Outside, desperate screams cut through the dark night. Footsteps. Hoofbeats. The town was alive in a mad search for the outlaw. They would not find him, she told herself, and tried to gather some courage from that fact.

Suddenly aware of the sick feeling in her stomach, Jo felt her head begin to spin. She tried to lean on the splintery wall, but toppled back onto the bench. An icy chill seeped into her veins and she began to shiver. She tried to calm herself, to take deep breaths to stop the shaking, but it was no use. She'd never felt so out of control.

She needed to get to a doctor. She stood, then staggered in the darkness, her trembling hands fumbling over bristly wood in search of the door latch.

Please, someone help me. I'm not going to make it.

Suddenly the door whipped open and she stared into another gun barrel.

"Mrs. O'Malley! You're bleeding!"

Jo couldn't look up until the gun lowered and dropped easily into a holster. A pair of hands were reaching out to her. Where was she? What was happening?

Arms encircled her and she fell into them. "Help me," she mumbled.

"I've got you. It's Deputy Anderson."

Relief poured through her as he hoisted her into his arms and carried her into the night.

Chapter

2

*F*LAT ON HIS BACK ON the examination table, Fletcher tried to focus on a small black spider crawling across the white ceiling, instead of the stabbing pain in his right thigh. Nothing against Doc Green, but the man seemed to be using a knitting needle to stitch him up instead of a surgeon's needle.

"You're a lucky man," Dr. Green said, pulling the needle through the bloody mess on Fletcher's thigh. "Bullet barely even grazed the muscle. This should heal in no time. It's your head wound that worries me. I want to keep you here overnight."

Fletcher grit his teeth. Some city marshal he was—shot in the leg and collapsing like a schoolgirl, right into Zeb's glass display case. Dead to the world before he even hit the floor. "Thanks for the concern, Doc, but that's not necessary."

"You were out cold when they brought you in,

Marshal. Even with guns going off like the Fourth of July, you didn't flinch."

What else had he missed? Fletcher wondered as he covered his eyes with one hand and sighed, trying not to wince when the doctor pierced the wound again with that aggravating needle. For all Fletcher knew, the kid in Zeb's store tonight might have killed ten men on his way out of town.

The doctor tied the thread and began to dress the wound. Fletcher's head throbbed where he'd knocked himself out, but it was his leg that ached the worst, even though he tried to withstand it.

It could have been a lot worse, he supposed. He'd seen other men shot before, and most times they didn't live to see the dawn, so in that way, the doc was right. Fletcher should count himself lucky.

Just then, the door opened. Startled, Fletcher leaned up on one elbow to see Deputy Anderson hurrying inside with a woman in his arms, looking like an anxious groom carrying his bride over the threshold on his wedding night. But this woman was no bride. She lay lifeless like a rag doll in the deputy's arms.

"Another casualty, Doc," Anderson said. "It's Mrs. O'Malley. I found her in the privy behind Zimmerman's. She must have gotten in the way of a stray bullet."

Dr. Green quickly cleared off another examination table. "Set her down here."

Anderson laid her on the table and her face tilted away from Fletcher. He saw the disorderly twist of honey-colored hair at the back of her head, then his gaze fell to the accompanying blood stain on her shoulder.

This was what happened when men didn't respect the law. Innocent, law-abiding folks got hurt, and if they weren't lucky, they got killed, too. He hoped this poor woman wouldn't be one of the unlucky ones.

Her long skirts fell over the side and touched the floor like a fancy tablecloth. Fletcher noticed with some interest that she wore men's work boots.

The doctor searched for a pulse at her neck. "Was she conscious when you found her?"

"Yes, but she fainted straight away."

Doc began to unbutton her bloody bodice.

Wanting to do something to help, Fletcher tried to sit up but felt suddenly nauseous and dizzy. He dropped back down and watched the ceiling spin over his head.

The deputy approached. "Marshal! Thank the Lord! I heard you were shot in the head."

"No, just the leg," he answered.

"What's this, then?" Anderson asked, pointing at the bloodstained dressing around Fletcher's head.

"Don't ask."

"He knocked himself out on the corner of Zeb's jewelry case," Doc answered.

"Well, I'll be," Anderson said. "Your first showdown in Dodge and you didn't even get to see how it ended."

Fletcher ignored Anderson's teasing tone. "Did anyone catch the guy?"

"Not yet."

"Who's the woman?"

Anderson walked around the table, watching Doc

examine the wound. "Josephine O'Malley. Her husband was killed about six months ago by some horse thieves. Right in his own barn."

Fletcher shifted uncomfortably. "Did anyone ever catch them?"

Anderson shook his head. "No witnesses."

Fletcher glanced at Mrs. O'Malley, her arm hanging limply over the side of the table. "Where was *she?*"

"In the house, I reckon. Now, she keeps to herself. A bit of a recluse. Doesn't even let her kid come to town. She lives out on her ranch with a bunch of cowhands and that causes a lot of talk in town, if you know what I mean."

The doctor glanced at Anderson with disapproval, then began unfastening the woman's corset. "Deputy, you'll have to wait outside."

Anderson left the office and closed the door behind him. The doctor gathered his instruments.

"Need any help, Doc?" Fletcher asked.

"No. But I suggest you look the other way if you're feeling queasy."

Fletcher lay flat on his back and stared at the ceiling, searching for the little spider that had distracted him last time, but as luck would have it, he was gone. So Fletcher turned his attention to the bookshelf, but reading the spines of all those medical books made his head pound harder than a steel mallet, so he resigned himself to staring at the empty ceiling again.

If he could've relaxed, he would have been fine, but all he could think of was the woman beside him, her delicate skin being sliced open, all because of a small-time thief who didn't seem old enough to use a razor.

Fletcher touched the blood-soaked dressing on his forehead and tried to fight his anger. He'd taken this job to try and stop the killing, to uphold the law, to be strong where his father had been weak. A fine job he'd done tonight. Gunfire in the streets and innocent people shot down.

The woman moaned and Fletcher couldn't help but turn to look. The doctor stood over her with a bloody scalpel in his hand. He set it down and began digging around with another instrument. Fletcher felt ill, but at the same time, he couldn't tear his eyes away.

The doctor soon began to work with a needle he held in a clamp.

The woman groggily turned her head, and at last, Fletcher saw her profile—her tiny upturned nose and her moist, full lips the color of a pale red rose. Her long, delicate lashes were swept down upon her cheeks, and she moaned again in a delirious stupor that seemed almost sexual to Fletcher, who immediately chastised himself for thinking such a thing. The doctor quickly reached for a bottle, tipped it over a white cloth and pressed it to her face. Within seconds, her head fell limp toward Fletcher. The moaning stopped and the doctor went back to work.

Seeing her face for the first time, Fletcher took note of how pale she looked, albeit tanned. Obviously she possessed an unfashionable preference for sunshine. And her tiny, rough hands told him she had not abandoned her husband's chores after he died. Fletcher couldn't help but feel sympathy toward her for all she must have endured.

Dr. Green cleared his throat. Fletcher looked up at

him and saw the perspiration dotting his forehead. "You okay, Doc?"

He nodded. "I've never seen such a close call. If the bullet had gone in any lower—and I'm talking the width of a thread—she would have bled to death."

The wound in Fletcher's leg throbbed as he leaned up on one elbow. "Will she be all right?"

"I hope so. There's always the risk of infection, but like I said, she was lucky."

Fletcher's blood burned at the thought of her suffering. It was so damned unnecessary.

He would catch the man responsible for this, he swore to himself. He would see him brought to justice in front of everyone in a court of law, and he would show this town that—where their new marshal was concerned—*the law was the law.*

He wondered if Mrs. O'Malley would remember what had happened to her. Fletcher closed his eyes and decided to be there when she woke to ask her that very question. If this woman survived, she would see justice.

He would give her his word on it.

Consciousness bloomed slowly, as if from an empty, black abyss. Jo heard the murmur of voices, but could only lie immobile, fighting to awaken her mind from its dazed stupor, all the while becoming more and more aware of a throbbing pain in her shoulder. She had to concentrate to force her heavy eyelids open.

Where was she? she wondered, trying to sit up. In someone's bed, no doubt, but whose? Nothing seemed familiar. Her sleepy gaze darted from the blue gingham curtains on the window to the unpainted pine washstand, then across the small room to a kerosene lamp flickering atop a tall chest of drawers.

She heard the voices again. They spoke quietly, probably in the next room if her ears were working properly. What had happened? Was Zeb still alive? And what about the lawman? Had she killed him?

Good Lord, she hoped not.

She began to sit up, but even the slightest movement gave way to her broken body's protest. She let out a low groan, squeezed her eyes shut and touched her injured shoulder.

"Land's sakes," she whispered, feeling the large dressing over her wound. Someone had tended to her and put her in a borrowed nightdress. Was she in the doctor's clinic?

Her ears suddenly tuned to footsteps and a man's voice just outside her door. Perhaps someone was coming to arrest her. Perhaps the world now knew that a vengeful heart had lived inside the breast of a desperate widow. What if a lynch mob was forming outside? What would she do?

Telling herself these fears were irrational at this point, Jo watched nervously as the brass knob turned. The white-painted door squeaked open and Dr. Green walked in. Jo let out a tightly held breath and prepared herself for whatever fate held in store.

"Mrs. O'Malley, you're awake," he said, closing the door with a light click behind him.

Jo wet her dry lips and tried to bring the approaching doctor into focus. She had to gather her wits, carefully plan her responses. Was it too much to hope that her identity had not been discovered? "Yes, I... what happened?"

Dr. Green approached the bed, his black sleeve stained with blood. Was it her blood? she wondered, worrying not just about her own wounds, but about whoever else might have been hurt because of what she had done.

"You were in the wrong place at the wrong time," the doctor said.

Jo paused, contemplating before she spoke. "Who brought me here?"

"You don't remember?"

"Not exactly."

Dr. Green cupped his fingers around her wrist and took her pulse, which was probably thumping faster than he could count. "You were shot. Deputy Anderson found you in the necessary behind Zimmerman's." He glared down at her, and Jo thought she saw suspicion in his brown eyes. "Do you remember?"

"I...I'm not sure."

The doctor looked closely into both her eyes, pulling each of her lower lids down with his thumb. "You were lucky. The bullet went straight through without too much damage. I closed the wound and it should heal just fine. I want to keep you here, though, for at least a day or two to watch for infection."

Jo barely heard a word the doctor was saying. All she could think of was how lucky she was to be alive, and what Leo would have done if he'd had to bury another parent.

"I've already sent word out to your ranch. Your son will want to see you, I reckon."

Jo smiled weakly at him. "Thank you."

How was she going to explain this to Leo? she wondered. She was supposed to have been running errands when all of this happened.

As the doctor turned to leave, Jo thought again of the lawman she had gunned down in Zeb's store. A mental picture of him, sprawled out on his back and bleeding onto the plank floor, made her heart wrench. "Wait, please, Doctor. Was anyone else hurt tonight?"

"Besides you? Why, yes. The new marshal took a bullet."

"He's not dead, is he?"

At that moment, a knock sounded. Dr. Green crossed the room and opened the door.

Jo suddenly found herself staring in stunned silence at the man she thought she'd killed. Her heart did a quick *pitter-pat,* then her mind was struck numb by the strangeness of it all—how she could be so plagued by him one moment, then so happy to see him the next.

"Why don't you ask Marshal Collins yourself?" Dr. Green suggested.

Leaning heavily on a cane, the marshal limped like a Civil War vet into the room. A white, bloodstained bandage was wrapped around his head. He wore black wool trousers and a white shirt with the sleeves rolled up, a dark brown vest, no hat, and his chestnut-colored hair was neatly trimmed.

"Ask me what?" he drawled good-naturedly.

Jo couldn't find words to reply. She was too busy trying to keep herself from spilling out her relief in a gigantic wave of apologies and confessions and useless reparations, all of which would land her in the county jail.

The marshal glanced questioningly at the doctor.

"She wants to know if you're dead," Dr. Green answered.

The marshal's lips parted with a grin that revealed straight white teeth and deep dimples around his mouth, and his eyes sparkled flirtatiously. "There are days, ma'am, when I think I might be. Thankfully, this ain't one of 'em."

The two gentlemen shared a chuckle, but all Jo could respond to was the charming, congenial glint in the lawman's eyes—so different from the threatening glare he'd produced in Zeb's store when he first burst through the doors.

When the moment of humor passed, however, the marshal peered at Jo, and his smile faded. She swallowed nervously, not wanting to think of all the things he could say to her at this moment, all the accusations she deserved to hear.

He limped a little closer, his cane tapping twice on the floor. "Are you well enough to speak with me, Mrs. O'Malley? Or would you prefer I come back later?"

She would have to face this man at some point, she knew. She might as well get it over with now and try to learn as much as she could about the situation. Jo tried to speak with a steady voice. "I believe I could manage it. Please, sit down."

He took a seat in the corner rocker, wincing subtly when he bent his knee. The doctor stood just inside the door.

"I'm very sorry about what happened to you," the marshal said, leaning his elbow on the armrest. "I can't help feeling responsible."

Knowing it was the most absurd thing for him to say—considering it was *she* who had shot *him* in the leg—Jo waited in silence for him to continue.

"As luck would have it, today was my first day on the job. It was my intent when I walked in on that holdup to disarm the man who shot you."

The marshal still believed the outlaw was a man.... "You must have been in the wrong place at the wrong time," he continued. "Where were you, exactly?"

"I was in the privy."

Marshal Collins stared at her intently. "But there were no bullet holes in the privy walls, I'm told."

"I mean, when they found me," she added.

"I'm aware of that much. I was here when Deputy Anderson brought you in."

So much had happened while she was unconscious. She was groping for an explanation in the dark with both hands tied behind her back. "What happened to you?" she asked, stalling. "Were you badly hurt?"

"Thank you for your concern, ma'am, but I'm fine." Dr. Green interrupted. "Rumors are going around that he was shot in the head and laid out cold as a wagon tire. But as you can see, he hasn't hung up his holster yet."

Marshal Collins shot the doctor a rankled glance, then looked back at Jo. "I was wounded, is all."

Jo gestured to the bandage on his head. "What happened there?"

"It's nothing serious—"

"He fainted," Dr. Green said.

The marshal shook his head. "I didn't faint, ma'am. I took a bullet in the leg and cracked my skull on the counter when I went down."

"The bullet just grazed him, actually," the doctor added.

"If you don't mind, Doc, I'm trying to interrogate a witness."

Witness. Jo felt some of the weight lift from her shoulders.

The marshal looked back at Jo, his expression sobering. "I'll have to ask you again. Where were you when you were shot?"

Jo did her best to answer sensibly. "I was late in running my errands today and I was on my way to the privy before heading home."

"A lady like yourself shouldn't be walking the streets alone after dark. In the future you might want to be more careful."

"A woman like me doesn't have the means to be careful, Marshal. I'm raising a son and running my late husband's ranch. If I need supplies, I get them. I don't pay much mind to whether it's the sun or the moon lighting my way."

Something unreadable flickered in the marshal's eyes as he digested her reply. He hesitated a moment, staring, before steering the subject back to where he wanted it. "Did you see the man who shot you?"

"I didn't see him. I only heard gunfire, stopped to look in the direction I thought it was coming from, then felt the bullet strike. I have no idea where it came from, or who shot me. Then I ran to the privy and locked the door. I was quite frightened."

"Of course you were." He narrowed his eyes and his inquisitive gaze routed some of Jo's resolve. "Would you excuse us for a moment, Doc? I have some questions of a private nature, and I'm sure Mrs. O'Malley would want her answers kept private as well."

She felt a rush of anxiety. What would this private conversation be about?

Jo nodded her consent at the doctor.

"I'll be right outside the door if you need me," he said. "But you go easy on her, Marshal. She's in a delicate state."

As soon as the doctor walked out, the pain in Jo's shoulder grew worse, if that was possible, but she tried to ignore it. She had to keep the situation in focus. Her future depended on the marshal's questions and what she might learn from them. She had to protect Leo from his father's killer, and if that meant skirting the law until she had a chance to meet Zeb again, then so be it. The most important thing now was to lead this marshal away from her masquerade.

He leaned forward in his chair and the muscles in his sun-bronzed forearms tensed, then relaxed, distracting her from everything. Accordingly, Jo tried instead to concentrate on his voice, but that wasn't much better. His slow drawl had the same calming effect it had in Zeb's store when he'd told her to lower her weapons. And she *had* lowered them.

Oh, if she wasn't careful, she would confess everything.

"You were on your way to the privy?" he asked again.

"That's right."

"Mrs. O'Malley—" he tilted his head "—I don't think you're telling me the truth."

Jo's heart began to beat faster until she could hear it pounding in her ears. "Of course I am."

"In order for me to do my job, I need you to trust me and tell me where you *really* were when you were shot."

How could he know all this? It wasn't possible. "I don't know what you're referring to, Marshal."

He watched her with discerning green eyes that told her she could hide nothing from him. "I know you weren't injured in the dress you were wearing when Deputy Anderson brought you here. After Dr. Green transferred you from his operating table to this room, I was curious about the extent of your wound. Please forgive me, but I examined the bodice of your dress. There was no bullet hole."

Jo stared blankly at the marshal, knowing she couldn't stand up to him much longer. Surely, she was done for.

"So let me ask you again, Mrs. O'Malley. Where were you when the bullet struck your shoulder?"

Chapter

3

MARSHAL COLLINS SAT WITH HIS forefinger resting on his temple, studying Jo and seeming to find her as guilty as the last fox who'd emptied her chicken coop.

All Jo could do was stare into those green-and-gold flecked eyes and scramble for an explanation. Why wouldn't she have been wearing her dress when she was shot? she asked herself. What possible reason could there be?

"Mrs. O'Malley, I only want to know the truth so I can find and arrest the man who shot you."

"The truth."

"Well, yes, ma'am."

She tried to imagine herself not wearing her bodice outdoors in the full dark of night, why any person would ever do such a thing. Anyone respectable, that is. At the same time, she knew what folks had been saying about her living on her ranch with all those cowhands in her bunkhouse, and those same folks probably wouldn't be the least bit surprised to hear she'd been out behind the saloons in her unmentionables.

Maybe those rumors might get her out of this—at least temporarily.

Jo pursed her lips. What did it matter if she told a little lie? After all the gossip, she couldn't possibly do any more damage to her reputation.

She tried to speak with conviction. "I...I was with someone."

"I'm not sure I understand."

"Marshal, this conversation is highly improper."

At that instant, he seemed to grasp her meaning and his elbow slipped right off the armrest. He quickly pulled it back and cleared his throat.

"This is awkward, I know," she said, lowering her eyes. "That's why I don't wish to speak about it any further."

The chair creaked as he shifted uncomfortably. "But perhaps whoever you were *with* might have seen something more."

"No, he'd already left."

"Left...left where? The privy? You were in the privy together?"

"No, we were in back of Zimmerman's. As I told you before, I was on my way to the privy before heading home when I was shot."

The marshal seemed reluctant to believe it. "Can I have his name? He might have seen something."

"Absolutely not."

"Mrs. O'Malley, this is a deadly situation. You have my word as a peace officer that I will do my best not to repeat what you tell me."

"I'm sorry, Marshal Collins, I can't say."

They lingered in a thick silence while Dr. Green paced the hall outside, his shoes clicking lightly across the plank floor.

After a few minutes, the marshal took in a deep breath and sighed. Jo braced herself for whatever he was about to say next.

"I'm sorry to tell you this when you're in such a state, but your refusal to answer my question is an obstruction of justice. Are you aware of that?"

Jo could only nod, still unable to look up at him after the lie she'd just told. She'd told so many lies tonight, they were all taking their toll on her conscience—a conscience that by now was wracked with guilt and regret and a dozen other things that could make her toes curl if she let them.

"I'd like to go easy on you," he went on, "given the circumstances, but when it comes to the law, I'm about as inflexible as a branding iron. I need to ask this person some questions, so if you don't give me his name, I'm going to have to take you to the jailhouse." By the firmness of his voice alone, Jo knew he meant every word. She had to put an end to this discussion, and fast.

"I'm waiting, Mrs. O'Malley."

"It's not what you think," she said, stalling. "It's not that I don't *want* to tell you, it's that I can't."

"I beg your pardon?"

"I can't because...I don't know his name." She was

digging herself in deeper and deeper. She just wanted it all to end.

He rubbed his stubbled chin with his big, manly hand—the same hand that had pointed a gun at her earlier that evening, and her skin prickled at the frightening image.

"I see. He didn't *hurt* you, did he?"

"No, no, it was nothing like that." Good Lord, what was she saying?

"So let me get this straight," the marshal said, rubbing his forehead in disbelief. "You were out behind Zimmerman's with a stranger, not wearing your bodice. The stranger left you there, you were shot, then you took the time to put your bodice back on and refasten all the buttons?"

"That's right."

"Why did you go to the privy? Why not just go straight to the doctor's office?"

Jo tried to stay alert, but it was proving more and more difficult with all these questions. "I was afraid of being shot again. I was in search of a safe place to hide." She met his gaze head-on. He wasn't going to outsmart her. "Marshal Collins," she said, in her best no-nonsense voice, "I don't know the man's name, I probably wouldn't even recognize him. It was dark. Now if you don't mind, I'd like to get some rest."

She swallowed hard, unable to believe what she'd just said, but knowing she'd had to come up with something to explain herself. Biting her lip, she heard the marshal rock back and forth in the creaky chair. Why wasn't he leaving?

"I don't mean any disrespect, ma'am, but I intend to

find the man who shot you, and if that means I have to ask questions that might dent your delicate sensibilities, well..." He shrugged.

Frustrated and exhausted, Jo closed her eyes. She wished with all her heart that this night had never happened, that she could go back to a day when her husband was alive and there was never anything more distressing in her life other than a damaged corral fence or a few too many chores to complete before breakfast. Those things, those little problems, seemed so insignificant to her now, so easy to mend and put away. Her life had been simple once. There had been nothing to fear.

Or at least that was what, in all her precious innocence, she had believed.

"I just want to go home and be with my son," she said.

"I understand that, Mrs. O'Malley. I'm...I'm just hoping you can help me out. That gunman broke the law, and with first impressions being what they are, folks are going to think their new marshal is a little soft, and that just ain't the case. To be frank about it, I got a score to settle here." He stopped rocking and locked his large hands together. "Besides, Zeb Stone wants the man brought to justice, and I owe it to my sister to see that it happens."

Jo's breath caught in her lungs. "Your sister?"

"She's married to Zeb."

"Zeb Stone is your...your brother-in-law?"

He nodded. "That's right. And besides being family, he's the one who convinced the town council to hire me. I owe him."

Jo could only stare in stunned silence as her enemy's kin rose from his chair to stand tall before her,
his words leaving her whole body chilled to the bone
with despair.

Fletcher gazed into Mrs. O'Malley's wide-open
blue eyes and struggled to keep his hopes from sinking. She'd given him nothing that would lead him to
the gunman. And now she was obviously going to be
ill. "Doc, could you come in here?"

The doctor hurried in to her bedside. "What's the
problem?"

Mrs. O'Malley put her hand over her mouth and
the doctor saw what was about to happen. He reached
for a pan and held it under her chin while she was sick
into it. Fletcher stared at his boots, shaking his head
with a note of irritation.

Not so much at Mrs. O'Malley, of course—she
couldn't very well stop herself from being sick after
what she'd been through. He'd just hoped for something more to go on.

"It's a reaction to the surgery," Doc said, then turned
to Fletcher. "You'll have to leave. She's answered
enough of your questions."

Hearing the doctor's chilly tone, Fletcher felt a
hint of guilt, then backed out of the room. He closed
the door behind him and leaned his weary forehead
against it. Perhaps he had been too hard on Mrs.
O'Malley, but when it came to tracking leads, he
found it difficult to see past his own nose.

Fletcher turned away from the door and took two
painful strides down the hall. Suddenly the image

of Mrs. O'Malley having a willing "encounter" with a stranger hit him like a brick in the face: Mrs. O'Malley, doing *that* in the dark of night, out behind Zimmerman's hardware store?

Fletcher stiffened uncomfortably. Was it really a stranger? he wondered, finding it almost impossible to believe. Had Mrs. O'Malley sought the man out or was it the other way around? She must have been as hot as a two-dollar pistol to risk such a scandal, especially with what people were saying about her. But why outside by the privy? Why not somewhere more private?

Fletcher started off again, leaning on his cane, reminding himself that he was an impartial lawman, and what Mrs. O'Malley did with her personal life, no matter how outlandish and risqué, was none of his concern.

He reached the doctor's front office and sat on the straight pine bench by the window, pulling the lace curtain aside to peer out into the predawn darkness. Except for a mangy rat terrier sniffing around the water troughs, Front Street was about as quiet as a turkey pen after Thanksgiving.

The sound of hoofbeats and a jingling harness alerted him to an approaching wagon. He leaned closer to the window as a rickety buckboard came to a slow stop in front of the doctor's office. A young boy hopped down and landed with a thud on the dry street. An older woman set the brake and tied the reins, and with some difficulty, wiggled her wide bottom down from the high seat.

Before Fletcher had a chance to stand, the door

opened. "Where's my ma?" the boy asked in a panic, pausing in the open doorway. "She was shot." Fletcher stared into the same wide-eyed, fearful innocence that had thrown him off balance in the back room a few minutes ago.

"I just met your ma. She's fine. What's your name?"

"Leo." His shoulders relaxed slightly.

The older woman appeared behind him. "Go inside and close the door, Leo. The mosquitoes are getting in."

As they moved into the dimly lit room, Fletcher managed to rise to his feet, silently cursing his sore leg. When the woman noticed him, she pulled her black shawl tighter around her shoulders and raised her chin. "You're not the doctor."

"No, ma'am. I'm the new marshal. And you are...?"

"Shouldn't you be out looking for the man who shot Mrs. O'Malley? From what I hear, and no thanks to you, he's roaming the town as free as a wild prairie dog."

Fletcher's annoyance doubled as he hopped to keep his balance. "It's being taken care of. And your name is...?"

Indignantly, she lifted her double chin even higher.

Her cheeks were fleshy and red like a couple of ripe tomatoes. "I'm Matilda Honeyworth. I work for Mrs. O'Malley. Where is she?"

Fletcher gestured toward the back room. "The doctor's with her."

"Can I see her?" Leo asked, his dark eyebrows drawn together with worry.

When Fletcher remembered the tragic details about

the late Mr. O'Malley, his heart went out to the boy. He must have been terrified when he heard about his mother. "You'll have to ask the doctor, son. He should be out in a minute or two."

Leo leaned into the front hall and tried to peer past the stairs. "So you're the new marshal?" He turned to Fletcher and held out his hand. "I'm a rancher."

"Is that right?" Fletcher replied, trying to suppress a smile that might insult the young man's proud spirit. "I'm Fletcher Collins." He shook the boy's hand.

"Did you see it happen?" Leo asked.

"If you mean did I see your ma get shot, no, I'm afraid I didn't."

"But you saw the rest of it? Were you there? Is that why you got that bandage around your head?"

"Leo! That's none of our business!" Mrs. Honeyworth scolded.

Leo ignored the reprimand. "Did you shoot anyone?"

"Leo!"

"Gunfighting's a serious matter, son. I do my best to avoid it. When I can."

Dr. Green walked into the room and stopped in the doorway. "Mrs. Honeyworth, it was good of you to come."

"How's my ma?" Leo asked.

The doc smiled down at him. "She's going to be fine, Leo. Would you like to see her?"

"Yes!"

"Come this way, both of you."

Fletcher watched them walk down the hall. He limped to the bench and sat down again, looking out the window at the slowly brightening sky, then he rubbed his tired eyes and listened to the quiet laughter coming from the back room. They seemed like a nice enough family. Obviously been through a lot lately.

Hell, he didn't want to tarnish Mrs. O'Malley's reputation any more than it was already, especially after meeting her son, but the lover she was protecting might have seen something that would help solve this case. Was Fletcher to set aside his personal oath to uphold the law because he felt sorry for her and her son? Wasn't that the same kind of thing that had caused his own father's tragic death?

Fletcher pinched the bridge of his nose, thinking. It was impossible to leave that rock unturned, he knew. The way things stood at the moment, he had nothing to go on, not a single shred of a clue, and that didn't help his present mood. It was the kind of situation that would grate across his nerves—and his conscience—until he caught that gunman and brought him to justice.

One way...or another.

Chapter

4

*H*EARING FOOTSTEPS IN THE HALL outside her room, Jo felt her pulse quicken. Had she left another clue somewhere? A trail of blood perhaps?

The doorknob turned, the door slowly squeaked open, and there stood her darling, dark-haired boy. He wore a plaid shirt with suspenders, and duck trousers that had recently become too short and now showed off his loose socks pooling almost comically around his ankles.

"Leo," she said with a rush of relief that could not compare to anything she'd ever known. The pain in her shoulder seemed to disappear momentarily as she regarded her son.

He ran in, his loosely laced work boots stomping noisily across the floor, and gave her the hug she so desperately yearned for. "Ma, are you okay?"

She loved him so much, her heart *ached* with it. She

squeezed his slender body and when she felt his boy-ish weight upon her chest, she wished that life could go back to what it had once been.

As she considered it further, however, she knew she could never go back, even if Leo's father could some-how return from the dead and take over his duties on the ranch. After what she'd gone through, nothing would ever be the same again: she was not the same person she was, not the trusting woman who took safety and well-being for granted.

She began to wonder uneasily how the change in her personality would affect her relationship with Edwyn, if he actually *did* come back from the dead. Would he even notice? Then she swept the thought away and squeezed Leo tighter. It was a foolish, fool-ish notion to imagine Edwyn ever returning to her.

Leo withdrew from her embrace. Reluctantly, she let him go and noticed Matilda standing just inside the door. The older woman smiled warmly, her con-cern showing. She hadn't known what Jo had set out to do, only thought she was running errands, and she must have been devastated to learn what had hap-pened. "We're very glad to see you," Matilda said.

"I'm happy to see you, too," Jo replied, wishing she could confide in Matilda about all of this, but afraid the knowledge might put her at risk. Matilda was a friend Jo could not do without.

"When can you come home?" Leo asked.

"The doctor says I'll have to stay here for another day, so he can keep an eye on me."

"But you're going to be all right, aren't you?"

"Yes, I'm going to be fine, but I don't think I'll be

gathering any eggs for a few weeks. I'm going to need you to take over some of my chores."

Leo considered that a moment, then sat up straighter. "I can do everything. Don't you worry about a thing, Ma. I'll take charge."

"Thank you, Leo. Matilda and I will be sure to depend on you."

He smiled proudly, then his dark brows rose with excitement. "It must have been some gunfight. The marshal got shot, too, and he's all bandaged up."

"You saw him?" Jo asked worriedly, then she tried to sound casual and unperturbed. "What in heaven's name did you talk about?"

"I asked him if he saw you get shot, but he said he didn't."

Matilda gazed at a framed sketch on the wall. "I didn't like the look of that lawman. There was something about him..."

"Oh?" Jo questioned.

"I'm not certain what it was. Perhaps the way he asked my name. As if I were some sort of criminal."

Jo shifted, trying to ease the pain in her back from lying still for so long. "Don't fret, Matilda. I believe he's suspicious of everyone. He told me quite plainly that he was inflexible and that Dodge would soon learn he was in charge."

Matilda adjusted the small, round spectacles on the bridge of her nose. "Just what our town needs— another power-hungry man running things. What's his background?"

"All I know is that he's Zeb Stone's brother-in-law. That's how he got the job." Jo wished she knew more.

"Strange. I hadn't heard anything about that. Whatever happened to Marshal Peavy?"

"I don't know. When he rode out to check on us a few weeks ago, he didn't mention anything about leaving Dodge, although folks have been saying that ever since he took a bullet in Caldwell last year, he's been wanting to retire to California."

Leo broke in. "What's everybody so surprised about? I knew Marshal Collins was coming to town. I saw Zeb Stone on the McCaffrey land the other day when I was fixing the fence. He came over to talk to me."

Jo winced at the sound of Zeb's name on her son's lips. "You didn't tell me about that."

"Sorry, Ma, but you didn't ask. You haven't asked about much lately."

It was true, and she regretted having become so obsessed with Zeb, that she had neglected the person she loved more than anything in the world. She tried to hide the fact that she was shaken, and got straight to the heart of the matter. "What did Mr. Stone say to you?"

"Nothing much, except that he was on his way to the depot to meet the new marshal."

"That's all? You didn't bother him with any questions about your pa, did you?"

For the past six months, Jo had tried to keep a low profile and steer clear of Zeb's watchfulness, but Leo's newfound interest in solving his father's murder had become such a dangerous problem it had driven her to desperation. *Good Lord, what was she going to do about all this?*

"No, ma'am." Leo lowered his gaze.

Jo's head was pounding. She knew Leo must have said something and was afraid to tell her.

Matilda gave Jo a nod. "We best be getting on home. Your mother needs her rest."

Leo moved forward to hug her.

"Be a good boy for Mrs. Honeyworth until I get home," Jo said, patting Leo's back and trying to keep her voice from quivering around the lump forming in her throat. Oh, she missed him so terribly much, and he was becoming a man so fast, changing every day, it seemed. She didn't want to let him go.

"I will." He gave her a carefree smile that only a child could muster, then walked to the door.

Matilda leaned down and kissed Jo on the forehead. When the door swung closed behind them, Jo looked at the window. Through a crack in the closed curtains, she could see the first glimmer of dawn, but sadly, the new day did not carry with it new hope.

With the morning sun uncomfortably hot on his back, his cane in hand, Fletcher limped down a Front Street boardwalk to get some breakfast. He could feel the curious stares from the townsfolk, ladies standing around with parasols, shopkeepers and barbers gathered in groups at their windows, chatting quietly. People wanted to get a look at the new marshal who had *fainted* in the middle of his first gunfight in town.

Fletcher clenched his jaw. What a circus. Now he had a reputation to fix. Hobbling around Dodge like a wounded dog didn't exactly strike terror into the hearts of the local criminal element. He tugged the brim of his Stetson down over his forehead to cover the bandage and wondered if he could manage without the cane.

When he reached the Dodge House Hotel, he walked into the wallpapered dining room, removed his hat and chose a table by the window to watch for Deputy Anderson and his posse.

"You must be the new marshal," the dark-haired waitress said, approaching. She carried a silver coffeepot and a newspaper, which she promptly set down on the white tablecloth. "Pleased to make your acquaintance. I'm Gert Bezel. My husband owns the place. Coffee?"

"Yes, thank you."

She turned over the flowery china cup already placed in front of him and poured the coffee. "It's a downright shame what happened to you last night. I saw them carry you off to the doctor. You looked like a big sack of flour. Most people thought you were dead."

Fletcher felt his cheeks grow hot. "I'm still breathing."

"Mr. Stone's done so much for Dodge. It's a pity he was robbed like that."

"He's a good man, for sure."

Mrs. Bezel smiled warmly, but Fletcher knew he had some fancy footwork to do if he was ever going to regain confidence in this town. He leaned his cane against the dark wood wainscoting under the window.

"What can I get for you this morning?" Mrs. Bezel asked.

He ordered a plate of fried eggs, bacon and corn-bread, and when Mrs. Bezel took her leave, he flipped open the newspaper, but the front page headline turned his appetite sour.

Frontier Fun

Dodge City's Newest Marshal

Swoons at Gunpoint

Fletcher dropped his forehead into his hand and read on.

> *Last evening, Zeb Stone's Dry Goods Store was held up by the man citizens are now calling "Six-Shooter Hank, Scariest Man Alive." Marshal Fletcher Collins took one look at Hank and grace-fully retired to the floor, not forgetting to introduce his head to the glass cabinet on the way down. For a few confused moments, it seemed as if the coroner and undertaker might have something to do, but a closer examination of the town's new guardian revealed he was merely resting his eyes. Collins continued his nap while gunshots flew freely in the street, injuring Mrs. Josephine O'Malley, wife of murdered rancher, Edwyn O'Malley. Six-Shooter Hank made off with unknown amounts of cash and a posse on his tail. Marshal Collins has awak-ened from his nap and sources say he is recovering affably.*

Fletcher leaned back in his chair and gave up trying to control his temper. He clenched his fists and hoped he'd be able to find a lead soon—anything to help him catch that outlaw.

Just then, four men on horseback rode into town, Deputy Anderson bringing up the rear.

Hopes rising, Fletcher slid his chair back and took his hat with him to the front door. "Anderson, any luck?"

The deputy walked his horse to the hitching rail. "Afraid not, Marshal. Didn't find a trace of anything."

"Did you talk to any of the cowboys out on the range?"

"Sure did. Nobody's been bragging about a gunfight, but I reckon nobody wants to be a rat, either."

Fletcher removed his hat and pulled the bandage off his head. With the posse's failure, it was up to him now, so he decided right then and there that he would spare nothing to catch Six-Shooter Hank. Fletcher's tarnished reputation depended on it. And as far as Hank being the scariest man alive? Well, Fletcher would just have to see about that.

Chapter

5

*G*ROWING MORE IRRITATED BY THE minute, Jo slapped yesterday's newspaper down on the bed. Marshal Collins had probably read the front-page headline and spent every waking hour since the alleged robbery trying to capture Six-Shooter Hank.

Six-Shooter Hank! Didn't people have anything better to do than invent nicknames for criminals who had no business with fame?

She tapped her hand repeatedly on her leg. Her criminal disguise had been nestled beneath a public privy floor for two days, just waiting to be discovered by a disgruntled city marshal. She huffed in exasperation. Where was the doctor? He said he'd be in this afternoon to change her dressing and check her wound before releasing her. It must be past three by now, and she had to retrieve her bag and sneak it back home before anyone found it and turned it in.

Finally she heard footsteps in the hall and the door opened. "Good afternoon," Mrs. Eisenbein said, walking in with a lunch tray. "How are you feeling?"

"I'm feeling fine. I'm ready to go home, if the doctor would complete his examination—"

"Yes, yes, I understand. The doctor will be in after he's seen his patients."

"His patients? Are there many out there?"

"A few." She set the tray down on Jo's lap and began to spoon-feed her the hot broth.

"How long will it take him? Because I really have to be on my way—"

"Open up," Mrs. Eisenbein said, not waiting for Jo to finish. Before she knew it, she was swallowing the hot, salty-tasting liquid.

Just then, Jo looked up to see Marshal Collins standing in the doorway, his walking stick gone, his bandage removed.

Her insides whirled with alarm as she stared at him. He wore a clean white shirt and black vest, his black leather gun belt buckled loosely on an angle over his narrow hips. Jo eyed the shiny silver bullets, each with their own tiny pocket on the belt, and imagined those dangerous hands meticulously inserting each bullet while he imagined all the gruesome ways he would like to settle the score with Six-Shooter Hank.

Mentally shaking herself to force the disconcerting image away, she sank back onto her pillow, hoping he wasn't here with her disguise already in hand.

"Is the patient giving you trouble, Mrs. Eisenbein?" he asked.

Jo wasn't sure if he was joking or not. He wasn't

smiling.

Mrs. Eisenbein, on the other hand, grinned and set the silver spoon into the bowl. "No, Marshal. She's just anxious to get home, is all, and the doctor hasn't tended to her yet."

Holding his tan-colored hat in his hands, the marshal leaned at his ease against the doorjamb. The steel badge pinned to his vest flashed brilliantly, reflecting sunlight from the open window. "Well, maybe I can speed the good doctor up a little. I'll just threaten to polish his head with my six-shooter."

Mrs. Eisenbein chuckled, but Jo was less inclined to see the humor. She was too busy trying to think clearly while battling her rapid pulse.

"And how are we feeling today?" the marshal asked, directing his gaze straight through her.

"Fine, thank you, Marshal. Any luck catching that outlaw?"

"Six-Shooter Hank? Not yet. But I'll get him."

Not if I keep my wits about me. "Did the posse come back?"

"Yep, but they didn't find anything. I'm not through with this yet, though. A man couldn't disappear into thin air."

"No, of course not. Could I have some more soup?" Jo asked Mrs. Eisenbein, trying to change the subject.

The woman gathered up the bowl and began feeding Jo again.

"So what's the hurry?" Marshal Collins asked, crossing one brown leather boot over the other. "If I'm going to convince the doc to see you before his other patients, I'd better have a good reason."

"Tea, please?" Jo asked.

"You don't like to answer questions, do you?"

She glanced up long enough to get the impression he found her responses frustrating, which was only natural, she decided. She *was* avoiding his questions. "I'm hungry and I'm in a hurry to get home to my son, who is probably taking years off Mrs. Honeyworth's life as we speak."

"They expecting you for supper?"

"Yes, and Mrs. Honeyworth serves it precisely at six."

"Well, we'd best get you on your way, then." He leaned back to peer down the hall. "Doc should be done soon."

Jo tried to sip her tea delicately, but was annoyed to find she couldn't stop her fingers from trembling. In the silence of the room, the fine china cup rattled against the saucer.

Self-consciously, she glanced up at the marshal and saw that he was watching her. What would he do if he knew he was staring at the person who had caused that ugly lump on his forehead and the scar on his thigh?

She glanced at that thigh, able to see quite clearly the broad expanse of muscle, the hard contours beneath his trousers. He was a large man and a strong one. No wonder Zeb wanted him as the city marshal.

She cleared her throat, telling herself to keep her eyes to herself, stop jiggling the teacup like a dunderhead, and get out of there and back to the privy.

"Just so you know," Marshal Collins said, interrupting the uncomfortable silence, "we'll be spending some time together this afternoon. I rented myself a buggy and I'm going to take you back to your ranch myself."

Jo tried not to choke on her tea. "But Mrs. Honeyworth is supposed to come for me."

"I told her *I'd* get you home."

"Why would you want to do that?"

"Maybe I enjoy your conversation."

Mrs. Eisenbein's playful gaze flicked up at Jo.

"What is it that you want to discuss with me?" Jo asked pointedly. "Whatever it is, you can ask me now."

"There's nothing to discuss. I just want to see that you get home safely. Mrs. Honeyworth isn't coming, and your ranch is four miles outside of town, I hear. That's at least an hour's walk and it's powerful hot out there. Not a good risk in your condition."

"Thank you, but it's not necessary. I wouldn't want to trouble you."

"On the contrary, it would trouble me if you refused." His eyes darkened with a cast-iron message that Jo understood all too clearly. He could see through her charade and he wanted to knock her off balance. Get her to say something incriminating.

She set her cup and saucer on the side table and looked to Mrs. Eisenbein for help, but the woman lowered her gaze and began to gather up the tray.

"Something tells me you won't take no for an answer," Jo said to the marshal.

"Something tells me you're right."

She stared at him, considering her options. If she refused, he'd become even more suspicious than he was already, and probably follow her to the privy. But if she said yes, she'd have to leave her bag there for another day.

Without waiting for her response, the marshal backed into the hall. "I'll go get that buggy and fetch the doctor." He placed his hat on his head and disappeared from sight, the rhythmic sound of his boots lingering on the surface of Jo's frayed consciousness.

"That was kind of the marshal, don't you think?" Mrs. Eisenbein said, the dishes clinking on her tray as she stood.

But Jo knew with plunging hopes that the marshal's offer had nothing to do with kindness.

After the doctor came to the room and checked Jo's wound for infection, Mrs. Eisenbein entered with Jo's laundered gown and helped her slip into it. A few minutes later, Jo was at last being escorted down the hall to the front office.

While she arranged payment, the door squeaked open and the distinctive rhythm of the marshal's heavy boots rattled her nerves as he came up behind her. "All set to go, Mrs. O'Malley?"

She faced him. "Yes, but it really isn't necessary for you to take me. I'm perfectly capable of walking. I do it all the time."

"Not with a bullet hole in your shoulder."

"The marshal's right," Dr. Green said. "No sense taking chances. It's best to have someone with you, in case anything happens."

Marshal Collins settled his hat onto his head. "There, you see?"

Why did he have to be right all the time?

They walked onto the sunny porch and the marshal took her elbow as she descended the stairs. Feeling the stability of that hand on her arm only made her more uneasy, but she fought the urge to pull away. She had no choice but to allow him to assist her. Any hostile behavior might alert him to her apprehensive feelings, and she had to keep a calm head if she wanted him to leave her alone long enough to retrieve her bag from the privy. She only hoped it would remain there untouched until she could return for it.

"Careful now," the marshal said, helping her into a black canopied buggy with a shiny red seat. The leather creaked as she slid across. "It's been a while since I've driven one of these." He climbed in beside her and gently flicked the long leather reins. "I'm usually in a saddle." The buggy lurched forward and the harness jingled as the horse flicked his ears at the flies hovering around his head.

They rolled smoothly down Front Street in silence, the round buggy wheels grinding two straight tracks down the dusty street. The marshal paid the fare to cross the toll bridge over the river, then they drove onto it and faced the wide-open prairie, speckled with longhorn cattle as far as the eye could see. The buggy wheels rattled over the wooden bridge, the horse's hooves clopping while Jo mentally went over the alibi she'd given to the marshal the other day. She only hoped she would remember it correctly if he asked about it again.

Once the buggy rolled off the edge of the bridge, the ride grew rougher. Jo hugged her arm to her chest to keep her sore bones from knocking into each other.

"You okay?" the marshal asked, then they leaped over another bump.

"Ouch! I'm fine."

He bounced toward her and his knee touched hers. She felt a keen awareness of it and slid away.

"I could slow down," he offered.

Going slower meant spending more time with him in this confined space, and she wasn't sure that was such a good idea. "I told you, I could have walked. And slowing down won't make the ruts in the road go away. Why don't you stop and let me out?"

"I don't think that would be wise, ma'am."

"You can follow along behind if you like."

"It's a long way."

"I know how far it is. I'll be fine. I feel wonderful right now." They bounced one more time and she winced noticeably. "Except for the bumps."

He drove another few yards, then pulled the lumbering horse to a halt with a gently spoken "whoa." They were surrounded by hundreds of longhorn cattle, idly grazing. The horse nickered and shook beneath the harness.

"You don't want to talk to me, do you?" Marshal Collins said, all too perceptively.

"Where would you get such a notion? I simply prefer to walk, that's all."

He stared at her a moment, his eyes calculating. "All right. You can walk if it's easier for you. I'll drive behind in case you get tired, but don't overdo it."

"I won't get tired." She tried to step down, but had some difficulty holding on to the thin steel rail.

Before she knew it, the marshal appeared with his hands around her waist. Her insides did a flip as he lowered her to the ground, her calico skirts billowing upon the wind. He remained there looking down at her for a moment.

"Thank you," she said politely, staring at the short, stubbly grass with the pretext of examining the toe of her boot, all the while relieved that she could hide her eyes beneath the brim of her sunbonnet.

"You're welcome. Just watch where you're walking and don't hesitate to get back in the buggy if you feel ill. You've been through a lot."

Stepping back out of his arms, she struggled to gloss over the awkward feeling that was niggling at her, telling herself that she had merely *imagined* he was looking at her lips just now.

"There's a cow about to sniff your boots," Jo said, more than grateful for the distraction.

Marshal Collins turned. "Go on now. Go back to your herd."

The animal shifted direction and plodded away without argument, and by the time the marshal turned to face her again, Jo had started walking. "Let's get going before we become fodder."

She didn't let herself look back. She only listened to the sound of the buggy's springs bouncing and squeaking, then the horse's hooves thumping over the grassy road. Marshal Collins was following along behind her and that was just fine as far as she was concerned. At least they didn't have to talk to each other, and she didn't have to make a fool of herself answering any more of his prying questions.

Chapter

6

NOT FAR TO GO NOW, Jo thought wearily as she forced one foot in front of the other along the narrow prairie road, the wind blowing her bonnet ribbons every which way. She couldn't wait to get home, rid herself of these heavy clothes and collapse onto her soft bed to sleep.

She just had to make it the rest of the way. She'd walked at least two-and-a-half miles and the marshal hadn't asked her any more questions, thank heavens. He simply drove behind her—but she could *feel* him staring—and he hadn't made a peep except when he clicked his tongue at the horse.

With a dizzying sense of apprehension, Jo eyed the next hill. If she could make it up and over the other side, she would be fine. The rest of the way was as flat as a cornmeal griddle cake.

She climbed the grassy rise and began to breathe

harder. Oh, this wasn't promising at all. Her nose was beginning to feel hot and sunburned, and when she reached the top of the rise, her vision grew blurry. Dizziness overtook her as the rolling, tawny hills began to fold into one another and take on a silvery hue. She stopped and touched her gloved fingers to her forehead. *Oh no, not now...*

She hesitated and heard the muffled hoofbeats behind her come to a slow stop. The horse jingled its harness. Her stomach exploded with nausea and she knew that if she didn't climb into the shaded leather seat in the next few seconds, she'd be on her back.

She turned around, but a fresh wave of nausea crashed over her and she staggered to the side.

Her gaze locked with the marshal's and she took some comfort that he knew what was about to happen and was going to do something about it. He leaped down and ran toward her, but all she could do was stare blankly, dimly aware of her knees crumpling beneath her and the sight of his leather cowboy boots as she fainted at his feet.

Jo's mind floated in a sea of blackness. She couldn't speak, couldn't open her eyes. She could only lie immobile in the stiff grass that was needling the back of her neck, while she listened to that slow, easy drawl.

"Mrs. O'Malley, wake up. Wake up, ma'am. You fainted."

Her eyes fluttered open to see the inside of the marshal's black hat, fanning in front of her face—back and forth, the cool breeze beating against her cheeks and eyes and lips. Jo tried to speak, but all she could do was let out an embarrassing guttural groan.

The hat moved aside and she found herself blinking up at the marshal's green eyes. Behind his head, a black hawk soared against the blue.

The marshal donned his hat and pressed it down tightly. "You feeling okay?"

She didn't want to answer. She only wanted to lie there a little longer and look up at him. Then all at once she remembered who this man was.

Angry with herself for letting down her guard, she jolted upright, but the sudden movement made her shoulder throb painfully.

"Hold on, now," the marshal warned, touching her good shoulder and laying her back down in the grass. "Not so fast. You need to rest."

Feeling a headache coming on, she tried to keep it at bay by rubbing her temple. "How long was I out?"

"Only a minute or two. You were strolling along just fine, then all of a sudden, whoosh." He knelt on one knee, his arm resting across his thigh. "You dropped like all your bones turned to the kind of oatmeal my mother used to make."

"What kind of oatmeal was that?" she asked warily.

"It was runny, ma'am. But don't get me wrong. It was tasty...in its way."

Jo sat up and allowed the marshal to help her to her feet.

"You sure you're feeling well enough to stand?" he asked. "You lost a lot of blood the other night. It's no surprise you took a fancy to the ground."

She held on to his hand for support and had to work hard not to fall completely into his ready arms. "I'm fine, but I think I'd prefer to ride with you the rest of the way."

"I reckon that's a wise decision." He led her to the buggy and helped her up, then climbed in beside her and they started off again.

Jo remembered how he had tried to convince her to stay in the buggy in the first place and wished she hadn't proven him right. At least he wasn't saying *I told you so.*

"It's not much farther," she mentioned, swaying from side to side.

He took his eyes off the road to study her for a moment and she felt vulnerable, as if her secrets were printed on her cheeks in bold red ink. "You're worried I'm going to ask you more questions about the shooting."

Jo tried to appear unruffled. "I said all there was to say about that."

"Uh-huh—then what's with the toe tapping? You've been doing that since you sat down."

Realizing he was right about one more thing, Jo stilled her boot. "I always tap my foot. It's a habit." She pulled her toe in to hide it under a petticoat ruffle. "If I'm worried about anything, it's about whether or not you're going to deliver me home in time for supper."

He glanced toward the western sun. "I reckon we'll pull into your yard just as Mrs. Honeyworth is spooning up the gravy." He licked his lips. "Mmm, gravy on just about anything would go down nice right now."

Recognizing the hint for an invitation, Jo didn't

bite. "Maybe you should get yourself a wife to cook for you."

The corner of his mouth turned up in a cynical grin and he chuckled. "I don't think so."

"Ah. I see," she said knowingly.

"What do you mean, *Ah, I see?*"

Jo knew his type well enough. She'd seen enough roaming cowhands to get a feel for the kinds of things they wanted. "Married life isn't good enough for you. Too dull, I suppose."

"Dull. No, I never imagined married life would be dull, especially on a ranch like yours, with kids around. The ranch I grew up on was anything but dull."

Jo was surprised to hear he'd grown up on a ranch. "If it was so interesting to you, why aren't you there now?"

His jaw twitched. "It's kind of personal, ma'am."

"I'm sorry, I didn't meant to—"

"No harm done."

They drove on in silence for a while and Jo felt like a complete fool for having been so ill-mannered.

After a few minutes, the marshal spoke up and his words nearly knocked her over. "My father was murdered five years ago. That's why I'm not at the ranch anymore."

Shaken, Jo took a few seconds to respond. "I'm sorry to hear that. What happened, if you don't mind my asking?"

He spoke offhandedly, revealing no sadness or regret, something Jo found strange. "My father was a judge, and a man named Garrett Robinson was on trial for murder in his court.”

“Garrett Robinson. I heard about him. He robbed trains and stagecoaches.”

Fletcher’s jaw twitched again and she wondered if maybe he *did* mind talking about it. “The night before my father was to hand down a guilty verdict, Garrett’s gang sent him a message saying that if he convicted Garrett, they would hunt down his family and do to us what Garrett did to all the people who got in his way. We didn’t know anything about it, of course. We were as shocked as everybody else when the verdict was ‘not guilty.’”

Jo shifted in her seat, needing to hear the rest. “If your father did what they said, why didn’t they just leave it be?”

Marshal Collins shook his head. “Men like that don’t know much about honor. They killed my father on his way home that day, three hours after he let them go free. I heard the shots from the ranch house and saw the gang ride off. They were hootin’ and laughin’ like a bunch of kids playing tag. I had to run a mile up hill, climb over three fences, and I knew I wasn’t getting there fast enough.” His Adam’s apple bobbed and he paused. “My ma died of typhoid that winter, leaving me and Elizabeth to run the ranch, but neither of us wanted to live there anymore. Too many memories. So we sold off the herd and Elizabeth went to college in Chicago. I’d always imagined I’d be a rancher, but I ended up a U.S. marshal.” With a shade of indifference, he added, “Funny how things turn out sometimes.”

Jo knew exactly how he felt. How many times had

she wanted to pack up and leave, to start a new life somewhere else and forget about the old one? She most certainly would have if she wasn't certain Leo would return someday to claim the land that was his birthright and avenge his father's death.

"What about Garrett and his gang?" she asked, wondering if the marshal and his sister had received the justice Jo herself was still seeking.

He flicked the reins. "I dragged each one of them back to jail and watched their trials, and those who hanged saw my face in the crowd. The others are still rotting in prison."

"You dragged *all* of them to jail? Without shooting anyone?"

"Oh, I used my weapon plenty. Knocked 'em over the head with the handle most times. So when I said 'dragged,' I meant it in the literal sense."

Jo stared at him, dumbfounded. "Oh my goodness. That was you? You're *The Bruiser*?"

He chuckled. "I reckon that's where the name originated. You heard about that all the way up here in Kansas?"

"Yes, and that you've never shot a man in your entire career." She couldn't take her eyes off him now, this famous lawman who sat beside her. She'd had no idea....

"I have too much respect for life to go around killing people willy-nilly," he said. "Though if I could turn back the clock, I might have shot the gunman who tried to rob Zeb the other night. Wounded him at least."

At the mere mention of Zeb and the shooting, Jo

quickly forgot her fascination. "Why is he different from the others?"

"He's not different. He's the same. They all are. Men who don't respect the law need to learn they'll get caught eventually. You see, I'm not like my father. I don't believe in bending rules. If he had been a stronger man and had done his duty instead of being afraid, those men wouldn't have killed him, wouldn't have gone free for another year, killing other innocent folks."

Jo thought about what she had done, or almost done, the other night. How she had felt there was no other choice left to her. Not surprisingly, she could sympathize with the marshal's father.

"Your father thought he was protecting his family," she tried to explain. "Someday, when you have children, you'll understand it better. You'll be ready and willing to walk through fire for them. You'll do anything to keep them safe. Even break the law when you feel the law can't help you, and frankly, the law isn't always able to help innocent folks around here. You can't begrudge your father for what he did."

Marshal Collins gave her a steely glare. "There's never an excuse for breaking the law."

"That's very idealistic."

"Maybe so. But you can't argue that that's the way things *ought* to be, and we owe it to this world to keep striving for what's right. My father could have protected us another way. Sent us somewhere safe until the rest of the gang was caught. He shouldn't have done what he did. He was a judge."

The marshal's voice had grown almost hostile.

"And to answer your question about last night's gunman, I wish I'd shot him because he made me look incompetent, and when it comes to the law, I rely on my reputation to help me run a tight ship. With it, outlaws are more likely to give up without a fight and no one gets hurt. Without it, all hell breaks loose, and hell ain't no place for decent folks. Tarnation, that man shot you, Mrs. O'Malley, an innocent bystander. And he shot me in the leg and tried to rob my sister's husband. She's been through enough after what happened to our parents. If she'd lost her husband, too..."

His voice trailed off and Jo saw how truly angry he was over all this.

"The town thinks their new marshal is a buffoon, and all because I wanted to avoid gunfire. It's going to take a lot of time and energy to earn back any respect, and who knows what might happen in the meantime? I should have known better than to think that gunman would lower his weapon, but I thought I saw something in his eyes. Something..."

Jo leaned forward, curious. "Something what?"

"Something frightened. Something..." He hesitated again, as if searching for just the right word. "Something woeful."

A lump formed in Jo's throat. The marshal had seen through her that night, and if Zeb hadn't raised his pistol, she *would* have lowered her weapon. She would have confessed everything to Marshal Collins.

Not knowing, of course, that he was Zeb's kin.

Desperate to change the subject, she cleared her throat and forced a smile. "Heavens above, I'm sitting beside the famous Bruiser. You're not what I imagined."

"No? And what was that?"

Jo felt suddenly uncomfortable. "I was expecting someone...bigger."

She saw humor dance across his face, then he laughed. "Well, it doesn't take size to whack someone over the head with a pistol. It only takes a sober mind."

"I suppose." They drove past a patch of white elderberry and pink clover, and in the distance, Jo recognized bright yellow sunflowers. She breathed in the deep aromatic scent of the blossoms and, with some surprise, felt the tension lift between her and Fletcher. He was gazing toward the sunflowers, too, the set lines of his face relaxing somewhat, so that he no longer looked like the rigid, vigilant lawman that he was.

Realizing she wasn't the only one letting down her guard, Jo decided to take advantage and ask some questions of her own.

"How did your sister get hitched up with Zeb Stone?"

"He met her in Chicago just before she finished school. They hit it off but he didn't stay around long, with his business back here. They only knew each other a few weeks before he sent for her, asking her to be his wife. You don't know her?"

Jo shook her head. She'd made it a point not to get to know Zeb's wife. "How long have *you* known Zeb?"

"Since the wedding this past spring." He didn't look at her when he spoke. "I thought I was the one supposed to be asking all the questions."

Jo clasped her hands together in her lap. "Just making conversation. It's a long drive."

"But not much longer." He nudged his hat back with his thumb and squinted up at the blue sky. "Looks like you'll be home in time for supper."

Jo settled into the seat and tried not to think about everything the marshal had just said. With all the tragedy he'd seen, it was no wonder he'd retreated from the ranching life he'd known to become a lawman. It was plain to see that he thought he could make up for his father's mistakes, and that he was dead set on protecting his sister's happiness. The way he saw it, she was the only survivor left in the family, the only one with any hope for the future. He wanted to protect his own, and that meant protecting Zeb Stone.

And Lord help Jo if the marshal ever discovered he'd rented a fancy buggy to escort none other than Six Shooter Hank straight home to her front door.

Chapter
7

B Y THE TIME THE MARSHAL drove the buggy up
the last rise, the wind had calmed and the meadowlarks were singing their hearts out. Though the ride
had been bumpy and painful at times, Jo was glad she
had decided to drive instead of walk. She only wished
she had come to that conclusion sooner and avoided
the unfortunate fainting incident.

The horse nickered softly when they crested the last
hill. Jo spotted the ranch, where a couple of the cowhands were leaning against the bunkhouse, sipping
water. One more was shaving, and she heard their
easy laughter in the distance, along with the clucking
chatter from the henhouse. Wood smoke rose from
the kitchen chimney and melted into the sky.

She sat forward when the front door of the house
swung open and Leo ran onto the covered porch. He
clutched the corner post and waved, then called for

Matilda, who promptly came out, wiping her hands on her long white apron and waving. Jo waved back.

The marshal drove the buggy into the yard and pulled the horse to a gentle halt next to the white plank corral fence.

"Ma!" Leo called out, leaping off the porch and hurrying to take hold of the horse's harness. "You're all better!"

"Not quite, Leo, but I'm on the mend and happy to be home."

The marshal hopped down and walked around the buggy, appearing at Jo's side to help her down. She reached for the marshal's hand, but he took her by the waist and lifted her like a feather to the ground. "Wouldn't want you to fall," he said.

She quickly withdrew her hands from his shoulders.

Leo approached Marshal Collins. "Did you catch Six-Shooter Hank yet?"

"Not yet, but I will. And Leo, don't believe everything you read." He winked at him, and Leo smiled brightly.

Matilda approached.

"The marshal insisted on driving me home," Jo explained.

No one said anything for a minute or two, and the long silence was more than a little awkward. Surely everyone must be wondering what he was doing here.

Determined not to let her uneasiness show, Jo spoke up. "Well, thank you for the ride home, Marshal Collins." *You can go now,* she wanted to add, but of course held back the rude remark.

"It was no trouble at all." He moved to put on his

hat, but Leo stopped him.

"Why don't you stay for supper? We're having beef stew with dumplings."

If the last silence had been awkward, this one was downright painful. Matilda stared in shock at Leo, whose face colored sheepishly. Marshal Collins stood waiting for someone to say something, while Jo wanted to bury her head in the nearest haystack. If he stayed for supper, he'd have more opportunity to ask questions about the night of the shooting, or he might come to realize that she had a motive for murder where Zeb was concerned.

"Of course, you're welcome to stay, Marshal," Matilda said coolly.

He looked down at Jo, telling her with his eyes that he knew she wanted him to leave. "How can I refuse?" He patted his firm, flat stomach. "A man's gotta eat."

A short while later, Fletcher pulled off his shirt and washed up outside the bunkhouse, where the ranch hands kept their shaving equipment on a white painted shelf under the window. Leaning forward, he splashed cool, water from a wooden bucket onto his face and over his chest and arms, lathering himself with lye soap, trying to clear his mind.

He thought about the drive and how he'd gotten none of the information he'd wanted from Mrs. O'Malley. He'd been struck foolish with some kind of tongue-flapping disease, spilling out his soul to her about his father. He hadn't spoken about personal things to anyone in years, but her interest had seemed genuine. She'd been through something similar not long ago, and maybe that was why she'd wanted to talk, and why she seemed to think she understood certain things about him.

Which she didn't, of course.

Fletcher splashed more cool water on his face and rubbed his fingers over his tired eyes, trying to get his mind back on track. He straightened and looked across the yard at Leo, who was walking toward him with a folded white shirt in his hands.

"Ma said to bring you this to wear at supper," Leo said. "It belonged to my pa."

Fletcher toweled his hands and face dry, and eyed the shirt with some reluctance. "Much obliged."

Leo handed it to him and Fletcher shrugged into it. It was a bit small through the shoulders, but he managed to fasten all the buttons, and at least it was clean. He pulled his vest on over it and buttoned that, too.

He felt a little strange wearing a dead man's clothing, though. How would Mrs. O'Malley react when she saw him wearing it? Would it make her think of her husband?

Just as Leo was about to turn away, Fletcher stopped him with a question. "Tell me, does your ma spend much time in town?"

The boy leaned his back against the log wall of the bunkhouse. "Not since Pa died. She only goes for supplies when she has to, and even then, she'll put it off or get Mrs. Honeyworth to go for her."

"Does she stay out here alone when that happens?"

"Nobody's ever alone out here this time of year. I mean, there's always ranch hands around."

Fletcher knew that, of course, having been raised on a ranch, but he needed to steer his questions gradually. "What about in the winter? Is it just you and your ma and Mrs. Honeyworth? Any visitors?"

Leo kicked the dirt with the toe of his boot. "Not since Pa died."

"I heard about your pa," Fletcher said gently. "You must miss him a lot."

"Yeah. Things were different when he was around. He used to let me do more stuff."

"Like what?"

"Like helping with the spring roundup. It's different now, that's all."

"Your ma doesn't let you do that?"

"Nah. She barely lets me out of her sight sometimes. She won't even let me talk to people we don't know."

Fletcher tossed the towel over his shoulder. He could hear the frustration in Leo's voice—a boy desperate to be a man and stand in his father's empty shoes, and a mother who was afraid of losing him like she'd lost her husband. "I think you just need to give your ma some time, Leo. Things will get better."

"But she never used to be like this."

"Maybe that's because your pa made the decisions about you. Now your ma has to do a lot of things by herself. A lot of things she never had to do before, and I would guess that losing your pa broke her heart and she's real scared of losing you, too."

Leo's voice was quiet. "Maybe. I just..." He stopped talking altogether.

Fletcher rested his hand on Leo's shoulder. "If you ever need to talk to someone about your pa, I'd be happy to listen. I lost my pa, too, and I know what it feels like."

"Really?"

"Yes. It might not seem like it now, but it *will* get easier."

Just as Leo stared up at him hopefully, Mrs. Honeyworth opened the front door of the house and rang the tarnished brass dinner bell on the porch. The clanging echoed off the barnyard walls as four ranch hands left the corral, swung the wide gate closed behind them and headed toward the house.

Leo pushed away from the wall and brightened a bit. "Supper's on."

"Everybody eats in the house?" Fletcher asked, watching the dusty cowboys climb the front steps. Back at his old place, the hired help ate in the cookhouse.

"Yeah. Unless they're out at the range camps. Then they settle for the chuck wagon. Pa always wanted it that way, and I guess it makes Ma feel like some things haven't changed. Even though they have."

Leo walked off and Fletcher stood for a moment, feeling a deep sense of sadness for this boy who had lost his father at such a tender age. At least Fletcher had been a man of twenty-five when it happened to him.

But as he considered it more, he doubted that age made much of a difference. Grief was grief. At least Leo still had his mother. And this land.

Fletcher let his gaze wander the rolling fields beyond the fenced corral and felt a pang of regret. He looked at the windmill behind the barn, listened to the purr of its wooden blades as they sliced the wind. A large herd of cattle grazed quietly in the front pasture.

There was much to remind him of the home he had once had, the ranch his family had owned back in Texas when life was simple and cheerful and filled with luxuries he, for one, had taken for granted. He wasn't talking about the luxuries money could buy, either—though they had plenty of those. What came to mind now was the laughter and the sense of belonging, the warmth of the big house on stormy winter nights when the fireplace was roaring and the wind was whistling down the stone chimney, and they all sat in the front parlor talking and laughing and reading aloud to one another.

But that was another life, he thought wistfully. Another time. Those days were gone and nothing could bring them back. He was a lawman now and he was devoted to something else. He went where he was needed, and if that meant the idea of "home" had to be modified a bit, then so be it. There was no point reminiscing about it.

Leo turned back and yelled across the yard, "You coming, Marshal?"

Startled from his thoughts, Fletcher replied, "On my way!" Then he looked toward the small creek that babbled near the road, the wooden barrels stacked outside the barn, and the smokehouse next to the chicken coop. This place was probably already engraved on Leo's soul, Fletcher thought with some melancholy, just like *his* Texas home had once been engraved on his, and Leo probably didn't know it. Fletcher decided he would make a point very soon to tell the boy how lucky he was to have this place as his birthright.

He tossed the towel over the side of a half-full water barrel and started walking toward the house, laboring to force all thoughts of lost dreams from his mind, and keep only two others.

Beef stew and answers.

"So what brings you to Dodge City, Marshal?" one of the ranch hands asked, as he passed a plate of thickly sliced rye bread down the large table. The red-checkered tablecloth was barely visible beneath all the serving bowls full of steaming potatoes, corn and green beans. Forks clinked against plates as eight hungry men chowed down, as if it were their last meal.

Knocking elbows with the man, Fletcher accepted the china plate and picked up two slices for himself. "My sister, really—Elizabeth Stone. She came here this past spring and I thought it was high time I live near my kin. At least for a while."

Mrs. O'Malley sat next to him at the head of the table. Her gaze remained lowered as she ate her stew. "Bread?" he offered.

Without looking up, she took the plate. The pads of their fingers touched beneath it. Fletcher tensed at the swift surge of awareness and wondered if she had felt something, too, and if that was why she refused to make eye contact with him.

Bowls passed from one end of the table to the other and Fletcher was glad when the conversation picked up again. "Where are you from, Marshal?" one of the men asked.

"Texas. My family owned a ranch there, but after

my folks passed, Elizabeth and I sold the place."

"That don't make a lick of sense to me," the man said. "A place like that is worth a—"

Mrs. O'Malley interrupted. "Mr. Birk, I'm sure the marshal has his reasons, and it's really none of our concern. Pass the lemonade, please, Marshal, and would you be kind enough to pour it for me?"

Fletcher was grateful for her interruption.

During the remainder of the meal, he thought about what her life must be like on a daily basis. Judging by the faces at the table, he could see that she held everyone's respect as head of the household. She was intelligent and strong, to be sure. He could tell by the condition of the ranch. She'd kept things going efficiently around here, and done it without a husband. Most women probably would have packed it in by now and gone back to their families. Did she have a family to go to? he wondered. He wanted to know so much more about her.

With a hint of unease, he realized that he wasn't curious because it was his job and she was witness to a shooting. Something more personal was stirring inside Fletcher now. He wanted to make up for what had happened to Mrs. O'Malley the other night and make sure it didn't happen again. She already had enough pain to deal with in her life. Anyone could see that.

One of the cowhands handed the plate of bread down the table and Fletcher passed it to his hostess.

"Thank you, Marshal," she said, and he felt something friendly pass between them.

"Thank *you*, ma'am, for inviting me to supper. The

stew is delicious."

"Sure beats beans and bacon!" someone said, and the whole table cheered.

After that, Fletcher's mood lightened and he settled in to eating. It was a busy meal, bowls and pitchers being passed along for second helpings. By the time everyone finished their stew and there was nothing left of the bread and vegetables, Fletcher was stuffed. Mrs. Honeyworth gathered up the plates and disappeared into the kitchen.

At the opposite end of the table, sitting at the head, Leo leaned back and laced his fingers together over his full belly, like some middle-aged banker after a hearty meal. Fletcher couldn't help but grin to himself, and when he glanced at Mrs. O'Malley, he caught her doing the same thing, trying to hide it as well. They smiled at each other.

The kitchen door swung open and Mrs. Honeyworth swept into the dining room with a tray of desserts and served Mrs. O'Malley first. Then she set a glass pedestal dessert cup in front of Fletcher, filled with what smelled like raspberry cream custard, and finally she poured coffee for everyone from a shiny silver pot.

"What's it like to be a lawman, Marshal?" Leo asked, delving into his dessert.

Fletcher was grateful for the conversation to distract him from thinking about his hostess. "It can be dangerous, son, if you're not careful. But I try to be careful most of the time." He considered the question some more over a sip of hot, black coffee. "I reckon the best part is when I help somebody." He felt Mrs.

O'Malley studying him but didn't look up.

"If I were a marshal, I'd catch all the outlaws," Leo said, playing with what was left of his dessert. "Especially the horse thieves who kill—"

"Leo," Mrs. O'Malley firmly said, cutting him off.

Fletcher saw the look of shock on her face, then saw a similar emotion dance across Leo's.

"May I please be excused?" the boy asked.

Mrs. O'Malley stared at her son, her womanly facial features tightening, then her authoritative tone vanished. Clearly, her love for her son was her number-one weakness. "Are you finished your dessert?"

"Yes, ma'am."

"Then yes, you may be excused."

He shoved his chair back and walked quickly from the room, which had gone deathly silent.

Fletcher glanced at Mrs. O'Malley. She made a move to rise, but winced with pain and touched her shoulder.

"I'll go," he said, lightly touching her hand.

"That's not necessary."

"Someone needs to."

"But not *you*," she whispered, looking up at him with eyes, both pleading and commanding.

Fletcher hesitated, confused by her desperate expression. "Just trust me, alright?" he said simply. Then he walked out, feeling every eye watch him as he left the room.

Chapter

8

WITH MATILDA'S HELP, JO ROSE from the table and said good-night to the other men. She had to follow the marshal and prevent him from talking to Leo, from getting too close to him. Leo was vulnerable now. He needed a father figure, and a lawman sworn to protect Zeb Stone was the last person her boy should turn to. Just the thought of it made her stomach turn.

Walking quickly, she reached the front hall, peered out the window and listened for voices on the porch. She heard nothing but crickets chirping and cows lowing in the distance. She pulled the door open. The moon hung like a lantern in the clear black sky, lighting the barnyard.

She knew where Leo had gone.

A wave of apprehension swept over her. Ever since Edwyn's death, Leo had chosen the barn as his private

hideaway, the place he went to think. Jo's heart ached
with the painful realization that he chose it because
he knew it was the one place his mother would not
go.

As she crossed the yard, she tried to calm her erratic
pulse. After everything she'd lost, was she losing her
son, too?

She reached the barn door, which had been left
open a crack, and stopped outside to listen. Hearing
the faint murmur of voices, and seeing light from a
lantern coming from the tack room, she tried to find
the courage to go inside, but icy terror licked at her
flesh.

It had been six months since she'd been in the barn,
and if not for Leo and the other men, the animals
never would have survived. Each time Jo went near
the huge gambrel-roofed building, she could still
smell death, hear the rope creaking as it swung back
and forth like a pendulum. She could see Edwyn's
well-worn boots suspended only a foot above the
hay-strewn floor, his body limp, his bare hands bleeding from trying to defend himself against Zeb's two
hooded henchmen, who had beaten Edwyn before
dragging him inside.

She wished she had heard Zeb say *why* he had murdered Edwyn. Then there might have been a way to
convict him.

Squeezing her eyes shut to force the memories away,
she tried to listen to the voices inside the barn, but
could hear nothing clearly from where she stood. She
worried about what the marshal might say to Leo. Or
worse, what Leo might say to him. But should she go

in? *Could* she go in?

She sucked in a deep breath of air to fill her tightening chest. She'd had the courage to confront her enemy with a loaded weapon a few nights before. Why couldn't she face the spot where her husband had died? Why must it continue to haunt her with such vengeance?

Feeling defeated, she rested her head against the timber wall of the barn and closed her eyes. She needed a moment to think, and began to make excuses, as she always did: Perhaps she didn't *need* to go in. More than a few things the marshal had said to her during the day had surprised her and cast doubt upon his involvement with Zeb. Maybe he wasn't such an adversary after all. She wished she knew. Maybe what he was saying to Leo privately would reveal something. Give her hope that some lawmen could be trusted. That Zeb didn't own everything in Dodge City.

Hearing laughter from the tack room, Jo knew she would not be going into the barn tonight. And though it would drain her already depleted patience, she would have to wait to find out what the marshal with the questionable integrity had said to her son.

Precisely fifteen minutes later by her pocket watch, Jo sat on the porch swing, tapping her foot. What was taking them so long? What could they possibly be talking about?

At last, the light from the barn went out and the door swung open. Jo stood up, pressing her palm to her chest, relieved to see her son appear from the dark and silent interior where Edwyn had gasped his last breath.

Leo stepped into the moonlight, then the marshal walked out and closed the barn door behind them. As they approached the house, he rested a hand on Leo's shoulder. Leo laughed at something. It made Jo feel disturbingly territorial. Until tonight, Leo would not speak to her—or anyone, for that matter—when he disappeared into the barn. What was it about the marshal that he admired so much? Was it because Fletcher had lost his father, too? Had he spoken of that to Leo?

They reached the porch, and only then did the marshal look up and notice Jo sitting there with her watch in her hand. She forced a smile, stood up and walked to the top of the steps. "Is everything all right?"

"Yes, Ma. Can I go to bed now?" Leo replied.

Jo swallowed the urge to ask him anything more. "Yes, you may."

"Night, Marshal Collins. Night, Ma."

"Good night, Leo."

Jo watched her son go into the house and listened to his footsteps tap eagerly up the stairs. She took a deep breath and turned to face the marshal, not knowing what to expect.

When their eyes met, her emotions dipped alarmingly. He stood at the bottom of the porch stairs with one boot resting on the second step, his hand on his raised knee. He gave her a subtle, reassuring smile and she found herself knocked slightly off kilter by how devastatingly handsome, muscular, and manly he was.

*That smile…*It was an absolute killer.

"What happened?" she asked, fighting to breathe

steadily and not get lost in the whirlwind of his good looks.

"Nothing much. We just talked."

Just talked. Leo hadn't *just talked* to anyone in six months. "What about?" She tried to sound nonchalant.

The marshal didn't answer right away. He walked calmly up the steps, moved around Jo, sat himself down on the porch swing and leaned back. "Care to join me for a minute or two?"

The invitation—the thought of sitting so close to him—made her insides grow hot with nervous excitement. She tried to smother the reaction and stiffly made her way to the swing and sat down, keeping her backside perched forward on the wooden seat to avoid touching his muscular arm, which rested across the back of the swing.

"How's your shoulder?" he asked.

"It still pains me a great deal. I'm anxious to retire."

The corner of his mouth turned up, as if he were amused by her constant attempts to get rid of him. "I see. Can you stay awake long enough to hear what your son had to say?"

"Of course." She met his gaze directly. "I'm always interested in what Leo has to say."

"I'm sure that's true. Only problem is, he doesn't think so."

Jo felt as if she'd been blasted by another pistol, this time straight through the heart. She knew she and Leo had been having problems since Edwyn died, but she didn't want to hear it from Marshal Collins, of all people.

"He'll come around in time," she said, working hard to be guarded and abrupt with this man who seemed to be pushing to get closer, to understand her and Leo. Could that be true? Could he be as sincere as he sounded?

The marshal leaned forward, rested his elbows on his knees and laced his fingers together. "He told me what happened to your husband."

Jo let her eyes follow the erratic flight of a bat overhead. But he didn't tell you the truth. *I'm the only one who knows what really happened.*

The marshal continued. "You can't let that stop you from letting your son grow up. He thinks you don't trust him with things. That you don't have any confidence that he can take over the ranch."

"He's just a boy. Taking over the ranch is a long way off."

"Not in his mind. He feels he's ready to be a man. He wants some freedom."

Jo knew this already. She'd known it for a long time. She just couldn't bring herself to give that kind of independence to Leo. How could she, when she knew he only wanted to be out from under her protective wing so that he could investigate his father's murder?

Part of what angered her now was that she was being told this by a man who had no business with her family. In fact, he was the last person on earth she wanted involved.

"Did he talk to you about Edwyn?" she asked, hoping desperately that Leo hadn't tried to elicit the marshal's help in finding his father's killers.

"He said things were different when he was alive."

"Of course they were different—" She heard her angry tone and cut herself off before she spilled out all her woes to the marshal right then and there.

But oh, how she needed to spill her woes to *someone*. It had been so long since she'd had anyone to trust with the workings of her heart—her doubts and fears in the middle of the darkest nights....

And what was it about this man that made her feel safe, even against her better judgement?

"I know how you feel," he said gently, and his kindness, which she had been working hard to deflect, nearly broke her.

She had to move away from him. She stood up, and the swing twisted to and fro. The porch planks creaked beneath her feet.

"Just try talking to him," Fletcher said. "Let him know why you're prudent, and maybe you could relax the rules a little. Let him do the things he used to do."

A chilly evening breeze blew her skirts as she stood resting her hands on the white-painted porch rail, gazing across the dark hills. "I can't," she whispered, feeling as though the ground was slipping out from under her.

"You have to. Or you'll lose him."

Jo swallowed a sob that rose up in her throat. Either way, she would lose.

She heard the swing creak behind her as the marshal rose and approached. Jo closed her eyes, feeling his nearness. He was going to touch her. She sensed it. Her heart was racing and her body was growing warm at the mere thought of it.

Oh, God, how long had it been since she'd been touched? Since she'd felt any sort of sensual pleasure?

Fletcher laid a hand on her good shoulder. She felt his breath on the back of her neck, knew he was smelling the orange flower water she'd splashed on before supper.

Her skin tingled with desire and she wanted to touch his hand. To thank him, oddly enough, for wanting to help Leo, even though she'd not wanted him to. It had been a while since Leo had looked to anyone for advice. None of the ranch hands seemed wise enough. Mature enough.

But the marshal...he was so much of a man.

He gently squeezed her shoulder and she sucked in a shaky breath. She could respond to him now, turn around and...

Oh, she wanted to. She longed to touch him. Her heart was beating wildly in her breast, imploring her, pushing her...

She bowed her head, fighting the urges and desires she hadn't known she was capable of feeling. She felt so wildly confused and physically tormented. Even if the marshal was ignorant of Zeb's crimes—and she couldn't be sure of that—he would still feel some duty to protect him. Zeb was his sister's husband, after all. Why was she feeling this burning attraction to him? It made no sense.

A few seconds later, Fletcher withdrew his hand from her shoulder and stepped back. Jo felt a chill of disappointment move through her.

"I should be on my way," he said in a low and husky voice that slid over her like velvet. "I'll just get my hat."

The door squeaked open and Jo looked up at the starry sky, so impossibly distant. She heard Fletcher thanking Matilda, then the door squeaked again and he stepped onto the porch. The evening crickets chirped a steady rhythm and she clung to such normal things, to distract herself from her unexpected desires.

He stood behind her for a moment, and she realized he had not asked her any more questions about the shooting. Had she managed to convince him she'd said everything there was to say? Or had Leo simply distracted him from it?

Or had he felt the same things she had felt? Was he fighting desire?

Jo turned around and faced him.

He donned his hat. "Thank you for supper, ma'am. I'm much obliged. Good night, now."

With that, he breezed by her and walked to the rented buggy. It bounced as he got in, and the horse nickered. Fletcher flicked the reins and turned the buggy around in the yard, gifting Jo with one last look as he passed by the house.

For a long moment, she felt as if she were floating in a lake of erotic bliss. He touched the brim of his hat, staring a little longer than would be considered proper, but Jo stared back all the same, wishing she could trust him to take care of all this for her, to make it all go away.

Confused, she stood on the porch watching the back of the buggy until it disappeared over the moonlit hill. The relief she was expecting from his departure eluded her. All she wanted, strangely enough and in the most unsettling way, was for him to return and touch her again. To whisper softly in her ear so that she could feel his hot, moist breath upon her neck.

Fletcher drove away from the O'Malley ranch, fighting the urge to turn back and take that reclusive widow into his arms and satisfy the rampant flood of desires he'd been trying to fight all night long. He was certain he'd seen something in her eyes that suggested she didn't want him to go, that she was aroused physically, as he had been. That she wanted him.

He drove over the hill and simply *had* to pull the horse to a halt. His body was on fire with yearning, and after that pleading look in her eye just now, he began to wonder if there wasn't something more going on here—besides an obvious attraction he couldn't be mistaken about. But maybe she'd actually seen the gunman the other night, and that's why he'd shot her. Maybe that's why she was so secretive. She was afraid the gunman might come back to finish her off if he knew she could identify him, and she wanted Fletcher to know.

But it still didn't explain why there had been no bullet hole in her dress, he thought with some irritation. After spending time with her, he was finding it harder and harder to accept the explanation she'd given him, despite the rumors about her.

Come to think of it, he was finding it harder to accept the rumors, too.

Unable to make sense of this, Fletcher sat alone on the dark prairie, squeezing the soft leather reins in his hands. He wanted—needed—to protect her from whatever danger he sensed she might be in.

But how was he to stay on his toes and maintain his professional impartiality when all he wanted to do now was put his hands on her body, taste those sweet lips, and carry her off to his bed? He hadn't wanted a woman with such extreme desire in a very long time, and he certainly didn't want anything like this to happen *now*. It would never work to take a wife. He'd known that when he chose this career path. He shouldn't be having these thoughts.

He took a deep breath and tried to think rationally. If he went back there, it would be personal—that much he knew—and it made him clench his fists in frustration.

But despite it all, he flicked the reins and began to turn the buggy back around toward the ranch, with no idea what he would say or do when he got there.

The fragrant prairie breeze cooled Jo's flushed cheeks as she stood on the porch, watching the dark horizon. All she could think of was the intimate conversation she'd just had with the marshal when she knew he was a man she could not trust—the brother-in-law of her husband's murderer and the man her son had confided in instead of her.

Why then, was she staring after him? Why was her body thrumming with heat and passion for something she had no business wanting? She was a widow. Her husband hadn't been dead long enough for *that*.

She waited a few moments, then sighed heavily and went into the warm, lantern-lit house where all was quiet. Leo was in bed, Matilda was in the kitchen, and the ranch hands had retired to the bunkhouse.

Jo stood in the front hall staring at Edwyn's large tilting portrait. The black-and-white photograph had captured him well—his brown eyes serious, brows in a straight line, mouth covered by a long bushy mustache that made him appear to be frowning, even though he wasn't.

She reached out to straighten the gilt frame, trying to remember the long-ago days when they were first married. Had he ever made her body respond with fluttering, breathless desire as the marshal had tonight when he touched her shoulder and she had felt his breath on the back of her neck?

No, she did not remember anything like that with Edwyn. Ever. He was a kind man. A decent man. That was why she had married him, and they'd had a good life together all these years. But there had never been passion for either of them in their union. Her husband's touch had never inflamed her senses like Fletcher's had tonight. She hadn't even really known such a thing was possible for her.

She stepped back and stared a little longer, feeling guilty for so many things.

Of course, Edwyn must have had his share of guilt, too...

She walked into the parlor and sat on the sofa, letting her fingers roam idly over the deeply buttoned crimson upholstery. She thought about the marshal, and imagined her fingers roaming over the strong lines of his jaw, through the wavy hair at his nape. Though she tried to chase the thought from her mind, she wondered what it would feel like to kiss him. Heaven help her, if he came back in this moment and she found herself looking up at him in the doorway, she would be done for...

Fletcher sat quietly in the buggy in Mrs. O'Malley's front yard, wishing he had not returned to see what he'd seen through her front door—a young widow staring so intently, so longingly at her dead husband's portrait, she'd not noticed the man in her yard.

Perhaps it was best, he told himself as he flicked the reins to head back to town. Maybe that's why fate had urged him to return here just now—so he could see the way things *really* were, and put an end to this attraction before it gained any momentum. Before it turned into something he sure as hell would have to be crazy to want.

Chapter
9

*L*EO BLEW OUT THE LANTERN by his bed and snuggled down under the patchwork quilt. He stared at the ceiling for a few minutes, then out the window where the moon shone brightly onto the hills in the distance. He looked at a star, the brightest one, and watched it flicker.

Listening to the sounds of cattle far away, he closed his eyes and thought of the things Marshal Collins had said to him in the barn. *Your ma loves you very much. She just misses your pa.*

He tried to remember the last time he'd seen his ma laugh, but couldn't. He tried to remember the last time he'd seen her cry, but couldn't. Where had his tender mother gone? Why was she always so angry with him?

Leo wished Marshal Collins were here so he could talk to him some more. Then he thought of his pa, and he clutched the quilt in his fists.

"Pa? If you can hear me, I want you to know that I'm gonna take care of Ma. She's been sad since you left us, but I think part of it's because she's afraid of losing me, too. At least, that's what Marshal Collins said. Marshal Collins is a real nice man. He promised to show me the jailhouse someday."

Leo thought carefully about what to say next. He wanted to get it right.

"I'm gonna take care of things, Pa. I'm gonna see that the men who robbed us get taken to jail, and then Ma will feel better and not worry so much about losing me, too. Maybe she'll start smiling again."

Leo turned onto his side and looked at the star out the window. It flickered brightly in the sky, and he watched it shine until he couldn't keep his eyes open any longer.

Today was a day for new beginnings, Jo thought, feeling more optimistic than she had in a long time. Heading into town, she sat beside Leo on the squeaky, bouncy wagon seat, heeding some of the marshal's advice by letting her son drive.

She'd also told him he could run the errands for her in town—all by himself—which gave him a reason to eat breakfast in a hurry instead of fiddling with it endlessly just to prove a point. This way, Jo could accomplish two tasks at the same time: patching up some of the lost love between her and her son, and sneaking her bag out from under the privy floor.

Of course, there was a third very important task. "Tell me, Leo, what did you and the marshal talk about in the barn last night?"

Elbows to knees, Leo held the reins loosely. "Some talk between men is private."

Jo pulled her shawl tighter around her shoulders, realizing her optimism was a bit premature. "I didn't mean to pry."

He hesitated a moment, as if considering whether or not to continue the conversation. Jo waited, determined to prove she could give him the space he desired. After a few more minutes, Leo leaned back and said, "Fletcher told me you were just worried about me, and that you miss Pa. He said you were lonely for companionship, having to run the ranch all on your own."

"Lonely for companionship?" she blurted out, then wondered why it should matter what the marshal thought about her. "Of course, I'm lonely for your pa," Jo said, trying to sound casual, "but I have everything I need in you."

His eyes beamed briefly. "Did you know the marshal has sent more than sixty men to prison? Some of them were horse thieves. He's a real good tracker. He chased some of them for weeks."

"Leo, we have to put what happened to your pa behind us," Jo said, "otherwise it will eat away at us forever. The men who robbed us are long gone and the trail is cold. We did what we could."

He shook his head and spoke softly. "No, we didn't."

Her heart throbbed at his words. She knew Leo felt powerless and understood his frustration, but she just couldn't let him act on it. Not while it was still so dangerous. "Yes, we did. You know I spoke to the sheriff about it. I told him everything and he looked into it. There was nothing that could be done to catch those men."

"But maybe Marshal Collins can help us."

"No, Leo."

"Did you ask him?"

"Of course not."

"Well, I did." Leo shifted in his seat, as if he knew how angry Jo would be, and was preparing himself.

She stiffened and strove to control her voice. "What did you tell him?"

"I told him what those horse thieves did and that the sheriff couldn't find them. Fletcher said *he* wouldn't have stopped hunting them until they were brought to justice."

Jo swallowed hard. "Is that all?"

Leo cleared his throat nervously. "I asked him to see what he could do."

"You what?"

"Why won't you let me do anything?" he asked pleadingly. "I want things to be right again!"

It was bitterly ironic that Leo had no idea how much she wanted that, too, and how far she was willing to go to get it. If only she could explain it to him. But if he knew what she knew, he would not survive the day.

"You're all I have left, Leo, and I don't want you getting mixed up in that sort of thing."

"But Fletcher said he'd do all the work. He's going to look into it for us. You don't have to worry."

"There will be no looking into it, do you understand?"

God, oh, God! Did Fletcher even *know* his brother-in-law was a killer? Was he here to protect Zeb, or was he about to start sticking his nose into places in didn't belong, and would he wind up dead, too? She honestly had no idea what sort of man he was. Could he be trusted? Or was he as smooth and seductive as silk, just trying to learn what she and Leo knew about Zeb?

Leo flicked the reins and said nothing more.

Stunned to speechlessness, Jo stared straight ahead. As desperately as she'd wanted to mend the broken feelings between her and her son, what he was asking of her was the very thing she could not give him. Trusting Marshal Collins to investigate Edwyn's murder was too great a risk. What if he was with Zeb right now, telling him that a young rancher boy was dead set on finding the man who had killed his pa?

Jo needed to stop Zeb on her own, without anyone's help, particularly the marshal's. Her son was growing more and more determined every day, and the new marshal with his shiny revolver was giving Leo false hopes he'd do better without. On top of that, she'd actually thought about *kissing* the man. She'd lain awake half the night imagining exactly what it would feel like.

Very well, then. Her choice was clear. The best thing for everyone now was for her to stay as far away from Dodge City's handsome new lawman as possible.

After finally retrieving her gunman's disguise from the privy, Jo returned to the wagon and hid her bag under a worsted blanket in the back. She stood for a while under the hot sun, fighting to recover from the day's activities because she was still weak and sore from the bullet wound.

Oh, where was Leo? She wanted to get home and crawl into bed.

When she heard people cheering at the other end of Front Street, she turned to look and saw a crowd gathering near the water tower.

Jo picked up her skirts and walked curiously along the boardwalk past the saloon and mercantile, her boot heels clicking a steady rhythm over the uneven planks until she reached the far end of town where the smell of burnt pastry wafted out of the bakery.

Jo stood on the boardwalk shading her eyes, squinting up at the raised platform, and when she saw the speaker, her heart began to race.

There, in a black suit and top hat, his dark mustache waxed into curls, his deep eyes gleaming with the charisma that had gotten him everything his black heart had ever wanted, stood Zeb Stone.

What was this? He was announcing his candidacy for mayor?

His eyes lowered and he spotted Jo in the crowd. For the briefest of seconds their gazes met, and she saw the sparkle of recognition, the hint of a smile. Her stomach clenched with white-hot rage.

The crowd erupted in applause and Jo looked around without the slightest idea what he had said to gain such approval. She hadn't been able to hear anything above the thundering rush of blood through her veins.

Then she remembered Leo and tried to spot him. He was probably watching from up front. A sea of colorful feathered hats and Stetsons blocked her view, so she stepped onto the street and circled around the audience, going by the tall water tower, still searching. Then, one word from Zeb caught her attention. *Family.*

She stood off to the side, watching.

Zeb's voice gentled. "I want to introduce my beautiful wife, Elizabeth, whose support has been, and will continue to be, my greatest bounty."

"Isn't she lovely?" the woman next to Jo said, her gloved hands muting the sound of her clapping.

A warning voice whispered in Jo's head telling her not to look, but she couldn't help herself. A suffocating sensation squeezed around her chest.

Elizabeth Stone was lovely, without question, but that was not what nearly knocked Jo over onto her backside. The young woman with the dark features possessed an uncanny resemblance to her brother.

Elizabeth smiled down at the citizens of Dodge, making shy eye contact with them. It was not surprising that Zeb had chosen her for his wife. She was any politically ambitious man's dream.

Zeb bowed before her and kissed her white-gloved hand, a well-thought-out spectacle that made the crowd cheer and whistle. Elizabeth blushed sweetly.

"And I must also introduce," Zeb went on, "a man I am confident will bring pride and dignity and restraint to our growing city. My brother-in-law, Marshal Fletcher Collins."

The audience held back their applause, murmuring with gossip about the shooting and the way their marshal had collapsed decorously before the gunman. A flicker of anger passed across Zeb's face. Jo rose up on her toes to see Fletcher.

He climbed the platform steps, appearing relaxed and confident despite the crowd's quiet chatter. Jo felt the tension for him, as if it were she who was up there facing the difficult crowd. He didn't speak, only touched the brim of his hat. He and Elizabeth said something to each other with reassuring smiles.

"And I wish to take this opportunity to clear up some misconceptions about our new marshal," Zeb said. A hush fell over the crowd. "Whatever was reported in the newspaper about Tuesday night's shooting was grossly inaccurate. I witnessed the event, and allow me to assure you, the marshal did not flinch or cower. He walked into my store with his weapon drawn, ready to fire, and that gunman had agreed to surrender. He was, in fact, shaking in his boots!"

A hum of approving laughter filtered through the crowd. "Marshal Collins was wounded in the line of duty because that outlaw was so terrified, he shot his pistol off by mistake!"

People began whispering to each other. Some laughed, and Fletcher shifted his weight, clearly uncomfortable being the focus of so much attention.

Zeb added, "But what this city needs to know, is that I did not bring this man here because he is my brother-in-law. I brought him here because we need someone to clean up our town's distasteful element. I have brought to you, good people of Dodge—The Bruiser!"

The roar of merriment nearly shook down the water tower. Jo was bumped on either side by men unable to control their excitement. Hats were being tossed into the air.

She looked up at the platform where Zeb was shaking Fletcher's hand. Smiling, they patted each other on the back like true blood brothers, hearing the cheer below them and feeling their power grow.

Searching for Leo, Jo circled the crowd and spotted him up front, clapping his hands over his head, leaping up and down.

"Leo!" she called, sidling along the platform. She reached him and grabbed his hand with her weak arm. Gritting her teeth against the pain, she pulled him through the crowd, out into the open.

"Ma! What are you doing? Didn't you hear? Marshal Collins is The Bruiser!"

"Let's go, Leo." She started off toward their wagon down the street, but Leo didn't follow.

"Don't you want to hear the rest of the speech?"

She turned back, her temper rising and overflowing. She'd never been so furious with Leo. He'd never given her reason to be. "Leo, you have disobeyed me enough. Come with me now."

"But Ma!"

Just then, Zeb raised his hands to quiet the crowd. "As president of the city council, I can report that the election for mayor will be held one week from today. The election for county sheriff will be held as usual in November, and I believe..." He paused, then his voice took on a humorous tone. "I believe, judging by the enthusiasm I hear today, that we may have a suitable candidate in our very presence!" He gestured toward Fletcher, and Jo shook her head in disbelief.

"I must thank you all for your support, and I'll see you on election day!" The crowd applauded and cheered.

"All right, Leo, it's over. Come with me now."

"But Ma! If Mr. Stone's going to be mayor and Marshal Collins is going to be county sheriff, maybe they can help us find the men who killed Pa!"

Before Jo could stop him, Leo turned and ran into the crowd toward Zeb.

BREATHING HARD, JO FOLLOWED LEO into the crowd. She pushed her way to the center of the shifting mass, but others were eager to brush elbows with the future mayor. Ambitious businessmen butted ahead of her, bumped her in the shoulder, which caused her no shortage of pain, knocked her off balance and into other equally aggressive money-grubbers.

"Leo!" she called out, but the noisy mob smothered her voice.

Forcing her way forward, she found herself stuck somewhere in the middle of the hubbub, not sure which way to go. She grunted and pushed at someone, then felt a hand squeeze her arm and pull her back.

"Are you looking for Leo?" the familiar voice asked as they emerged from the mob. Jo whipped around to face Marshal Collins.

"Yes. Have you seen him?"

Fletcher lifted his chin. "Over there."

Jo looked up at the platform. Zeb was down on one knee, the tail of his long black coat laid out behind him, while he spoke to Leo, who stood in the front row.

A flash memory of the night in the barn filled Jo with panic. She saw the unmistakable eyes that peered out from holes in a black hood while she'd watched everything from a shadowy stall, knowing she would die if she showed herself.

Jo knew she must show herself now and retrieve Leo if she was to make a difference this time. She squared her shoulders and stepped forward, but Fletcher stopped her.

"Wait, I'll take you. There are a lot of men wanting to be first." He donned his hat and guided her toward the platform steps, his hand on the small of her back.

Oddly enough, and despite the camaraderie she'd just seen between him and Zeb, she was glad he was here to escort her to the front. His touch and his presence made her feel less alone, less powerless as she made her way to face Zeb.

She picked up her skirts and climbed the steps, until she stood behind him, looking down at his clean black coat stretched tight across his back, hearing his laughter as he spoke to her son.

"Zeb, there's someone here to see you," Fletcher said. Jo put on her most captivating smile.

Zeb tousled Leo's hair and idly rose to his feet. He turned to face Jo. "Why, Mrs. O'Malley, it is a sincere pleasure, indeed, to see you again. It has been too long."

Jo answered in a light tone that masked what she truly felt—nauseous from being so near to him. She held out her hand and he shook it. "Congratulations on your campaign for mayor."

He focused his steely gaze upon her. "I understand you were wounded the other night. How are you faring?"

His question caught her off guard, and she had to remind herself of the role she must play. "I'm much better, thank you."

Zeb rested his hand on Fletcher's shoulder. "I have every confidence that this man's presence will discourage such crimes in the future. It's why I brought him here in the first place."

Fletcher responded in good humor. "I thought it was because my sister missed me."

Elizabeth approached from behind. "Oh, but it was, dear brother. You have no idea how I hounded my husband about it. He had no choice but to finally give in."

Fletcher walked to the edge of the platform. "Leo, come and meet my sister." The boy ran around to the stairs while Fletcher began the introductions. "Mrs. O'Malley, this is my sister, Elizabeth Stone."

Too much was happening at once. Jo had not wanted any of this. She had only wanted to get her bag out of the privy floor and return home again. How had she ended up here, shaking hands with the woman she had tried to make a widow? "It's a pleasure, Mrs. Stone."

"No, it's *my* pleasure, Mrs. O'Malley. My brother

spoke to me about you, and I can assure you he plans to do everything in his power to apprehend the man who shot you. I was beside myself thinking of it. You, my brother and my husband, all nearly killed in one shootout."

Jo found it increasingly difficult to look into this woman's kind eyes. She seemed so different from Zeb. How had she ended up as his wife? She could not possibly know the truth.

Fletcher affectionately rested his hand on Leo's shoulder and introduced him to Elizabeth. They shook hands, then Elizabeth turned to Jo.

"Will you come for tea sometime? I'm starting an embroidery club on Tuesday evenings if you would like to join us. Tonight we're meeting at the Presbyterian church on Central Avenue at seven o'clock."

Scrambling for a polite reply, Jo smiled. "I shouldn't commit myself. Things are busy on the ranch this time of year and so much has fallen upon my shoulders...." An awkward silence ensued until Leo offered a needless explanation. "My pa died last winter."

Elizabeth nodded serenely. "I'm very sorry about that. Unfortunately, I know what it's like to lose someone you love." She directed her gaze at Jo, who felt shaken. "Will you at least stop by for tea when you are in town next?"

After a long pause, Jo gave in. "Of course." She felt Zeb's inquisitive stare.

Elizabeth kissed her brother on the cheek. "We'll see you at supper, Fletcher? We missed you last night." Smiling, she headed for the stairs. "I must go and speak to Mrs. Jennings about this evening. Excuse me.

It was a pleasure meeting you both." She descended from the platform and met an older woman at the bottom. Jo watched them converse, envious of such a simple existence where the greatest concern was in acquiring the proper color thread.

She glanced back at Leo. "We must be getting home. There's work to do." She turned to go, hoping the departure would not be difficult.

"But wait," Leo called after her. She halted, closing her eyes with sinking hopes. "I need to talk to Mr. Stone."

Jo wheeled around, and felt the impatient crowd listening and staring, waiting for her response. "I'm sure he's very busy, Leo. Perhaps another time."

She stood tall and silent, willing Leo with her eyes to follow, but knowing she would have to remain and control the damage to come.

"What is it, son?" Zeb asked, resting his hand on Leo's shoulder. The intimate gesture made Jo's skin prickle.

Leo looked up at him hopefully. "The men who killed my father were never caught. Now that you're going to be mayor, I thought you might be able to do something about it."

Revealing nothing, he replied, "Such as?"

"You could spread word around. Marshal Collins said he'd help, and if he becomes sheriff, then—" Zeb's eyes darted suspiciously at his brother-in-law. Jo saw the subtle annoyance and knew she had to interrupt. "Leo, you have to let it go. Those men left no trail."

Zeb's left eyebrow rose a fraction while he peered

down at her curiously. "How do you know there were more than one?"

Jo tried not to let her anxiety show. "I don't. I was only guessing."

Zeb continued to stare at her, saying nothing, and Jo made the mistake of trying to fill the unbearable silence with an explanation. "There must have been more than one because of the tracks I saw."

"But as I recall, you told the marshal you saw *no* tracks. You said they'd been covered by snowfall." He frowned down at her and she knew, somehow, that he saw the truth in her eyes. "Perhaps you saw more than you lead people to believe."

Jo tried to backtrack. "They were very clever to have gotten away without being seen."

"How clever do you have to be to hang someone?" Leo asked.

The retort shocked everyone into silence.

Fletcher knelt down. "If it means that much to you, Leo, why don't we go on over to the jailhouse now. If it's okay with your ma, we could look up the report. I'll tell you what was done about your father's death."

Zeb's jaw clenched visibly, but he said nothing.

Jo couldn't believe what she was hearing or seeing. There were no reassuring looks between Fletcher and Zeb, no winks or nudges. Only Zeb's uneasiness and the marshal's sincere interest in seeing the report.

Whatever suspicions Jo had held about Fletcher Collins dissolved right there. She was certain that, for all he knew, her husband *had* been murdered by horse thieves.

Not that any of that mattered. Zeb knew the truth

now. That was obvious. And she feared she was in grave danger.

Fletcher rose to his feet. "Is that all right with you, Mrs. O'Malley?"

Jo knew the answer had to be yes, but she felt suddenly ill-equipped to see what was written about Edwyn's death. She barely remembered the things she had said to the old marshal about it. She had been in such a state of shock, shaking and winded after the midnight ride through the snow all alone. So much of that night was a blur to her now.

"Mrs. O'Malley? Would it be all right?" Fletcher's voice startled her, and she realized suddenly that she had been staring blankly at him. His eyes were intense with concern for her, and she found she wanted to leave with him now. It didn't matter where they went, she just wanted him to take her away from the crowd.

She cleared her throat, feeling Zeb studying her. "That would be fine. I'll come along, of course."

"Zeb, I'll see you later," Fletcher said.

They descended the steps. Jo couldn't resist the temptation to take one last look back at Zeb. He stood watching, his eyes shaded by the dark brim of his hat. He glared with brows drawn together, eyes so dark it sent chills skittering across her skin.

She was glad she and Leo were with the marshal.

As Fletcher followed Leo and Mrs. O'Malley around the back of the two-story city clerk's office, he noticed that she checked over her shoulder every few seconds. She seemed nervous. He wondered if it was because her husband's killers had never been caught.

Maybe by checking into it, he would find something that would change that, and help her move on with her life.

He was not completely comfortable with how much he wanted her to move on—to be free from the tragedy that seemed to haunt her so intensely—because it wasn't out of the goodness of his own heart.

What he *really* wanted was for her to look at him and see more than just his badge. He wanted her to see him as a man—a man who desired her—and he wanted her to remember what her *own* desire could feel like, if she surrendered to it.

They climbed the back stairs on the outside of the building to the second floor that served as city offices and police court. Fletcher removed his hat and fought to struggle free of the sticky web of attraction he was caught up in. He had to focus on his job instead of wishing his potential witness was wanting him to take her into his arms and start unbuttoning her blouse.

Later, of course. After dark. When her son wasn't around....

He hung his hat on a hook by the door, and raked his fingers through his hair to distract himself from the heat in his blood. He went around the back of the largest desk and unlocked the top drawer to retrieve a second set of keys that jingled between his fingers.

All the while, Mrs. O'Malley stood quietly by the door—seemingly unaware of how much her presence affected him—while Leo walked around the room, looking at the "Wanted" posters on the walls.

"Is it true what Zeb said?" Mrs. O'Malley asked curiously. "That you plan to run for sheriff?"

Half laughing, Fletcher replied, "No. I reckon Zeb was just trying to make up for what happened the other night, to give folks something new to talk about." He set down the report he was looking at and added, "I'm not the political type, nor am I interested in anything that permanent."

"But it's a very prestigious position."

"Doesn't matter much to me. I don't plan on stayin' in Dodge forever. I'm only going to hang around long enough to establish some law around here and clean up the town's reputation. Make sure Elizabeth's okay."

"Why wouldn't she be? She's married to the future mayor." Mrs. O'Malley stared into Fletcher's eyes with a scrutiny he didn't quite understand but wished he did.

She seemed to be searching for something, waiting for him to say something....

Then she grew uncomfortable for some reason and turned away, joining Leo, who was still reading the posters.

Fletcher took a moment to clear his desk, then changed the subject. "I know this can't be easy for either of you—" he crossed the room to a tall cabinet and unlocked it "—but I'll need to know the exact date your husband was killed, Mrs. O'Malley."

"It was the night of February 26," she replied, facing him. She clutched her small reticule in both hands in front of her. "Twenty minutes past ten." Fletcher hesitated at her exactness, and felt his mood grow suddenly somber as he reached for the police court dockets. He flipped through the papers, but didn't find what he was searching for. "February 26 of *this* year?"

"Yes," Jo answered.

He closed the drawer and opened another. "The report must have been misfiled. Has anyone looked at it recently?"

Leo eyed his mother, questioningly.

"Not that I know of." She didn't seem all that surprised by this.

Fletcher closed the last drawer and walked to his desk. He searched for the report there but found nothing. "You're sure that was the day?"

Mrs. O'Malley tilted her head at him.

"Of course it was. Forgive me."

Leo's voice filled with panic. "You mean you can't find it? The evidence is gone?"

"There was no evidence, Leo, that's the point," Jo said. "There was only the information I gave to the marshal that night about what I saw."

Fletcher sat down. "Was that Marshal Samson?"

"Yes. He was only here a few months, and left town shortly after Edwyn died."

"I know. This city seems to have trouble holding onto their lawmen. Care to tell the story again, Mrs. O'Malley? Leo gave me the rundown, but you were the one who found your husband." Fletcher gestured to the chair on the opposite side of his desk, knowing this wouldn't be easy for her.

Hesitantly, Jo sat. "Thank you, Marshal."

"Call me Fletcher."

She gave him a look, then cleared her throat and began, but her tone was surprisingly dry and emotionless. Fletcher wasn't sure what to make of it.

"Edwyn was in the barn late that night because one of the horses was delivering a foal. I had been reading in the parlor when I heard hoofbeats and went to the window to look. It was very dark and I didn't see anyone, but for some reason I felt concern—call it a woman's instinct—and decided to go out to check on Edwyn. I put on my overcoat and went to the barn. My husband was dead when I got there. They'd hanged him."

Fletcher leaned straight back in the chair. "I'm very sorry, Mrs. O'Malley. I wish I had been here then. Maybe I could have—"

He stopped himself. *Could have what? Held her? Comforted her?*

Mrs. O'Malley only nodded.

"And they took horses?" he asked, trying to focus on the crime and not easing the heart of the beautiful, grieving widow across from him.

"Yes, they took two, I discovered. I ran back into the house to wake Matilda, then I saddled a horse and rode straight here without thinking."

Leo interrupted. "Ma told me the next morning." Fletcher nodded compassionately. "And what was done about it, Mrs. O'Malley?"

"A posse went after them at dawn, but a heavy snowfall covered the trail. The posse came back two days later with nothing. The horses were never recovered or seen again. No one even had any idea which direction the gang had gone."

"Do you feel confident that everything that could have been done for you was done?"

Mrs. O'Malley considered the question for a long time, then answered, *"With the information I provided that night about the events? Yes."*

He studied her a moment, and knew she was holding something back. But then again, he *always* seemed to feel that way around her. Always wanted her to give him something more.

"Did the marshal examine the barn for evidence?" he asked.

"Yes, but he didn't find anything."

Fletcher stared intently at her. Where was the desperation? The desire for justice he had expected to see in her eyes? He saw it only in Leo's.

Fletcher couldn't help probing a little further. "And there's nothing else you can tell me? Nothing for me to look into?"

Mrs. O'Malley seemed frozen in her chair, the question hanging between them on a thread. *What was she hiding?*

Leo touched her shoulder again. "Are you all right, Ma?"

She covered his hand with hers. "I'm fine, but we've done all we can do today. We should be going."

Abruptly she stood and held out her gloved hand. Fletcher shook it, and noted the direct and purposeful way she looked at him. He was aware of everything about her—the moisture on her lips, the pace of her breathing, the clear dewy softness of her complexion and the reflection of sunlight in the pupils of her eyes.

Feeling downright aroused by her touch, Fletcher said goodbye to Mrs. O'Malley and Leo. Then he stood at the second-floor window, watching them cross Front Street. Mrs. O'Malley kept checking over her shoulder. She tried to hold Leo's arm a few times, and each time, the boy pulled away from the protective gesture, like any boy his age would do.

When they disappeared into Wright's store, Fletcher leaned his shoulder against the window frame.

Why in hell was he so drawn to this woman who obviously didn't want anyone to get close to her? And was he only interested in this case because he couldn't stop thinking about how she smelled so fresh, like sweet orange water, and how he wanted to touch her curvy, soft body, slide his hands around her waist, press his lips into the crook of her neck? Hear her sigh with pleasure? See her with her hair down and tousled, smiling up at him? Her shoulders bare?

Stop it, Fletcher, he thought, turning away from the window and taking a deep breath to wrestle his urges under control.

Think about the case...the case.

Yeah, that's better.

Something about it was, in fact, niggling at him. The fact that Mrs. O'Malley hadn't seen much of anything didn't bother him so much as the look she had given him just now when he asked if the marshal had done everything he could at the time to catch the thieves. It was almost a challenge. A plea for him to see the truth in her eyes, to hear more than what she was actually saying.

With the information I provided that night about the events...

Was there something else she hadn't told anyone? Maybe something she later remembered? And why were the misfiled papers bothering him so much? Was it the fact that Mrs. O'Malley hadn't seemed surprised they were missing?

Fletcher went to the cabinet to lock it, then dropped the key into his desk drawer and locked it, too. He shouldn't be thinking about a six-month-old murder case when everybody in town was expecting the speedy capture of the notorious Six-Shooter Hank. But he couldn't help it. He couldn't keep his mind off *anything* that had to do with Mrs. O'Malley.

Ironically, she was the only potential lead he had to Six-Shooter Hank at the moment anyway—a good excuse to go out to her ranch again tonight.

Well, so be it. Perhaps some unexpected tidbit of information might fall into his lap. With any luck, it would be Mrs. O'Malley herself.

Chapter
11

$\mathcal{S}$HORTLY AFTER DINNER, ZEB WALKED out of the
house to find himself a poker game and some
good whisky. He climbed into his shiny black carriage,
which was waiting for him just outside the door, and
cracked the whip to get the animals moving.

As the horses' hooves clattered down his stone
driveway, he thought about the best way to eliminate
both the widow O'Malley and her meddlesome son
without creating any suspicious gossip. He wondered
with amused curiosity how she'd managed to keep
herself hidden that night in her barn, what she'd seen
exactly, and how the blazes she had been so dim-wit-
ted to let it slip this afternoon. More proof that you
couldn't trust a woman to control a tongue that was,
by nature, created to flap.

Zeb supposed it didn't matter what she'd seen or
if she had any proof of it. He simply couldn't afford

gossip with the election coming up. He would have to discuss a solution with MacGregor, his hired man, pay him a little extra to see that the "solution" was carried out properly.

How many ways were there, exactly, to kill a man? Jo wondered uneasily. She felt sick about the things she was thinking. Over the past five hours, she had considered poison, strangulation and a house fire. She'd even fantasized about a public stoning, but nothing seemed as quick and reliable as her Colt .45.

She only wished it didn't have to be so violent. The last time she'd attempted this, she'd discovered she was not the killer she thought she was. Oh, yes, she'd spent countless nights imagining pulling the trigger, but when it came down to it, she couldn't do it.

Now, standing in front of her bedroom mirror and staring at the fugitive known only as Six-Shooter Hank, she told herself she would not think of her morals. After what happened with Zeb today, her life depended on it.

At least she had managed to convince Leo and Matilda to get on the evening train out of Dodge City. It hadn't been easy, but she had told Leo that Matilda needed some time away from the ranch, that she was in need of rest, and Leo had believed the story and was eager to take care of Matilda in her time of need. Jo only hoped Leo didn't tell Matilda that.

Reaching for Edwyn's brown hat, Jo pulled it down snugly over her knotted hair and tied the red bandanna around the back of her neck. Edwyn's old trousers and shirt were a perfect disguise, and the long slicker she'd

worn the other night conveniently covered her feminine curves. She was unrecognizable.

The only things missing were her holster and guns.

She turned around. There they lay on her bed—the
place Leo was conceived. A disturbing thought at this
moment.

Jo fought against the sickening lump forming in her
stomach as she picked up her weapons. She buckled
the brown leather belt around her hips. Slowly she
withdrew one pistol and squeezed the smooth walnut
handle. She sat on the edge of the bed and clicked
open the cylinder to check it one more time.

Five bullets. She clicked the cylinder closed and
thumbed back the hammer. The cylinder rotated; the
trigger was set and in working order. She reset the
hammer to rest on an empty chamber again and slid
the gun back into the brown leather casing.

After repeating the inspection with the second
weapon, Jo stood by the bed and took one last look in
the mirror. Six-Shooter Hank gazed back at her from
beneath the wide brim of his hat. He was turning
out to be a useful character. When Zeb's body was
discovered, everyone and their dog would be searching for the elusive gunman, and Jo would be sitting
assuredly back at home in her tight corset and blue
gingham day dress. She only hoped she would be able
to live with herself.

She inhaled a deep breath and walked out of the
room. Dressed like a man, it felt natural to walk like
one, to stomp down the stairs instead of float down,
to grip and squeeze the railing instead of skimming
her delicate gloved fingers over it. Down the stairs

she went, full of purpose and conviction, and determined—this time—to crush her conscience if it threatened to intervene.

She straightened Edwyn's portrait in the front hall and glanced at the clock on the mantel in the parlor. Seven-thirty. Time to go. She'd worked out every detail of her plan right down to the minute, sending all the ranch hands on errands to each of the cow camps, so that no one would see her leave the house.

Swaying back and forth in the creaky leather saddle and listening to the ghostly sounds of cows lowing in the distance, Fletcher walked his horse up the last gentle rise on the way to the O'Malley ranch. Phoebes and mockers made short sweeps across the fields, skimming the ground and chirping into the dusk. The sun had dipped behind a field dotted with cattle, and the long shadows of twilight were fast disappearing.

When he reached the crest of the hill, he gently pulled on the reins. The horse paused, snorting, then lowered his head to munch on some buffalo grass at the roadside.

Fletcher crossed his wrists over the saddle horn and sighed. He could see the ranch now, tucked cozily in the small valley. There was a puzzle-like pattern to the corral fences, and the windmill was spinning sleepily, silhouetted against the darkening sky. The buildings seemed so grand in the middle of this vast, empty prairie.

Was this the right thing to do? he wondered uneasily. Ride down there and pretend to ask more questions about the shooting, when he knew darn well it was just an excuse to see Mrs. O'Malley again—and explore what might occur if they were in the same room together again. *Alone.* Because he darn well couldn't get her out of his head.

As if coming here would help. It would likely only make things worse.

He sat there another moment, considering it, then leaned back in the saddle and considered it some more. But instead of a clearheaded deliberation about his duties as a lawman, he imagined her standing on her covered porch, smiling knowingly at him as he rode up, fully aware of why he had come...

Feeling a fervor in his blood that he couldn't contain any longer, Fletcher tapped his heels against Prince and started off down the hill, because Mrs. O'Malley—just the idea of her—was pulling him like a magnet.

At the bottom of the hill however, he caught sight of a man walking boldly out of the widow's house and mounting an awaiting horse.

His stomach dropped. Was this Mrs. O'Malley's secret lover? The man she had told him about the night she was shot?

For a moment, his heart sank with disappointment, until a closer look at the man made him sit up straighter in the saddle. He reached for the rifle from his saddle scabbard.

This man was no lover. He was Six-Shooter Hank.

With significant effort, on account of her wounded shoulder, Jo pinned her foot into the stirrup and mounted her horse, Mogie. At least everything was easier without her corset to restrict her movements. She reached for the reins, kicked her heels into Mogie's firm belly and—with a plan to cut across the fields rather than risk meeting someone on the road— Jo steered him toward the north pasture.

About ten minutes later, as she rode Mogie along a fence, a gunshot shattered the silence. The noise spooked Mogie, who reared up and forced Jo to grab on to the horn for dear life, the muscles in her legs tightening around the frightened animal. Her wounded shoulder throbbed painfully with the sudden strain. Mogie skittered sideways, then bolted across the field.

Another shot rang out. Jo turned quickly to see where the gunfire was coming from, and a mere glance from the corner of her eye told her. She recognized that familiar slicker sailing on the wind and the black hat pressed forward on the man's head. It was Fletcher.

Shock choked her as she shifted in the saddle, joining Mogie in his flight of terror. She kicked in her heels. "*Yah! Yah!*"

Hooves thundered behind her, then Fletcher shouted, "Stop! You're under arrest!"

What was he doing here?

They raced across the open fields, the sharp wind stinging Jo's cheeks and threatening to sweep her hat off her head. There was nowhere to go, nowhere to hide, and Mogie was breathing hard. He wouldn't last much longer. She was surely done for.

Fletcher was gaining. The drumming hooves grew louder, pounding in Jo's ears. Was there no way out of this?

He fired the rifle again. Was he shooting at *her*? She hadn't thought he'd ever killed a man. Would she be his first?

Heart racing with desperation, she knew there was no escape. Mogie wouldn't make it and she had to do something. Her life and Leo's safety depended on it. With a muttered oath and hands that shook uncontrollably inside her loose gloves, she pulled her bandanna up over her face and drew her weapon.

Racing across the darkening fields after searching Mrs. O'Malley's house and finding no one there—which had come as a relief, because he was worried what Hank might have done to her—Fletcher cursed the outlaw trying to outrun him. What was he doing at the O'Malley ranch and where was Josephine? If that gunman so much as plucked one hair from her head, Fletcher swore he would track him to the ends of the earth.

Fletcher kicked in his heels, but Prince was winded. Damn, he couldn't lose now.

The outlaw drew his gun, turned in the saddle and took aim. Fletcher steered Prince in an arc, attempting to become a faster-moving target, but it gave the gunman the advantage of speed. The distance between them grew, and Fletcher knew the time for firing warning shots was over. If the rider wanted a gunfight, he was going to get one.

Fletcher reined Prince to a skidding halt, raised his Winchester, shut one eye to take aim, but hesitated. The gunman had lowered his weapon.

Confused, Fletcher watched the rider grow more distant. Hell, if he was going to stop Hank from getting away, he'd have to do it with a bullet and do it fast. He shut one eye, focusing...*don't miss, don't miss.*

But the rider disappeared suddenly, out of Fletcher's sights. The fool had fallen off his horse!

"*Yah!*" Fletcher yelled, dropping his rifle back into his scabbard and breaking into a gallop. The outlaw's horse was idly trotting away and the man lay motionless on the ground. Fletcher had seen men take spills at that speed before, and most of them didn't come out of it too happily, if at all. He trotted up to the gunman's lifeless form and dismounted.

Slowly, cautiously, he approached. The man was sprawled on his back, the red bandanna covering his face, the hat pressed down over his eyes. Fletcher was finally going to get a look at the man who'd destroyed his reputation on his first night in Dodge. He couldn't wait to drag Six-Shooter Hank to the jailhouse and lock him up where he belonged.

"Hold it!" the outlaw yelled, sitting up and whipping a pistol out from under his coat, pointing it straight between Fletcher's eyes.

In a flash of movement, Fletcher drew his Peacemaker and took aim. "Here we are again."

The kid—*he was just a kid, damn it*—didn't reply. He slowly rose to his feet, never taking his aim off Fletcher. They stood under the moonlight, a few feet apart.

Fletcher's hand was steady. Hank's hand trembled.

"I didn't appreciate that leg wound," Fletcher said. "It still smarts."

The gunman nodded.

"Before this gets ugly, I'd like to know what you were doing at the O'Malley ranch," Fletcher asked.

The kid's voice was strained, as if he were trying too hard to sound older than he was. "Drop your gun."

"Not a chance." Fletcher rubbed the pad of his index finger over the trigger, ready to fire if he had to, but only if he had to.

"Listen kid, it ain't worth it. You're gonna get caught sooner or later. Better to give yourself up now and save yourself a murder charge."

The kid frantically shook his head.

"It ain't a suggestion. You're coming with me, conscious or not. Take off the scarf."

Without warning, Fletcher's horse stepped sideways and took his attention for one vital moment. The kid came at him, swinging his gun.

Fletcher knew the move all too well and wasn't about to get knocked out cold, not by this kid, of all people. Quick as a shot, he raised his arm in defense and swiped the weapon out of Hank's hand.

Next thing he knew, Hank was coming at him in a tackle. Fletcher maintained his footing against the kid's surprisingly light weight, but felt a second gun at his hip, so he did the only thing that made sense. He hauled back and punched the kid in the nose.

The squeal nearly struck Fletcher senseless.

While the kid staggered back, holding his nose, Fletcher swung a boot and kicked him off his feet, onto his back with a *thump*. Before the kid had a chance to realize he was seeing stars, Fletcher was on top of him, pinning him down and ripping the second gun from the holster.

Fletcher checked the weapon for bullets, then pointed it at Hank's face, right between the eyes. "You gonna cooperate now?"

Hank nodded and Fletcher couldn't wait to get his hands on that scarf. He reached for it, but Hank bit into the fabric and held it in place with his teeth. He was grunting and shaking his head until Fletcher tired of the game and finally yanked with all his might.

The bandanna came loose, Fletcher blinked a few times, then the breath sailed out of his lungs.

Her nose throbbing unbearably, and with her shoulder in no better state, Jo lay on her back, staring up at Fletcher's stunned expression.

"What the hell's going on?" he asked incredulously, swiping her hat off her head.

She'd never been punched in the face before. *God, it hurt!* Adrenaline sped through her veins, causing her to see red. Before she knew what she was doing, she instinctively balled up a fist and walloped Fletcher in the nose. He fell off her, onto his backside, and she was free at last.

Fletcher leaned up on one hand while he cupped his face with the other. Blood seeped between his fingers.

Jo scrambled to her feet. She examined her own hand for blood and found her glove stained crimson. "I'm bleeding."

"So am I." Fletcher gently pinched the bridge of his nose. "Hell, you broke it."

For a moment, they both sat suffering with their own wounds, until Fletcher looked up at her. "Jeez, look what I did. If I'd known it was *you...*" He rose to his feet and tried to take her hand away from her face to assess the damage, but she elbowed him in the ribs.

"Just let me look," he said, clutching his side. "It doesn't look broken, thank God."

At the sight of Fletcher's bloody nose, which now looked a little crooked, Jo's fear and fury began to wane. "I didn't mean to do that to you, either," she said. "But you had me pinned down, and you punched me! I didn't like it."

She touched his face, and he touched hers.

Between the gunshot wound, the fall from the horse, and the sore nose, she felt like she'd been hit by a train.

"Does it hurt very much?" Jo asked, regretting what she'd done.

"Yeah. But I reckon I had it coming."

"You were just doing your job."

"It ain't my job to hit women."

Jo shook her head and stepped back. "Not even if they're trying to shoot you?"

He let out a breath of frustration. "What in tarnation were you *doing?*"

She'd known that question was coming, and she should have been prepared for it, but she still hadn't the foggiest idea how to reply. Jo pinched her nose and tipped her head back. "You wouldn't understand."

"Try me." He tipped his head back, too.

How was she to tell this man that if he hadn't caught her just now, she would be killing his brother-in-law this very night? She could barely believe it herself.

Feeling suddenly cold in the chill of the evening,

she flopped onto the ground and sat on her knees.

Fletcher approached and handed the bandanna to her. "Wipe your nose with this."

Thankful for his caring, she took it and wiped the blood from her face.

Fletcher knelt down before her. "Was it you that night? In Zeb's store?"

She felt tears pool in eyes, which had been dry for many months, and knew exactly the reason why. This man's presence was shining an unwelcome light on what she had nearly become—a cold-blooded killer with a future full of remorse. Sadly she nodded.

"Why?"

"I had a reason. I just can't tell you what it is."

"You're putting me in a difficult position, Josephine."

"I know. Why do you think I tried so hard to outrun you?" The sharp, steely blade of shame stabbed at her, its sting made worse by the fact that it was Fletcher wielding it.

He stared at her for another few seconds, as if contemplating her answer, then rose to his feet. She felt his gaze boring into the top of her head and knew with hopeless dread what was coming.

"Get up, please, Mrs. O'Malley." His voice was cold and exact.

Jo looked up and saw the regret in Fletcher's expression. Heaven help her, she could not bear to think of him despising her so deeply. He was a man who valued integrity and the law above all else, and she respected him for that, more than he could ever know. It was precisely why it killed her inside to have strayed so far from his ideals, ideals that had once been her own.

Her heart sank with shame and a desperate need to explain herself, even though she knew it was hopeless. He wasn't a parent. He would never understand how far she was willing to go—as a mother—to protect her son.

"You're under arrest for the shooting in Zeb's store," he said scathingly. "It was attempted robbery and attempted murder. Of both Zeb Stone...and me."

Chapter

12

*J*O ROSE TO HER FEET to face Fletcher, her skin prickling with horror. "You can't do this. You don't understand."

He wrapped his hand around her upper arm. She began to struggle impossibly against his grip, to pry his iron fingers away, but they wouldn't budge. He dragged her toward his horse, then reached for his handcuffs while she twisted frantically so that her back was to him while she tried to squirm away.

"Please, Josephine," Fletcher said, his voice and body straining. "Don't make this more difficult than it has to be." He held her around the waist to keep her from slipping free.

Bending and struggling in her husband's loose clothing only served to make Jo more aware of Fletcher's hard body, pressed tight up against her backside. "Fletcher, please, listen to me..."

"I can't let you go," he said, his voice husky in her ear.

Jo continued to squirm in his hold. The more she struggled, the tighter he held her—until she let out a sob.

Suddenly his grip loosened and her body relaxed.

Then all at once, he was holding her close in an intimate embrace...with the front of his hard body pressed against the back of hers, his arms locked around her waist, his warm breath beating on the nape of her neck. She shut her eyes, wanting to turn around and face him, to wrap her arms around his big shoulders and beg for his help and forgiveness.

"Jo," he whispered hotly in her ear, sending ripples of gooseflesh down the length of her body.

She turned her cheek to the side, and his lips grazed the side of her mouth.

"Please, Fletcher..." She wasn't sure what she was asking for, because she was terrified and frustrated with him for getting in her way tonight, but at the same time, her heart was racing with desire at the feel of his body so tight and snug up against her.

Reaching around with her good arm, she buried her fingers into the hair at his nape, pulled him closer, and tipped her face up to the sky as he dropped wet kisses onto her tingling neck. It felt so good, so intoxicating, her knees nearly buckled beneath her.

But he wasn't going to take this further. Somehow she knew he would put a stop to it very soon. She could sense it. She felt it in his touch.

Sure enough, he spoke softly in her ear. "I'm sorry, but I have to take you in. It's my job."

She looked up at the starry sky and exhaled heavily as she dropped her arms to her sides. Everything inside her wanted only to surrender to Fletcher and put her fate in his hands—for good or bad, no matter the outcome. But then she thought of Leo and her conversation with Zeb that afternoon. She couldn't let Zeb win. She had to protect her son, and she certainly couldn't do that from behind bars.

Jo broke away from Fletcher's hold. She had to talk to him, to make him understand. Perhaps there was a chance she could trust him...

"It's not what it seems," she carefully said.

He stood motionless, not making a move to handcuff her at least. "I'm listening."

She tried to find the right words to explain, but there was no right way to talk of murder. And what if Fletcher's righteous talk about his father and the importance of upholding the law was all a ruse, and he was secretly in Zeb's pocket and on his payroll? Zeb was married to Fletcher's sister, after all. Surely Fletcher had to know what kind of man he was.

Still, she had to feel him out, because something in her wanted to believe he could be trusted—that he genuinely cared about her and Leo.

She licked her parched, throbbing lips. "I...I wasn't trying to rob Zeb's store the other night. It was more complicated than that."

"Continue."

Jo's ribs were squeezing around her heart. "I was there that night because I believed I had no other choice left to me. I had to protect myself. And Leo."

"You're not making sense."

"I know. Just give me a chance. The problems began long before the night I walked into Zeb's store. I...I lied about what I saw the night Edwyn was murdered."

Fletcher stared at her for a moment, then his eyes softened and he helped her to sit down in the grass, away from the horses. She felt the weight of his anger lift a little and prayed it would continue.

"I knew something was wrong today when you came to the clerk's office," he said. "I could see that you were scared. Please believe that I wanted to help you."

"You knew?"

She worked hard to keep her voice steady as he sat down in the grass beside her. When had anyone seen the fear she had fought so hard to hide, and known she needed help? Matilda hadn't seen it. Leo had seen a change in her, but he'd not understood what horrors were at the root of it.

She took Fletcher's hand, knowing with surprising certainty that it was time to confess the truth to someone. To *him*.

"I didn't find Edwyn murdered, Fletcher. I saw it happen."

He stared into her eyes for a long moment, then he whispered, "I'm so sorry." Then he pulled her close.

She let her forehead rest on his shoulder and recalled the dreadfulness of what had occurred that night. Only then did she realize that by keeping this secret bottled up, she had not let herself express all of her grief for Edwyn. It was a strange comfort to do so now.

"What happened?" Fletcher asked.

"We were *both* in the barn late one night," she explained, "waiting for a mare to deliver. There was some commotion outside, and Edwyn went out to see what was going on. I heard him yelling, and then it was just a lot of angry voices. I backed into a stall, not sure what was happening. Then the barn door swung open and three men wearing hoods walked in dragging Edwyn, who was weak and staggering. They must have beaten him." She began to feel sick as she connected with the memories. She paused a moment, searching for strength. "They tossed a rope over a beam, forced Edwyn onto a chair and into the noose, and without a second's hesitation, the leader kicked the chair out from under him. It happened very quickly and I watched everything."

Fletcher stroked the hair away from her eyes and kissed the top of her head. A cloud floated in front of the moon.

"The men stayed to watch until Edwyn stopped struggling, and I knew if I tried to stop it, I'd be dead too, and I had to stay alive for Leo. That's all I could think of. I couldn't move, I was so terrified. By the time they left, it was too late. I tried to cut Edwyn down and save him, but he was...gone, and I'd done nothing to stop it. *Nothing.* How could I have been such a coward?"

"You were outnumbered, Jo, and you were frightened, thinking of your son." She pressed her face into his coat, and felt a single tear soak into the thick fabric. "Believe me, you did the right thing," he added. "You can't blame yourself."

"But I do, *I do.*"

A deep well of tears—which she had not been able to shed before—overflowed. To her dismay, she realized that where she thought she had been winning a battle against them, she had only been postponing them, while they multiplied, every day, inside her. "I want to be strong, for Leo," she cried. "He's all I have left and I love him so much."

"I can see that," Fletcher said. "And I promise, everything's going to be all right."

"*How* can you promise that?" she asked hopelessly, sniffling and gazing up at him with tearstained cheeks.

"Did you get a look at the men?" he asked.

This was the difficult part—the truth about that night. Would Fletcher even believe her? If he didn't, there was no hope for her life, or for Leo's.

Nevertheless, she had to try. Jo sat back, wiped her eyes and whispered, "Yes."

Fletcher's astonishment showed on his face, and Jo knew he was connecting these events to the ones that had brought them both here. He was remembering the night in the store, when they'd first met and when Jo had shot him in the leg. He stared speechless at her, then he shook his head in disbelief. "Jo, you don't think that Zeb—"

He stopped midsentence and laughed skeptically, but it was void of humor.

"I saw it happen," she firmly said.

"But you said they were wearing hoods. How can you be sure it was him?"

Jo looked down at her hands in her lap. "I know it. I heard his voice, saw the way he moved. It was him."

Fletcher stood up and raked his fingers through his hair. "Zeb Stone is my sister's husband—a respected, prominent citizen of Dodge. You can't make accusations like that without some kind of proof."

"I realize that. That's why I'm not making accusations."

Fletcher turned away, staring across the dark prairie, the fast wind lifting his hair. "You can't do that, Jo. I won't let you. It's not right."

"Not right?" Jo stood up as well and pulled him around to face her. "You dare talk to me about what's right? My husband dangled from a rope and struggled for his life in front of my eyes, and all I could do was watch. Zeb forced me to choose between my husband and my son, and I made that choice, but not without a lot of pain. I've not slept a full night since. I've felt so much hate and anger and guilt...I'll never be the woman I was. Six months ago, I never would have even *considered* taking a man's life, but now, I just can't see any other way to protect my family, even if it destroys me inside. So don't tell me about what's right."

Jo let out a breath. The realization hit hard—that she'd been surrounding her heart with ice just to escape the voice of her conscience, and this was the first time the ice had broken. The truth was out. Finally someone knew what she had suffered and what sinful, shameful impulses now lived in her doomed soul.

Fletcher stared at her. She waited with sickening dread for him to say something, but there were no words. He took a step forward and gathered her into his arms again. She felt breathless and surprised.

"I'm sorry that happened to you, Jo. And I *do* know what it's like."

All she could do was press her cheek into the warmth of his chest. "Your father..."

"Yes, and there was nothing I could do either. Just like you, I was too late."

"That's why I have to do this *now*," she tried to explain.

Fletcher gently pushed her back a step so that he could look at her face. "No, you don't have to do it. Not *that*."

"Zeb is a dangerous man. He'll kill anyone who gets in his way. I've kept my secret all this time, knowing he would never let me live if he knew what I'd seen. But he knows now, Fletcher. Leo and I are in danger."

Panic flickered across his face. "What do you mean?"

"Today, I saw it in his eyes that he knew."

"Saw it in his eyes!" Fletcher waved an arm in frustration. "You can't base decisions on something as subjective as that. What if you're wrong? What if it was someone else who just sounded like Zeb? He's a wealthy man with everything going for him. Why would he kill your husband and steal your horses?"

"I don't know, and there's no way to find out without him getting suspicious. I have no other choice."

"Jo, you're not thinking rationally. You're driven by guilt. You're trying to do now what you couldn't do that night in the barn." His quick, concise and all too certain summary of the matter caught her off guard.

Was he right? she wondered, while she mentally squirmed to understand her emotions.

"Did you ever try to have Zeb investigated?"

Fletcher asked.

"A few tried before, and they ended up dead. I won't let that happen to Leo and me."

"You're saying that you think Zeb has killed others? Jo, I need proof before I can believe something like that."

"I know, I know. Proof. The impossible."

"It's not impossible."

"It is. Zeb's too smart. He knows how to cover his tracks and he has the whole town fooled into thinking he's a man they can trust."

There was no sign of surrender in Fletcher's eyes as he replied. "I can't just accept all this. Even if it's true, it still doesn't excuse you. You tried to kill an innocent man—"

"He's not innocent!"

"He is, in the eyes of the law, and that's how I see things. I'll take your suspicions about Zeb into consideration, but for now, the only person I know for sure is guilty is *you*. I'm sorry about this Jo, but I took an oath as a lawman. You tried to kill a man. I have to take you in."

All the explaining in the world, it seemed, wasn't going to change his mind. He couldn't understand, nor did he want to, and that fact alone made her want to shake him, to force him to see this through her eyes.

"Please come with me willingly." He closed his eyes for a moment. "I don't want to have to hurt you."

She could see that he was struggling with himself, but it didn't ease her frustrations or her sense of dread about what was to come.

The thought to escape and disappear with Leo filled her mind—as it had on many occasions before—but she knew she could not outsmart or outmaneuver Fletcher. He would find them. He would never give up. He had never in his career let any outlaw go free.

Instead, she asked something else of him—the thing that mattered most to her. "Just promise, if anything happens to me, you'll look out for Leo. There's no one else I can ask. At least not in Dodge."

He looked stricken by the request, and after a moment's deliberation, he nodded. Then he took her by the hand and led her toward his horse. She went without a fight, but not without hope. There was still one possibility—one more thing she could say—and it just might be the thing to get through to him.

Chapter

13

*J*O OFFERED HER BARED WRISTS to Fletcher and he
clicked the cuffs around them. "Is that too tight?"

With no effort at all, she slipped them off her tiny
wrists.

"I guess not," he said softly.

For a moment she thought she might be spared the
humiliation of being cuffed, until he reached into his
saddlebag and pulled out a small rope.

"I guess this'll have to do." He wrapped the prickly
rope around her wrists and tied it in a knot, then whis-
tled to Jo's horse. "Can I help you into the saddle?"

"I'm not going to fly up there," she replied.

He bent forward and weaved his fingers together
for Jo to step into his palms. He lifted her slowly and
it was painful, with her injured shoulder, to grab on
to the horn and swing her leg over the other side.
Before she knew it, she was sitting high in the creaky

leather saddle with her wrists bound together, trying to hold on to some shred of dignity when all she felt was hopelessness.

Fletcher rested his hand on her knee, and despite everything, she felt a shock of awareness over every inch of her body. She stared into his shadowed eyes and saw doubt and regret—felt the same things herself—because all she wanted to do was to put herself into his hands and trust him completely, which made no sense because he was determined to lock her up.

Fletcher's brows drew together with tension. "Do you know how hard this is for me? You've been through so much and I feel..." He stopped himself and looked away. "I wish you had told me all this sooner."

"I didn't know if I could trust you. I still don't."

He met her gaze again, and she felt like she was falling from a very high place. "I'm just trying to do the right thing, and it's not easy. If I were a different man, I would let you go. And right now, in this moment..." He ran his hand over the top of her thigh, and she quivered with an overwhelming rush of desire. "I would..."

He stopped himself again, and she wanted desperately to hear him finish.

He rubbed his hand over her leg and went on. "I was coming out to your ranch tonight because...I just wanted to *see* you, Jo. I thought maybe I could invite you to join me for dinner some evening."

She let out a sigh, knowing the opportunity for something more intimate between them was lost forever. "I would have said yes."

He gazed up at her for another moment, as if exploring in his mind any possible way out of this conundrum, then he withdrew his hand from her leg. She felt suddenly cold.

Fletcher gathered up the guns they'd dropped during their struggle. He stuffed them into his leather saddlebag, buckled it and yanked it tight, then reached for her horse's reins. He mounted, and they started off across the dark pasture with only the moon lighting their way.

Jo rode in silence behind Fletcher for a mile or so, until she felt compelled to try one more time to change Fletcher's mind. She cleared her throat and spoke up. "Is there nothing about Zeb that makes you uncomfortable?"

He didn't look back. "Being rich and upper-class doesn't make someone a murderer."

"Does Elizabeth seem all right?"

Fletcher stopped the horses and turned around. "What are you suggesting?"

Jo shrugged. "If *my* sister was married to Zeb Stone, I'd be concerned."

"My sister's smart. She's a good judge of character, and if there was a problem, she'd come to me."

"Maybe. Maybe not. Isn't there *anything* that makes you worry about Elizabeth? A gut feeling?"

"Gut feelings aren't enough." Fletcher faced front and continued toward town in silence. Jo's last hope for his support shattered into a thousand irretrievable pieces.

Feeling unnerved by Jo's suggestions about Elizabeth, Fletcher shifted in the saddle. Elizabeth hadn't exactly been herself since she came to Dodge. There was a time she was more rebellious and free-spirited than she was now, living in Zeb's big stone house on the hill. But Fletcher had assumed she was still mourning the death of their parents and maybe needed some time to adjust to married life, as any woman would in her circumstances.

The problem here was Jo. She could see through him as clearly as he could see through her, and she was dead right about the gut feeling. Hell, tracking outlaws over the years, he'd learned to use his instincts like a compass, and there *was* something about Zeb that rubbed him the wrong way. Always had been, from the first moment they met, but Fletcher had kept quiet about it because he had faith in his sister, and besides, she was in love with Zeb. He didn't want to spoil that for her.

But why couldn't he have confessed that to Jo just now, when she brought it up? He supposed he didn't want to give her any false hopes that might make all of this more difficult in the end. For her *and* for him.

Prince nickered softly and twitched his ears. There were still a few awkward miles to go, more time for Fletcher to sit and suffer with a throbbing broken nose, beating himself up about this impossible situation.

Again, for some reason, his thoughts floated back to Elizabeth and how strange it was to see her in silk and satin on a daily basis, when she'd always preferred cool muslin, and had made a noisy fuss the one and only time their mother had suggested she wear ornamental combs in her hair.

Not that *that* was any reason to suspect her husband of murder, of course.

Fletcher shook his head. All that aside, there was no denying that he owed it to Jo to uncover the truth. Must he be so hardheaded about arresting her right now, this very minute?

But if he didn't, she would likely make another attempt on Zeb's life, and Fletcher couldn't let her become a murderer. No matter how badly her grief and guilt tortured her, she didn't have the heart of a killer—that much he knew. He'd seen it in her eyes the night in Zeb's store.

Struck suddenly by the memory, Fletcher stopped his horse and turned around. "If you weren't shot by a stray bullet outside the privy that night, who shot you?"

She raised her bound wrists to push a loose lock of hair away from her eyes. "You didn't see Zeb pull out his gun, and you were unconscious when he fired. I meant to defend myself, but I panicked and missed, shooting you, instead. That's when he shot me." Fletcher hadn't thought to ask Zeb if he'd fired his gun at the outlaw that night, and for reasons that were becoming clearer, Zeb hadn't volunteered the information.

"So there was never any lover," Fletcher added, realizing uncomfortably that this was the information he'd been after all along.

"It seemed like a good alibi at the time," she replied, "especially with my reputation in town. It was the only thing I could come up with. I just wanted to distract you from the truth."

"You didn't shoot me on purpose, then."

"Of course not," she replied with a subtle smile he hadn't expected. "I only punched you in the nose on purpose. And that particular business I do *not* regret."

He saw humor in her eyes and heard it in her voice. Lord, she was one brave lady.

The sentiment made him stare through the darkness at her, her beautiful golden hair hidden beneath a man's hat, her woman's body cloaked by the long brown slicker. He had not felt a corset when she'd struggled in his arms earlier. Was there nothing beneath the man's shirt she wore? Nothing but her bare breasts against the lightweight fabric?

A hot ache began to grow inside of him. Damn, he just couldn't keep his eyes to himself, could he? He wanted to leap off his horse and pull her down onto the grass, convince her she was not a killer, then slide his hands up under those clothes and feel her soft, warm skin against his. To become the lover he'd imagined her with that night. To do all the things he'd imagined they'd done.

Instead, he bit back the urge and gazed forlornly across the flat, dark plains. The chilly night wind hissed through the grass and brushed over his cheeks. He pulled his collar up around his neck and readjusted the reins in his grip, his urges twisting like a knife inside him.

Fletcher walked his horse up next to Jo's and decided that maybe it was time, for once, to relax the rules a little. "Who are these other people you think Zeb murdered?"

Jo sat back in the saddle and let out a deep breath of relief. Whatever his reasons, Fletcher was willing to listen.

"It happened about a year before Edwyn died. A man named Hennigar was killed by horse thieves, and when his wife reported everything to the marshal, she told him that one of the killers looked like Zeb Stone. The marshal questioned Zeb, who of course had an alibi, but a few days later, Mrs. Hennigar was found dead at the bottom of her stairs. People thought she'd been so devastated by her husband's death, she'd taken her own life. Then the marshal who questioned Zeb was killed in the line of duty. Zeb had an alibi again, and mostly, people were sympathetic toward him, thinking he was wrongly suspected. I'm surprised you haven't heard about it. Hadn't Elizabeth mentioned it?"

Fletcher removed his hat and raked his fingers through his hair. "All that happened before she came here. Maybe she doesn't know."

"Most people have forgotten about it, I guess."

"But *you* haven't."

"No, *I* haven't."

He gazed away from her, his face turned into the wind, and seemed to be thinking about things. "I can understand how you need to blame someone for your husband's murder, but maybe you're making connections where there are none. If Zeb had an alibi, he may be innocent."

Jo rubbed a finger along her irritated wrist beneath the rope. "It was Zeb, I tell you. Even under the hood,

I knew it was him."

Jo's heart pounded wildly while Fletcher considered her story. He had to believe her, he just had to....

After a few minutes, he looked into her eyes. "There's not enough here to arrest him, and certainly nothing even close to what you'd need to convict." Fletcher put his hat back on his head. "We'd need more proof before anything could be done. A motive at the very least."

We. "Would you be willing to help me find that proof?"

"I'd be interested in the motive first of all. Why would Zeb want your husband dead?"

"I wish I knew."

"What about Hennigar? Did he know your husband?"

"All the ranchers know one another."

Fletcher crossed his wrists over the saddle horn. "Hennigar was a rancher, too?" Jo nodded and Fletcher sat back, shaking his head. "That's at least one connection between the murders, but I don't see how it leads us to Zeb. He has no interests in ranching. He's a little too *civilized* for that."

Jo rubbed her wrists again with her middle finger.

"Is that too tight?" Fletcher asked.

"A little."

He leaned across and untied the rope, then turned her palms up and looked at them. Her wrists were raw and chafed. "Why didn't you say something?"

"There were more important things to say."

He blew on the sensitive surface of her wounds. Jo stared transfixed at his handsome face in the moonlight, his eyes closed, his cool breath easing the rope burns. For a moment, she was tempted to lean in and press her lips to his, but the expression in his eyes sobered her intentions.

"This doesn't change anything, Jo," he said, his voice rippling with regret.

She pulled her hand away, reminding herself of his sworn duty and fighting to stay true to hers.

He leaned back in his saddle and the wind grew suddenly colder. "I reckon there's something more than horse theft going on here, but that doesn't mean I'm going to set you free. You're still charged with attempted murder, no matter what happens, and I'm going to have to lock you up when we get to town."

"What about the investigation?"

"That's *my* job, not yours. Give me your hands." He wrapped the rope around her wrists again. "I'll try not to tie it so tight this time."

By the time Fletcher led Jo into town on her horse, the nightly celebrations were in full swing. Music and singing from the vaudeville act in the Comique echoed in the street, and cowboys staggered around in the dust, laughing and hooting and dancing. Fletcher's watchful gaze always went to their gun belts to ensure they hadn't forgotten the city ordinance about carrying firearms in town, but usually they were merely swinging half-empty whisky bottles.

Fletcher led Jo around the back of the jailhouse, past the barred window that did not mask the sound of a raspy cough and someone spitting tobacco inside. Feeling more than a little uncomfortable about this,

Fletcher dismounted, deciding he would crowd all the men into one cell and give Jo the other cell to herself.

When he helped her down from her horse, he saw that her face was drawn and pale. "Fletcher, if I'm locked up, I'm a fixed target. I have no way to protect myself."

"Deputy Anderson will stand watch. You'll be fine."

"Take me with you."

"I can't do that. I have work to do."

"But isn't it your job to protect people? I'm in danger. I can feel it." Her voice was growing more and more desperate to the point of panic.

"You'll be safe in the jailhouse." He led her around to the front, but in all honesty, he wasn't comfortable with the idea of leaving her alone.

"Please, Fletcher. I can't trust anyone."

He made a move to go inside but hesitated at the door, his hand barely touching the latch. It was that need to protect her, niggling at him again. He certainly didn't want to admit it was personal, not to himself or to her, so he made up some foolish, incomprehensible excuse: "If anyone sees you in this disguise, the story will spread like wildfire, and I won't be able to investigate." He turned to face her. "So there you have it—I changed my mind. Come upstairs with me."

She looked so relieved, he thought she was going to throw her arms around his neck and kiss him, all over his face, to thank him. As much as he would have enjoyed her gratitude in a place more conducive to such expressions, he certainly didn't want her—in *those* clothes—to do it here, when his reputation was already in shambles because of the unfortunate fainting incident. So, for the sake of his reputation, he grabbed her collar in his fist and dragged her along behind him.

They climbed the stairs and went into the office, which was dark and empty. Fletcher lit a lamp, carried it across the room and set it on the tall cabinet. He forced himself to focus on business, and it sure as hell wasn't easy, now that he had her alone in a dimly lit room with a door that could be locked behind them—if he were inclined to make things more private. For purposes that had nothing to do with his job.

He stood facing her flushed cheeks and full lips and heaving breasts, felt an irrepressible surge of heated attraction, and somehow managed to utter, "Do you know the exact date Hennigar was murdered?"

He wasn't at all happy about the fact that he was flustered.

"It was last year, in early January."

Fletcher flipped through the files, squinting through the dim, flickering light, pulling papers out one by one, but he found nothing. "Are you sure?"

"Yes, but you can't find the report, can you?"

"Give me a minute. It might have been—"

"Misfiled. Just like Edwyn's report. What a coincidence." She sat down at one of the desks.

Fletcher soon gave up and closed the heavy drawer. "Okay, there's definitely something going on here, and I want to get to the bottom of it."

"What will you do?"

Fletcher paced the room and considered the situation, then began to untie Jo's hands. "I'll agree with you on one point. If Mrs. Hennigar *was* killed because she witnessed her husband's murder, you might be the killer's next matter of business once this investigation gets going. It's my job to see that you're safe. Come with me."

Fletcher held out his hand and she slipped hers into it. Judging by the intense shudder he felt as he closed his fingers around hers and held them tightly, he would have to dig deep tonight for the strength to stay true to his principles.

14

*F*IGHTING NERVOUSNESS, JO FOLLOWED FLETCHER to the door. "Keep your head down," he said to her, "don't make eye contact with anyone. I'll walk behind you about ten paces, keeping watch, and I promise I won't let anything happen to you." He stopped and faced her. "You look scared."

"I *feel* scared." But was it because she had to walk through town in this disguise, or was it a reaction to the sudden change in her alliance with Fletcher? He was suddenly bending the rules for her, acting as her protector instead of her jailor.

"Don't worry, you'll be fine. All you have to do is walk straight to Jensen's Boardinghouse and don't look back."

"I can't ask for a room. The Jensens know who I am."

He placed a key into her palm. "Go straight to

room number twenty-three on the second floor and let yourself in."

"Is that where you live? At the boardinghouse?"

Fletcher lowered the wick in the lamp and the room went black. "I wouldn't call it *living*, but it serves its purpose. Let's go," he said, his voice cool and authoritative.

"What about the horses?"

"I'll lead yours to the stable behind the boardinghouse. Now, get going."

"You'll be right behind me?"

"Of course."

She passed him in the doorway, her body brushing lightly against his, then she quickly descended the stairs on the outside of the building, stopping at the bottom when she heard Fletcher say, "Not so fast. You don't want to look like you just robbed the livery." The keys jingled as he locked the door behind him. Jo couldn't stop herself from looking up at his dark, imposing figure on the stairs. Above his head, in the night sky, clouds changed shape and dissolved like smoke from a chimney.

"You're wasting time." He dropped the keys with a *clink* into his vest pocket.

Quickly turning on her heel, Jo buried her hands in her pockets and, with the moon lighting her way, crossed over the railroad tracks and headed west on Front Street. Cowboys and businessmen lined the boardwalks in front of Hoover's saloon and the Long Branch. Alert and listening for the sound of Zeb's voice somewhere in one of the small crowds, Jo forced herself to move with an air of calm.

She walked past the post office and saddle shop, keeping to the middle of the street, but once she turned up Third Avenue, she couldn't help but quicken her pace. By the time she arrived at the boardinghouse, her pulse was racing. Head down, she went inside.

She took two steps at a time to the second floor, glancing quickly at the brass numbers on each door. Reaching room number twenty-three, at the very end of a narrow hall, she inserted the key into the keyhole. The lock clicked and the door creaked open. Wasting not a single second, she went inside, shut the door behind her and leaned against it, unable to see anything through the darkness.

Just then, a knock sounded, and Jo nearly leaped out of her skin. She cleared her throat to lower her voice. "Who is it?"

"Fletcher. Open up."

Relieved, Jo let him in, then closed the door again.

"You made it in one piece," he said.

"Yes. Now what?"

He crossed the room and closed the curtains. "We get some light in here."

Jo removed her coat and looked around the room while Fletcher replaced a blackened glass chimney onto the kerosene lamp next to the bed.

"Don't you own anything?" she asked, seeing empty surfaces everywhere she looked.

"I travel light. Makes it easier to do what I have to do."

"And what's that?"

"Be a lawman. I can't get bogged down with stuff. Makes it too hard to leave a place, and I like to go where I'm needed."

She wandered around the room, still looking. "If it weren't for Zeb Stone, we wouldn't have so much *need* for new lawmen."

Fletcher set the matches down on the bedside table, then moved swiftly and purposefully toward Jo. Startled by his fast approach, she backed up against the wall until she couldn't back up any farther and he was standing mere inches from her, grabbing hold of her wrists.

"What are you doing?" she asked. He was so close, she could feel his breath on her face.

He whirled her around and sat her onto the bed so quickly, she didn't have a chance to object. "Lie back."

Then he climbed on top of her, straddled her hips, and held her arms down, pressed tight to the mattress on either side of her. He held one wrist down with his knee.

"Hey, you're supposed to be protecting me...*ouch!* That hurts!"

"Sorry," he said, distracted by what he was doing, and when she tried to discern what, exactly, it was, she realized he was reaching down. His free hand was maneuvering about, fooling around down low as if he were unbuttoning his trousers. Outraged, Jo tried to struggle, but it was difficult to even breath under his weight. "Get off me, Fletcher!"

"You're not helping things any. Just relax." He pinned her tighter to the bed.

"I will *not!*"

The next thing she knew, a rope was twisting around

one wrist, weaving through the steel bed rail under the mattress. He ran it over the top of her, bound her other wrist, and tied that to the rail on the other side. "I can't trust you to stay put," he said matter-of-factly. And I would have tied your hands to the bedframe, but I'm minding that shoulder of yours."

Jo immediately went still, realizing only then what his intentions had been, and feeling foolish for having thought anything else.

"I can't risk you making another attempt on Zeb's life until I know what's going on," he continued.

"You're going to leave me here?"

He pulled the knots tight at her wrists and leaned over her. "You'll just have to forgive me, because it's the only place I know you'll be safe."

He gazed intently into her eyes for a few seconds. Jo wet her lips and noticed his breath hitch. She felt another unexpected stirring of desire in her belly, hot and quick, and couldn't move. She was completely captivated by him—by how handsome and manly he was, how he smelled like leather and horse and a hint of shaving soap.

I'm completely at your mercy now, bound to this bed. You could do anything to me that you wanted. You could kiss me hard, tear off my clothes, and have your way with me...

Heaven help her. Where were those thoughts coming from? It wasn't like her to think such things, to feel so wantonly aroused by a man. But how long had it been since she had been touched like that? Edwyn, in the *early* years of their marriage, had come to her in the night, but not often after Leo was born, and it was never very passionate. They had later moved to separate beds because of Edwyn's snoring. At least that was their excuse.

Even so, had she ever wanted Edwyn's husbandly advances the way she wanted Fletcher's now? And would she ever not feel guilty about that...about wanting another man?

She tried to focus her thoughts on the matter at hand. "I'll forgive you if you find something on Zeb."

"I'll try," Fletcher replied, "but...now that I've got you here like this, it's not so easy to leave." He looked torn, frustrated, his expression dark. All his painstaking discipline seemed to dissolve into nothing as he gazed down at her.

The words barely made it past her dizzied senses. Stunned, Jo stared up at his slightly parted lips, realizing all at once that he was feeling the same pull of attraction she was, and he wasn't even trying to deny it.

Nothing good could come of this, she thought miserably, then despite her mental warnings and her firm emotional objections, she found herself responding rather breathlessly. "*Don't* leave, then."

He considered it a moment, his gaze raking over her face, then his hand slipped slowly into her coat.

Jo's body began to quiver with excitement at the sensation of his fingers moving over her clothing. He ran his hand along her hip, then he lowered his mouth to hers.

A passionate fluttering began in her belly as his tongue slid between her lips and mingled with hers. Never in her life had she been kissed like this—so slowly and seductively. It was deep and wet and it filled her with wanting.

She should have told him to stop, but she couldn't help but kiss him back. She wiggled sensually on the bed, her wrists still bound and restricted, when all she really wanted was to be free to touch this man everywhere.

"Untie me," she pleaded, wanting to hold onto him, to slide her hands under his clothes and feel the full length of his body, heavy upon hers.

He went still, and she thought for a moment he had heard something outside, but when she looked at his face, she saw the conflict of his emotions, and it had nothing to do with anything outside the room. Slowly pulling back, he perched on all fours above her and she knew wretchedly what he thought—that she was just trying to trick him, to seduce him into setting her free.

"I can't untie you." He backed away and stood.

"Why not?" She squirmed and her wrists burned painfully under the coarse rope. "You don't have to *free* me. Just untie me. Temporarily. So we can..." She didn't know how to say it, exactly. *So I can rip off your clothes and you can make love to me?*

Fletcher shook his head. "You're my prisoner. It wouldn't be right." He glanced around the room, the lines on his forehead deep with frustration.

"What's wrong?" Jo asked, finally lying still.

"The problem with not having any belongings is that you don't have extra rope around when you need it."

Jo ground out a grumble, her body still reeling from the curtailment of her desire...from the memory of his hands and lips on her. "Trust me, I'm not going anywhere," she said. "These knots are as good as steel."

Once again, she tugged at them, releasing some of her own frustration, but it only served to chafe her tender skin even more. She decided to relax and surrender to an uncomfortable night in Fletcher's bed. *Alone.*

"What are you going to do?" she asked.

He pulled on his coat and settled his hat on his head. "I'm going to talk to Zeb."

"Oh, that's smart. You're just going to walk up to him and ask him if he's a murderer?"

"Whatever it takes. Try to get some sleep."

Jo watched him leave the room and close the door behind him. She stared up at the unpainted plank ceiling with the beams exposed, and knew it was going to be a dreadfully long night.

Standing just inside the door of the smoky Long Branch saloon, surveying the crowd of cattlemen and gamblers who were listening to the five-piece orchestra, Fletcher wondered if he should have dunked himself in the water trough before coming in here. He had work to do, he had to stay focused, but he was still distracted by the memory of Jo's scent and the seductive sound of her voice and the feel of her lush, passionate body beneath him.

Kissing her had been a big mistake. Now there could be no denying that he wanted her, and that he was conflicted about his responsibilities as a lawman, here in Dodge.

He cleared his throat and walked to the white-paneled bar, leaned on the dark mahogany countertop and shouted over the music. "Zeb been in here tonight?" he asked the bartender, who was standing on a chair, straightening the ornamental rack of horns above the mirror.

"He's in the back room as usual."

Fletcher thanked the man and walked toward the back, past the billiard table and coal stove, then pushed open the door to the private gambling room. Zeb and three other men sat around a table under a hanging lantern, their money piled in the center, their cards close to their chests and their chips stacked like small buildings in front of them. Smoke from the tips of their cigars snaked in serpentine streaks toward the ceiling.

"Well, well, well," Zeb greeted, looking up from his hand. He set his cards face-down on the table and slid his chair back. The half-empty whisky bottle in front of him teetered. "Did you come to join us, Fletcher, or to dance to the magnificent orchestral arrangements only the Long Branch can provide?"

"Didn't think they allowed dancing in here," one of the men blurted out, as if he'd been missing out on something.

Zeb glared at him. "It was a joke, my dear man. Now lay down your cards, all of you, and go get yourselves some drinks. I want to talk to my brother-in-law."

All three of the cowmen rose from the table without argument. When the door closed behind them, Fletcher sat down. "They all friends of yours?"

Zeb tossed back a shot of whisky. "Not really. They're just a few transient fools willing to part with their hard-earned money, and I can never say no to that." He dragged on his cigar until the tip flared red. "Do you know that they only make thirty dollars a month on a drive? I have to wonder if they're all imbeciles."

"Maybe they can't do any better," Fletcher replied, keeping his thoughts to himself. "Maybe they don't know the right people."

Zeb eyed him speculatively, then nodded. "You're absolutely right. It's all about who you know, isn't it? What happened to your nose?"

Fletcher touched it lightly, and felt that it was still swollen and slightly crooked. "Saloon brawl."

"I hope the other man looks worse than you do. Did you bruise his head?"

"I gave it a tap."

"Good for you." They stared intently at each other for a moment, then Zeb reached for the whisky bottle in front of him and poured Fletcher a drink. When he slid it across the table, Fletcher accepted it and raised it before swallowing a bitter mouthful.

"I came to talk to you about something," Fletcher said.

Zeb leaned back in his chair and crossed one leg over the other. "The sheriff's office. You want to settle in Dodge, I hope."

"How'd you guess?"

"Never let it be said that women are the only intuitive creatures God put on this earth." Zeb flicked cigar ashes into a dish. "Before we get down to that bit of business though, where were you tonight? I wanted to talk to you."

Fletcher relaxed back in his chair, wondering how to answer that. He decided to make something up. "I went to meet a fellow who said he knew something about the shooting the other night."

"Indeed. Was he helpful?"

Fletcher thought carefully before he answered. "He didn't show."

"No? That's suspicious. Must be hiding something. Maybe he knows the identity of our enigmatic Six-Shooter Hank." Zeb's speech was slurred.

"Maybe."

"Or better yet, maybe he *is* Six-Shooter Hank." He laughed at his drunken wittiness. "It could be anyone, you know. The night he came into the store, he was well covered-up."

"Any ideas?" Fletcher asked. "I'm all out of suspects."

"I'd be willing to wager it's someone right under our noses, yours being the bigger one this evening."

Fletcher humored Zeb, who was clearly drunker than a lord. "What makes you say that?"

"My punctilious instinct. What I'd do without it, I cannot begin to imagine." Zeb raised his glass and downed the whole of it, as if celebrating something. "Instinct aside, you really have to apprehend *someone* if we're going to get you into the sheriff's office."

Fletcher managed a devious smile. "Anyone will do?"

Zeb laughed. "Now you're starting to sound like a man who's going places. Elizabeth will be pleased to hear you're thinking of settling here. What changed your mind?"

"I figured my prospects are good, with family around."

"Yes, yes, indeed. Family loyalty is important. You can always be sure of it. Having said that, if you're going to stay, I'd like to set you up more comfortably. You won't get far on seventy-five a month. Your salary is pathetic. How does an additional hundred sound?"

Fletcher wondered if Zeb would be saying any of this if he were sober. "Sounds good to me, but you might have trouble convincing the city council."

"I'm not talking about city funds. I'd put you on *my* payroll."

Raising his hands, Fletcher laughed. "No offense, but I never saw myself in the mercantile business."

"Rest assured, I don't see you there, either. You have talents that we could put to better use than counting bags of flour."

Fletcher leaned forward. "And what business are we talking about?"

Zeb seemed to consider his reply with great care. After a long pause, he blinked his bloodshot eyes. "The business of being family, of course. Elizabeth wants you to stay here, and if more money will keep you, then that's what you'll get. For now."

For now. Fletcher knew there was something more to this than just being family. Unfortunately, Zeb wasn't ready to trust him with it yet.

"I like to *earn* my keep."

"Be patient. You will."

Someone rapped at the door, then one of the cow-men peered in. "You want to finish the game, boss? 'Cause Billy wants to meet a lady across the street."

"Tell him if he wants to back out, he'll have to pay me what he owes me."

The cowman disappeared briefly, then returned. "He said his money's on the table, but only if you say it's okay for him to go."

Zeb shook his head at Fletcher. "Sheep," he whispered, then turned to the cowboy. "Tell him to go meet his lady friend, and you can go, too, but don't forget you have a job to do."

"Yes, sir." The cowhand closed the door and Fletcher heard them hoot as they left the saloon.

"What's this *job* all about?" he asked.

Zeb stared blankly, in a stupor, then spread his arms wide. "The job of getting the whores into bed, of course!"

Trying not to reveal his aversion for the distasteful reply, Fletcher stood up and walked around the table to help Zeb up. The future mayor wobbled to and fro as he gathered up his cash and stuffed it into both his breast pockets. "You'll be by for supper tomorrow evening?"

If Fletcher was going to gain Zeb's trust and find out what was really going on with this so-called family business, he had best accept the invitation. Even if it meant tying Jo to his bed again for another night.

"I'll be there," he answered, then he walked Zeb all the way home, just to make sure he made it back to Elizabeth in one piece.

Chapter

15

*I*T WAS NEARLY THREE-THIRTY IN the morning
when Fletcher returned to the boardinghouse and
led his horse into the small stable. He'd spent the night
on duty, asking casual questions about the Hennigar
murder Jo had told him about, to anyone who seemed
willing to talk. He learned nothing that Jo hadn't
already told him, and discovered that Zeb Stone had
held the town's sympathy back then—a man wrongly
accused.

Maybe he was. Maybe he wasn't. Fletcher had wrestled with the idea all night long, wondering what
kind of work Zeb had planned for him, now that he
was on his so-called payroll.

Fletcher was beginning to see that Jo was right to
be suspicious of Zeb about something, considering
the shady characters that were calling him "boss," but
with the information Fletcher had gathered so far, he

wasn't ready to arrest Zeb for murder.

Exhausted, he fed and watered his horse, then dragged himself up the boardinghouse steps. With any luck, Jo had managed to sleep a little. He thought about what lay ahead for them, and he still couldn't consider making an official arrest and locking her up in the city jail. People would want to know why, and if he told them, he would thwart his own investigation.

He just hoped he could convince Jo to cooperate. If he was going to uncover the truth, she had to go on with her life as if nothing were out of the ordinary. Otherwise, Zeb would suspect something. At the same time, Fletcher had to keep her safe from a potential murderer—whoever that might be—and safe from becoming one herself.

He unlocked the door and went inside, relieved to find Jo still secure on his bed, her body quiet and still with sleep. Trying not to wake her, he removed his coat and draped it over the foot of the bed, then unbuckled his gun belt and laid it gently on the chest of drawers. How she managed to sleep tied down on her back like that, he couldn't imagine. She must have been dog-tired.

Needing sleep himself, he carefully moved closer, but paused by the side of the bed when he caught sight of Jo's face, illuminated by the moonlight coming through the window.

Good Lord, she had a black eye. What had he done?

Wanting to kick himself clear across town, he sat on the bed beside her, trying not to create a stir while he let his fingers hover in the air above her bruised eye. Better not to touch it, he reasoned, when she was so peaceful in sleep. He'd done her enough harm already.

He considered the gentlemanly thing—curling up on the floor, but when he thought of what he and Jo had been through together so far, propriety seemed far beyond repair.

Or maybe he was just telling himself that. He might as well admit that what he really wanted was to be close to her. What damage could it do at this point?

Fletcher lowered his weary body down, on his side with his back intentionally to Jo. Feeling her warmth, even through his clothing, he considered the floor again, thinking he might in fact sleep better there, but when his eyes fell closed, there was no hope in getting them open again.

Jo woke from a deep slumber when she tried to turn over onto her side, but couldn't.

Flat on her back in the darkness, feeling the muscles in her back cramping into corkscrews, she wiggled uncomfortably on the lumpy mattress. Her hip struck something and her groggy mind suddenly cleared. Fletcher was sleeping soundly beside her, his head resting in his hands, his backside connecting with her hip.

How, she wondered with senses now buzzing to life, had this situation spun so impossibly out of control?

Through fading hope, Jo looked toward the window to estimate the time, and hearing meadowlarks chirping a full symphony, she guessed it must be between four and five in the morning. It wouldn't be long before her ranch hands woke and came looking for their breakfast. What would they do when they found the house empty?

Fletcher breathed deeply and rolled into her. He stirred and opened his eyes, as if her anchored presence in his bed was the most common thing in the world. "You're awake."

"Yes, no thanks to these ropes. My arms have fallen asleep and it feels like a hundred-thousand pins and needles."

He sat up and began to tug at the knots. "I guess I can untie you for now. You're not going anywhere while I'm here."

"I guess not." Finally she could rub her sleeping arms and hands and scratch all the places that itched. "What happened last night? Did you talk to Zeb?"

Fletcher sat up on the edge of the bed and lit the lamp. "Yes."

"What did *he* say? Or more importantly, what did *you* say?"

The room flickered with a dim, golden light, and Fletcher's large shadow loomed against the wall as he stood. "Nothing to suggest he killed anyone, though I didn't exactly ask him that, specifically."

"Couldn't you have hinted at something?"

"You know as well as I do that Zeb is an intelligent man. I don't want him to know I'm checking into his affairs. It's best if he trusts me. That way, he might let down his guard."

"So you *do* suspect him?"

Fletcher settled back against the wall, one ankle crossed casually over the other. "I didn't say that, but he's got something going on that he's being real vague about. Some kind of business. I'd like to know what it is, considering I'm an employee."

"An employee?"

"Yes ma'am," Fletcher replied. "If he even remembers saying it, that is. He was a little inebriated. He told me he'd put me on his 'payroll,' calling it a 'family thing.' He's going to pay me to stick around for Elizabeth's sake. Maybe that's all it is, but—"

"He's trying to make you feel like you owe him something. To trap you."

Fletcher watched her in an intent way, and she felt as if he were forming judgments about her in his mind. She wished she knew what they were.

He took his time to reply. "I'm not jumping to any conclusions, but I'm not ruling anything out, either." He pushed his disheveled hair away from his face. "Did you get enough sleep? How's your nose?"

"My nose is fine, and sleeping's not my first concern right now. I'm worried about my ranch hands, and what they'll do when they discover I'm missing."

Fletcher went to the window and looked outside. The faint light of dawn graced the smooth lines of his sculpted facial features. "That's a good point. They'll probably go looking for you, or worse, report your disappearance to the deputy." He reached for his gun belt on the chest of drawers and buckled it around his waist. "What about Leo and Matilda? They must have already noticed."

"I sent them away last night, for obvious reasons," she told him. "They went to Newton. The house is empty."

Assuming she and Fletcher would be leaving soon, Jo crawled off the bed and went to look in the small mirror on the wall over the washstand. "Good gracious, look at my eye."

It was puffy and ugly, her shirt was wrinkled and coming untucked, and her hair, still in a bun, looked like a hornet's nest.

Fletcher moved toward her, his voice soft and apologetic. "If I'd known it was you last night..."

"Don't worry about it," she said despondently.

She tucked one tangled strand of hair here, another there. "So what are you going to do with me? If it doesn't make any difference to you, I'd like to stay out of sight—Zeb's sights, in particular."

"Zeb's at home with Elizabeth until noon every day," Fletcher explained, "and I imagine he'll be sleeping extra late this morning."

"You're not hearing me," Jo said, facing him directly. "I'm in danger."

Fletcher strode toward her and pulled a hairpin from her hair, letting the whole mess fall onto her shoulders. She shivered at the silky play of his fingers around her neck. "I *am* hearing you. I said I wasn't ruling anything out. That means I'll keep you safe. You need to fix your hair."

Unmoving, Jo stared up at him. "I asked you what you were going to do with me."

He stroked her cheek with his thumb, and she shivered pleasurably at the contact. "I'm going to take you home."

"I thought you were going to lock me up."

He shook his head. "Not today."

She swallowed uneasily, not sure why he had changed his mind. "But I won't be safe at home."

"You will be, if I'm watching over you."

She tried not to acknowledge the one teasing finger that traced the outline of her ear.

"And just how do you plan to investigate Zeb's affairs from my front parlor?" she asked.

"I'm only taking you back to avoid a panic and a search for you," Fletcher explained. "You'll fix breakfast for the men just like always, while I look through some of Edwyn's things. I might be able to find something that will shed light on all this. You can make up some excuse to be away from the house for the day. I don't want anything to seem out of the ordinary until I can get some answers."

He turned to face her, and a stress-induced haze wiggled into her brain as she looked up at him, waiting for him to say that it was time to go. A muscle quivered at his jaw and she wanted desperately to step into his arms again, to feel his hands on her body and his lips on her mouth.

He gazed down at her for a moment, then he seemed to wake from some sort of trance. He turned his back on her, pulled out his gun and checked it for bullets. The clicking sound was like a bucket of cold water on Jo's frazzled nerves.

He dropped the weapon into its holster and strode to the door. "Put your hair up and get your hat on, Jo. We have to get you home before sunrise."

She did as he asked, but it didn't change the fact that she still wanted to feel his mouth on hers.

The prairie grass glistened like diamonds with morning dew, reflecting the first light of dawn. Warm beneath her coat, Jo watched Mogie's panting breath coming in little puffs like steam from a train as she urged him to trot over the last rise. She and Fletcher had decided to circle the long way around the corral to avoid waking anyone in the bunkhouse. They would hide his horse in the chicken coop where the cowhands never ventured.

Fletcher reached the top of the hill first, stopping on the road when Prince grew skittish.

"What is it?" Jo asked. "What's the matter?"

"I thought you said the house was empty."

She caught up to him and reined in her mount. "I did say that."

"Then what's that light in your parlor?"

Jo stood up in the stirrups, squinting through the hazy dawn. Her bones went limp at the sight. "I don't know."

"I'd better go down there. You wait here." Fletcher reached for his gun.

"I'm coming with you."

"No, you're not. It's too dangerous."

"I know," Jo replied. "That's why I have to go with you. You might need me.

He glared at her as if considering all options, then reached into his saddlebag. "Take this, then." He moved closer and handed her her own weapon from the night before. She checked the chamber for bullets.

"You're giving a loaded gun to a prisoner?" she asked with a raised eyebrow.

His eyes told her he trusted her, and she couldn't

deny that she was pleased about it.

"Just come on," he said. "Stay behind me and wait outside while I check the house."

They trotted down the hill, but as they grew closer, Jo noticed the light in the parlor window growing brighter. She stopped. "Wait a minute."

Fletcher stopped, too.

"That's no lantern light," she said.

"You're right. It's a fire."

Jo and Fletcher kicked in their heels and galloped to the house just as the lace curtains went up in flames.

"Fire!" she screamed, leaping off Mogie.

Five men from the bunkhouse ran outside looking flustered and sleepy, some wearing their clothes, some wearing only their undershirts and drawers. It took only seconds for all of them to bolt to the barn in their bare feet and grab buckets.

Fletcher hopped down from the saddle, ripped off his coat and dunked it in the water barrel by the bunkhouse. He was the first to enter the house, slapping at flames in the window with his wet slicker. Jo followed his lead, dunking her coat, running inside and striking the fire that was consuming the sofa.

Smoke burned her eyes and stung her throat. She covered her mouth with one sleeve, coughing, while she whipped her coat mercilessly through the smoke-filled air.

The ranch hands all ran in with buckets of sloshing water, dousing the flames that were eating the rugs and walls. Jo saw her wedding picture simmering on the mantel, and the fact that she made no move to rescue it sat for a while in her brain as if waiting to be comprehended, until she forced her attention to fix on more urgent matters, like saving her home.

While Fletcher ripped down the curtain rod and smothered the flames it carried, she slapped ruthlessly at the hot blazes that nipped perilously close to the bottom of his trousers.

Men ran in and out, tossing water through the air in long silver streaks. Jo coughed and sputtered. Her lungs felt tight as she gasped for breath. Fletcher turned and grabbed her arm, dragging her toward the front door. "You have to get out of here!"

"No!" She shook his hand away.

They stood in the front hall. The bright fire crackled and hissed behind him. "Just go outside and breathe a minute, or you'll suffocate!"

"What about you?"

"I'll be fine!" He ran back into the parlor and fought the flames that were devouring Jo's rocking chair and mantel. Jo ran outside and dunked her coat in the barrel again. She sucked in a few essential breaths, then ran back toward the house with her dripping cargo.

John, her foreman, ran past her in his scarlet knit drawers and matching undershirt, carrying two buckets. He met her at the door and halted. "Mrs. O'Malley! Your eye!"

She didn't stop to explain. "Hurry, John! Help Fletcher!"

He hesitated a moment, then ran in with his two buckets and threw water onto the flames at the mantel. Fletcher was wheezing, covering his face with a sleeve while he battered the fire. Three men came in at once and a torrent of water covered the floor and walls. The blaze winced and recoiled, gasping its last breath in one fatal hissing sizzle.

Coughing, Jo looked at Fletcher, who began to stagger. She ran to his side as he collapsed his heavy frame onto her tiny one. She struggled to stay upright, grabbing his arm and pulling it around her sore shoulder to support him.

"Someone help me!" she shouted.

John came running. On each side of Fletcher, they helped him through the front hall and down the porch steps. He dropped to his knees in the dirt, fighting for breath. Jo dropped down beside him with her hand on his back. "Are you all right? John, get him a glass of water!"

John ran back to the house.

Fletcher drew in one long, deep breath that sounded hideously thin. "Is the fire out?"

"Yes. It's out." She looked back at the house. "Are you men all right in there?"

One came out, waving. "We're okay. Just making sure it ain't gonna start up again."

She turned her attention back to Fletcher, who was rubbing his eyes. "You were lucky," he said.

"I know. We caught it just in time."

"No, I mean you were lucky, because that fire was set to get rid of *you*.

Jo sat back on her heels in disbelief. "Do you really think so?"

He leaned forward, coughed a few times, then cleared his throat. "The curtains were doused in kerosene. I smelled it, and the can was tossed into the fireplace. A shoddy job, really."

She'd expected something like this, but the reality of it infuriated her far beyond any imagining. A stranger—no doubt one of Zeb's hired men—had found his way onto her land and into her home. She looked all around, then rose to her feet. "We have to go after Zeb."

"Oh, no, we don't."

"He's not getting away with this!"

She strode purposefully to her horse, grazing by the fence, and took hold of the reins. Before she could lift her foot into the stirrup, she felt a hand on her shoulder.

"You're not going anywhere."

"Let me go, Fletcher."

"Not on your life."

"I said let me go!" She tried to struggle free of him, but he held her tight around the waist.

Growing more angry by the second, Jo elbowed Fletcher in the ribs.

In an instant, her feet were swept out from under her and she landed hard on the ground with a heavy *thump*. The cool handle of a Colt .45 came down to rest gently on her forehead, its light pressure a clear message not to move. She blinked up at Fletcher's irate gaze.

"I don't want to knock you out, Jo, but I will if I have to."

Relaxing the back of her head on the ground, she let out an exasperated breath, then noticed John's bare feet in the dirt beside her. He was holding the glass of water she had asked for.

"What the hell's going on here?" he demanded. He

glared at Fletcher. "Did *you* give Mrs. O'Malley that black eye?"

Jo tried to get up. "John, you don't understand."

His gaze moved up and down her manly attire and settled on her eye again. "I think I do, ma'am. I know the house was empty last night, and seeing how you're riding back here so early with the marshal..."

John passed the glass of water to Jo and balled his hands into fists. "What kind of lily-livered vermin are you, hitting a woman? If you can dish it out, Marshal Collins, you sure as hell better be able to take it."

Chapter

16

*B*ARELY ABLE TO GET A full breath into his tight lungs, Fletcher dropped his gun into his holster. He took in John's snug-fitting red underwear and bare toes. "Now, listen here..."

"Don't you '*now listen here*' me!" John shouted. "I'm about as savage as a meat ax over what you did!"

"It's not what it looks like," Jo tried to say.

"You stay out of this, Mrs. O'Malley."

"It is *my* business, not yours!" she replied.

Before Fletcher had a chance to explain anything, a tight fist came hurling through the air, straight for his nose.

"No, wait!" Jo cried.

The crack of bone against bone cleared Fletcher's lungs in a hurry. His cheekbones vibrated with agonizing spasms of pain that shot straight to his brain until his whole head hammered. "Ah, hell! Not again!" He cupped his throbbing nose, feeling blood flow out of his nostrils.

"John! Stop it!" Jo yelled. The other ranch hands emerged from the house and gathered on the covered porch to watch.

John pounced away like an amateur boxer. With both fists drawn, he bobbed up and down on the balls of his bare feet. "Face me like a man, Marshal."

"Let's talk about this," Fletcher said, holding up a hand to try and calm the situation.

"What's there to talk about?" John asked. "Somebody's gotta stand up for the lady."

Furious, Jo ripped off her hat and threw it onto the ground. "I can take care of myself!"

"No lady should have to take care of herself against a man like him," John said. "Preying on this lonely widow—listening to the gossip about her, no doubt. You're a disgrace to your badge!"

Fletcher bent forward, still holding his nose. "Jeez, what next?"

"If you weren't such a bastard, I'd force you to marry her!"

"Marry her?" Fletcher replied, looking up.

"Marry me!" Jo echoed.

Not sure what to say, Fletcher tried to stand up straight. He wiped his bloody nose on his sleeve. John bounced like a March Hare toward him and threw another punch. Fletcher dodged it.

"But you ain't good enough for someone like her. So if you ain't gonna honor her by proposing, I will!" Another punch flew past Fletcher's ear. He wiped more blood off his throbbing nose, his nerves just about at the breaking point.

"Nobody's marrying anybody," Fletcher said.

John bounced around the barnyard, then made one more lunge forward. "Oh yeah? We'll see about that!"

Enough was enough. Fletcher went for his gun.

The very next second, John was flat on his back, blinking up at the sky and rubbing his bruised noggin. Fletcher dropped his gun back into the holster.

"Damn, that was fast," John mumbled.

Jo set the glass of water down on the ground and knelt beside him. "My word. Are you all right?"

"I think so," John replied in a daze. She helped him sit up. "I feel a little dizzy, though."

Jo gave Fletcher an irritated look.

"What—he was going to punch me again!" Fletcher insisted.

"You didn't have to hit him so hard."

"I wasn't about to get my nose broken a third time."

Jo parted John's hair to examine his head. "I don't see any blood."

"Plenty of blood over here," Fletcher pointed out, feeling around the bridge of his nose.

Jo ignored him. "John, why don't you go and get dressed. We'll talk later."

He rose to his feet and Fletcher had to strain to hear what John said privately to her: "I meant it about marrying you, Mrs. O'Malley. If that's what you need, you can depend on me. I'm your man."

Jo only nodded and tapped him a few times on the arm. The sheepish foreman made his way awkwardly to the bunkhouse, rubbing the top of his bruised head.

Jo turned to the others on the porch, all staring in

silence. "Thank you for your help, gentlemen, but you can get to work now. Breakfast will be a little late this morning."

A general murmur of acknowledgment floated down the steps as they moved past, all glaring irately at Fletcher.

"You okay, Mrs. O'Malley?" one of them asked. "You want someone to stick around?"

"I'm fine, thank you. This is all just a misunderstanding."

When they were gone, Fletcher tipped his head back to stop the blood from dripping onto his boots.

"I'm sorry about that," Jo said swiftly, picking up the water glass and rising.

"Yeah? You don't look too sorry to me."

"What's that supposed to mean?"

Fletcher hobbled to the house and up the porch steps, hearing Jo pick up her hat and follow behind him. "You just got yourself a marriage proposal."

"As if I wanted it!" she argued. "I don't want to marry *him*. Or *you*, for that matter!"

"No?"

"No!" Face-to-face on the covered porch, breathing in the scent of singed carpet, they glared angrily at each other. Jo slammed her hat onto her head. Fletcher could feel all his pent-up frustrations exploding at once.

"Well, I don't want to marry you, either," he said, holding his painful, swollen, crooked nose.

"So you said already."

"No, I didn't."

"Yes, you did! You said, 'nobody's marrying anybody.'"

He stood quietly, trying to remember what, exactly, he had said, then he gave up on it and tipped his head back again to stop the blood that was dripping onto the porch floor. Throat burning, he coughed dryly. "I need a drink of water."

"Here!" Jo threw the water she held straight into his face.

Feeling the cold slap against his dry, sooty skin, Fletcher shut his eyes. He kept them shut a moment, trying to rid himself of the shock before he opened them to meet Jo's surprised gaze.

She covered her mouth with her hand. "I can't believe I just did that."

Fletcher wiped a hand over his wet face and flicked the water into the air. "Feel better?"

"As a matter of fact, I do," she replied, all rage gone from her voice.

He wished *he* felt better, but since he didn't have a glass of water to pour over *her* head, all he could do was keep struggling against the impossible cravings that had been torturing him ever since he'd made the mistake of touching her on the bed last night.

Feeling hot all of a sudden, he stared down at her blushing red cheeks and full lips and noticed a spot of soot smeared across her chin. Her golden hair was falling in stray tendrils onto her dust-covered shoulders. The hat she wore was wrinkled and rakishly askew, and she hardly seemed aware that she still held an empty drinking glass in her hand.

Without thinking, Fletcher grabbed her by the wrist and dragged her into the house. "Come in here."

"Why? What are you—?"

Once inside, he slammed the door behind them, pushed her up against it, and smothered whatever she was about to say next with his mouth.

Jo dropped her hat and the glass onto the floor. Fletcher barely heard the smash as it shattered into tiny pieces. All he could comprehend was the sound of his own breathing, deep and labored. Her tiny moan of pleasure made his body ache for the rest of her. She wrapped her arms around his shoulders and opened her moist lips to meet his fevered kiss.

"I want to take you upstairs," he whispered roughly against her neck as he nibbled the soft flesh.

"No, not with the men just outside. They'll know." Her leg came up to wrap around his hips, and he thrust against her, wishing their clothing wasn't stopping him from what he really wanted to do to her, right here, up against the heavy oak door.

"They'll be looking for their breakfast," she mumbled in a drawn-out whisper.

"Let them eat the roasted curtains."

Jo threw her head back as he kissed her neck, just beneath her collar.

"Maybe you should lock the door," she whispered.

Eyes closed, he clumsily felt around for the key in the lock, found it and turned it. "No one's getting in."

Just then, someone knocked upon it.

Fletcher stopped kissing her.

Jo's eyes flew wide open. "Who is it?" she asked in a melodic voice.

"It's John. Do you need any help with breakfast, Mrs. O'Malley?"

Her face paled as she squeezed Fletcher's shoulders. Fletcher raised his forefinger to his lips to keep her from sounding as if anything was out of the ordinary—he certainly didn't want his nose to get broken again—then he nodded for her to reply.

"No, thank you, John." Her voice seemed strained, out of breath. "I'm fine."

Silence swelled on the porch.

Then John asked, "You okay in there?"

"Yes. I'll ring the bell when breakfast is ready."

Still, there were no departing footsteps.

Growing impatient and sexually frustrated while staring down at Jo's wide-eyed gaze, Fletcher kissed the top of her head. His body throbbed with need, and he couldn't stop himself from pressing his lips to hers again, slowly, gently, as quietly as possible, letting his tongue drift inside her mouth.

Jo's little moan of pleasure soon made Fletcher forget about John, even as he heard the footsteps tap down the porch steps.

Quieter now, they finished what they had begun so hastily—a chain of kisses as long as the Santa Fe Trail, each one melting hotly into the next. Before long, Jo buried her face into Fletcher's neck, clutched at his shoulders, and told him in whispered words, "Take me upstairs."

Damn, how he wanted to hear her cry out as he knew she would if he made love to her. Just the idea of it made his blood race until he could hardly make sense of anything. He had to mentally shake himself to see reason.

He continued to hold her, to kiss her lips, cheeks

and neck, trying to think of a way to make himself refuse what she was offering. He took her trembling hand in his and pressed the soft, warm palm to his lips.

"I can't do that, Jo," he said softly.

He felt the weight of her stare and saw her expression change from heated arousal to feminine umbrage. *"You* can't do it?"

"I didn't mean to—"

She yanked her hand away and he closed his eyes in defeat. Sometimes he could be so unimaginably *stupid.*

"You're not the only one who's risking something here," she said. "I have reasons to stay away from you, too, and let me assure you, they're infinite."

"Jo, let's not do this now."

"No, I think we should. If not now, when? I'll be in jail before long, so we won't be able to have much of a conversation there."

"Jo, don't—"

"Why not? I'm still your prisoner, aren't I? And I wasn't kissing you to get you to change your mind about arresting me, if that's what you think."

"I didn't think that."

"It sounded like you did."

"I didn't mean it the way it sounded."

"How *did* you mean it?" she asked. "No, never mind. There's no point discussing it. When I suggested we go upstairs...well, that was rash of me. I've been confused about a lot of things lately, but I wasn't trying to trick you."

She was rambling now, and Fletcher had the feeling

it was her pride talking. She was trying to hold on to her dignity.

She bent down and picked her hat up off the floor.

"I'm sorry," he said, "but this is complicated." He backed away and sat on the bottom stair, resting his forehead in his hands, feeling more confused now than ever. For a long moment, he just sat there.

"I don't understand," Jo said despondently.

He looked up at her, his eyes burning and blood-shot. He didn't want to talk about this now, or tell her how he felt about her, but with things the way they were, he probably owed her at least that before he locked her up and called in the judge.

"The fact that I *want* you is simple enough," he said after a great deal of painful deliberation. "It's the way I *feel* about you that's complicated."

Jo sank down to sit on the floor, her legs stretched out in a V in front of her.

"This isn't at all how I'd planned things," he went on, "and I *always* plan things." He moved forward to kneel between her legs, and found himself revealing more than he'd intended to.

"When John told me he would marry you if I didn't, I wanted to flatten him."

"You *did* flatten him," she reminded him with a hint of a smile that eased the tension between them, but only a small bit. "John's a kind man," she added, "but I'm not going to marry him."

"I know it's none of my business," Fletcher replied, "but I'm glad." He took her hand in his. "I'm sorry for all this, I really am. I do care about you, but you know *I* can never marry you. I'm a US marshal, and I don't plan on changing the way I live."

Jo stood up, catching him off guard, and glared down at him. "I never asked you to marry me."

She moved around him on her way to the stairs, but stopped to straighten Edwyn's portrait on the wall. A mixture of fatigue and sadness passed over her features and, watching her, Fletcher felt a heaviness center in his chest.

"If you'll excuse me," Jo said, forcing all emotion from her voice and telling him in no uncertain terms that she was shutting him out, "I have work to do. And I believe you do, too."

When she turned her back on him and started up the stairs, he dropped his head into his hands, and wished that he could somehow change the man he had become.

Chapter

17

FLETCHER ROSE TO HIS FEET in the front hall and touched the tender bridge of his nose, still throbbing painfully. Right now, his whole body was aching, but mostly from the icy tone in Jo's voice when she'd turned away from him.

He had to admit, though, she was right. They'd become too damn close, and her shutting him out was the best thing for both of them.

What was he thinking, anyway, kissing her again like that? He'd taken advantage of her—that was certain—in her very own house after it nearly burned to the ground, up against her front door and under the watchful gaze of her dead husband's crooked, smoke-stained portrait. It was a stupidly selfish thing to do.

Feeling guilty and more out of touch than ever with the part of himself that was supposed to be a lawman, Fletcher looked up the staircase and heard the floorboards creaking under Jo's angry footsteps.

Her harsh tone reverberated inside his head. *I never asked you to marry me....*

What had possessed him to bring up marriage? It was the furthest thing from his mind—with any woman—and Mrs. O'Malley was hardly ready for marriage. Hell, the way she constantly straightened that damn picture....

Fletcher went to the kitchen, found a rag and managed to wet it under the forceful flow of cold water from the indoor pump. As he wiped the dried blood from under his nose and pressed the cool cloth to his burning eyelids, he struggled to remember who—and what—he was. *A lawman*. The sooner he took Jo to jail and left her there for someone else to deal with, the sooner he'd be back in control of his life and better able to do his job.

He winced when he touched the cloth to his broken nose.

Returning to the front hall, he decided it was time to find the men who killed Jo's husband and finish this investigation. That was the only way to be free of her. It was time he looked more closely into her and her late husband's affairs.

He glanced once more up the staircase and, hearing nothing, decided to take a look around. He walked down the hall toward the back of the large ranch house, and let himself into what, as luck would have it, appeared to be Edwyn's study.

The room was small and plain, painted green with chairs upholstered in a slightly darker green leather. A collection of rifles hung in a balanced display on the wall opposite the gray stone fireplace.

Fletcher glanced at the floor-to-ceiling bookcases with the books organized by author, but was more interested in the black walnut roll-top desk under the window. He closed the door behind him and strode across the room, his footsteps muted over the braided rug.

Taking a seat in the oak chair, he rolled up the bowed desktop. The contents were neatly arranged— the ledger and account book standing in one corner, ink jar and pens set back in the other, and correspondence stuffed tightly into a small cedar box on the desk shelf.

Beginning with the account book, Fletcher flipped through the pages to check the postings, but found no amounts out of the ordinary, nor any of the account names suspicious.

Reaching for the ledger next, Fletcher pulled out the thick black book and opened it. The silvery light of morning shone through the window and onto the long pages, which revealed typical journal entries—a debit to cash here, a credit to revenue there. All the amounts seemed reasonable for an outfit this size.

The only thing that made him stop and stare was the change in penmanship.

Sometime in February, the entries went from a small, dull scribble to a larger, more graceful, right-slanting script. Fletcher knew it was Jo's handwriting, for it matched her style—smooth and elegant, yet clear and strong—no fancy, curly swirls and loops in her letters.

He ran his finger over it. Tragic, that she'd put this ink to the page only weeks after her husband's death.

How hard it must have been for her to look at his script, a personal mark of his existence still living inside the book. She had probably run her dainty fingers over it, too, just like Fletcher was doing now, and what a task, he thought soberly, to undertake her husband's role as master of this ranch while the grief was still so fresh. He wished she would talk to him about it.

Realizing he was sliding off track of his duty again, Fletcher slammed the book shut and looked out the window at the rolling pasture, at rest beneath the white, overcast sky. He had to stay focused.

Setting the ledger back in place, he reached for the cedar box of letters on the small shelf and began reading. Unfortunately, all the letters were dated over the past six months, personal correspondence addressed to Jo from various friends or relations. Fletcher found nothing suspicious, just a lot of continuing condolences about Edwyn's death...*how lonely you must be,* a hundred times over.

Reminded again of Jo's recent sorrow—her problems, her vast responsibilities, her heartbreak over losing the man she loved—Fletcher tried to shake away the jealousy he didn't want to feel, and the regret about what had just happened between them. He stuffed the last letter back into the box, steepled his fingers together, and rested his forehead on them.

Concentrate. If this was Jo's workplace now, where were Edwyn's business papers and correspondence from the past few years?

Swiveling in the chair, he glanced around the small room. On the floor beside the bookcase, he spotted a small oak sea chest.

He crossed the room and knelt before it, but found it locked tighter than a bank safe. It was just as heavy, he discovered, upon trying to move it away from the wall. What in God's name could weigh so much?

He jiggled the lock a bit, but nothing budged. He jiggled a little harder, but froze when the door to the den suddenly swung open.

Fletcher rose to his feet to face John's skeptical gaze. "What are you doing in here, Marshal?"

Hell, he couldn't tell John he was investigating Edwyn's murder. He couldn't tell anyone. So what, exactly, *was* he doing in here?

At Fletcher's hesitation, John's eyes narrowed. "Where's Mrs. O'Malley?"

"Upstairs."

"Nonsense. I'm right here." Wearing a white cotton apron over a yellow calico bodice and skirt, Jo walked in and stood beside John. "What seems to be the problem?"

"Marshal Collins weaseled his way in here, ma'am. I found him lurking around like a bandit."

Jo cupped her hands in front of her. "Well, of course he's in here. Where else is he to wait for breakfast? In the burned parlor?"

"But I saw him jiggling the lock on Mr. O'Malley's private box right there."

"I was just admiring it," Fletcher said. "I like old sea chests."

Jo cleared her throat, looking shaken. "John, if you'll wait for me in the kitchen, I'd like to speak with you. I'll be along directly."

"Sure thing, ma'am." He glared irately at Fletcher before backing out of the room.

Jo moved inside, her skirts whipping between her fast footsteps. "Here's what you're looking for." Impatiently, she rose up on her toes and retrieved a brass key from the highest shelf over the chest. Her tone had never been so cold, and Fletcher felt the chill clear down to his boots. "Though I don't know what you're after," she went on. "It's just full of Edwyn's personal letters from Ireland. They're old, they were written before he even came to America. He was sentimental and brought them with him."

Fletcher's finger touched hers as he took the key from her, and she immediately jerked her hand back. Trying not to let it bother him as much as it did, he knelt down and turned the key in the old lock. The rusty hinges squeaked as he opened the chest.

"Yep. Letters, and lots of them." He flipped through a few.

"I wouldn't lie about it." There was something odd in her tone. Something that struck him.

"I didn't think you would." Fletcher closed the box and stood. "But is there something you're not telling me, Jo? Something about these letters?"

"I assure you, they're just personal," she replied. "So what *were* you looking for?" She returned the key to its hiding place, and seemed anxious to change the subject.

"Edwyn's business papers and correspondence. I didn't find anything in the desk."

"You searched my desk?"

"I thought we agreed I'd look through Edwyn's

belongings," Fletcher replied. "It seemed like a wise place to start."

Jo moved to the collection of rifles on the wall and pulled another key from behind the Winchester on the mantel. "You'll find everything over there." Pointing to another larger chest covered by a green plaid blanket, Jo handed the key to him. "I've looked through it all and didn't find anything unusual, but you have a go at it. Shall I bring your breakfast on a tray?"

He took the key. "It would get me out of here faster."

Jo lifted her chin. "Yes, of course. You don't like to stay in one place for too long, do you?" She turned to leave.

Too late, Fletcher realized how insensitive his words had sounded. "Jo..."

But in a whisper of petticoats, she was already out the door.

Jo walked down the wide hall, her hand on her stomach. She paused at the bottom of the staircase, her other hand resting on the newel post. The parlor to her left was blackened and smelling of scorched fabric, kerosene and smoke. Someone was trying to kill her, and Fletcher was itching to take her to prison.

Why, oh why, then, was she fantasizing about kissing him again, about making love to him, all problems forgotten? Why was she so completely heartsick and tormented by the fact that that would never happen?

She took a breath, trying to find the heart to move. Ridiculous, that she could be falling for such a soulless, heartless man who could kiss her one moment, tell her that he cared, yet not deny that he would toss her in jail the first chance he got? And why was she letting herself care for him when she knew that the law meant more to him than she did?

As she considered it more, she found herself remembering the things he had said to her on the dark prairie, how he had reacted when she'd confessed her sins and secrets—that she had lied about what she saw the night Edwyn was killed and, after that, had taken the law into her own hands.

Of course, Fletcher did what his duty demanded of him—he'd arrested her—but at the same time, he had listened and understood and consoled her. He had told her that Edwyn's death was not her fault, that she had done the right thing, to stay hidden. He did not condemn her for the thing that mattered most in her heart—the thing she believed was her greatest sin.

How then, could he be soulless? How could a man with no heart manage to touch hers, when she thought she'd cloaked it in ice?

It was all so frustrating. She could no longer deny how desperately she wanted and desired the man beneath the badge, the man she knew existed but could not have.

She supposed that if her heart was to be broken, she had only herself to blame for confiding in him, for entrusting her life to him, and for letting him kiss her and touch her the way he had.

It would not happen again.

Dropping her hands to her sides and forcing herself to stand tall, she glanced toward the kitchen where

John was waiting—after having offered to marry her in front of everyone—and she dreaded talking to him about this. She hoped it would not be too awkward.

Working hard to focus on what had to be done, she squared her shoulders and walked with purpose into the kitchen. There he sat, hands clasped together in front of him, full of hope when he knew nothing about all of Jo's reprehensible sins and failings.

He stood as soon as he saw her, and she felt a twinge of guilt.

"Good morning, John. Thank you for waiting. Please sit down."

Jo sat across from him. Unable to meet his gaze, she let hers fall to his rough, callused hands. "I...I want to thank you for what you tried to do this morning, after the fire was put out. I know you were concerned for my well-being."

"Yes, ma'am. I am concerned."

She tried to smile. "There's really no need to be. I'm quite capable of taking care of myself."

Before she had a chance to finish, John was leaping out of his chair and dropping to his knees before her, clasping her hands in his. "Mrs. O'Malley, that man in Mr. O'Malley's den is no good for you, no good at all."

"John, let me—"

"No, please, let me talk first. I reckon I can guess what he did to you, why your eye looks like that, but I promise not to ever mention it again if you'll just let me and the boys throw him out of here."

"John, this is all a misunderstanding." She hated herself for keeping the truth from him.

"No need to make up stories for me, ma'am. I'm just glad to see you popped him one in return."

She couldn't believe this was happening, and closed her eyes while she shook her head. "It's nothing like that, John—"

"I'm glad I popped him one, too."

By now, her head was throbbing with frustration. She pulled her hands from John's and stood up. "Fletcher did not intentionally hurt me. It was an accident."

"Then why'd you hit him back?"

"That was an accident, too."

John hesitated, his forehead crinkling. "I sure hope you're not going to marry him."

"Of course I'm not, and I would appreciate it if you would not speak of it again."

John's chest heaved with a deep breath. He stood and approached her. "Then my offer still stands, ma'am. I don't know what happened between you two last night, and I'm willing to forget about it. I won't mention it again if you'll just consider my offer."

"John..."

"Please, listen first." He dropped to one knee and held her hand. "I know you've had a rough year. We all have, after what happened to Mr. O'Malley. He was a good man and a fair boss, but you shouldn't have to be all alone and run things by yourself. Folks are talkin' about you living out here with all of us—"

"I know that, John, and I really don't care what they're saying."

"Maybe you don't love me, but you might in time. I'm a nice enough fellow, I'd always treat you decent, never raise a hand to you or Leo. I ain't like that."

Jo didn't know what to say. She had a million reasons not to marry him, but the only one that seemed
to reveal itself to her now was an impossible infatua-
tion for a man who cared only for the steel badge he
wore on his vest. "John..."

"It would be sort of like one of them marriages of
conven—conven—"

"Convenience," she finished for him.

"Yeah, yeah, one of them. You'd get your reputation back, and I'd get a ranch out of it."

Jo slowly pulled her hand away. "A *ranch*...?"

"Yes, ma'am. And a damn good one. Is something
wrong?"

She sighed heavily. "John, to be frank, you don't
know the first thing about me. If you did, your feelings might be different."

"Ma'am, a ranch is a ranch."

Turning her back on him, she cupped her pounding
forehead in her hand. *Oh, dear, sweet, simple Edwyn.
Nothing was ever this complicated with you.*

"Maybe we should talk about this later," Jo suggested, setting aside the sharp edge to her voice and
replacing it with a gentler tone that took significant
efforts to produce. "The men are waiting for their
breakfast."

He stood in silence behind her. She heard him
breathing hard and it made her uneasy, so she faced
him squarely and spoke firmly. "Wait outside, John."

Finally his boots thumped across the floor and the
front door creaked open and slammed shut behind
him.

Good God, was there no one she could trust?

Feeling angry and disillusioned, she collapsed into the chair and wondered how in all the world her life had plunged into such depths of misfortune, and how she would ever claw her way out of it.

Chapter

18

WHILE THE RANCH HANDS BURROWED into their breakfast plates in the dining room, Jo stood at the stove in the kitchen, serving up a large helping of fried eggs and bacon for Fletcher.

Perspiring over the hot stove, she reached for two slices of corn bread that Matilda had made before she left, dropped them onto the plate and set the heavy cast-iron frying pan aside. She reached for a jar of molasses to set on Fletcher's tray, and wondered why she was taking such pains with his food. It wasn't as if her cooking was so stupendous, it would convince him to let her go.

She poured a cup of black coffee for him and arranged everything on the tray. Untying the strings of her apron, she draped it over the kitchen chair, picked up the heavy breakfast tray and walked down the hall toward the den with caution on her mind.

When she set eyes on Fletcher, she would not—absolutely not—let herself think about how it felt to kiss
him. She would focus on her purpose: to ensure her
family's safety and see that Zeb paid for what he did.

With that, and only that, in mind, she pushed open
the door to the den and entered.

Fletcher sat in one of the leather upholstered chairs
reading a letter. Both his eyes were black from being
punched in the nose so many times, and Jo felt a
twinge of guilt about that. She stared at his focused
expression, then at his big, manly hands, and a flurry
of disloyal butterflies created a disturbing breeze
inside her belly. Why wasn't her body listening to
what her head was telling it?

Standing like a dazed ninny in the doorway, Jo tried
to concentrate on moving her feet, one in front of
the other. Somehow, she managed to fully enter the
room. She set the tray on the center table, brushed
her hair back from her perspiration-dampened forehead and looked toward the window, all in an effort
to fight the memories that would not retreat from her
mind.

She thought of Fletcher giving her back her weapon
that morning, of the way his eyes told her that he
trusted her with it; she recalled how he had coura-
geously fought the fire and how he'd insisted that
she leave the smoke-filled parlor to go outside and
breathe clean air.

He did those things not because it was his job, but
because he sincerely and genuinely wanted to protect
her. That's just the kind of man he was.

Fletcher lowered the page he was reading, and the

sound startled her from her thoughts.

"Did you know that Edwyn reported cattle theft to the city council more than once?" he mentioned with interest.

So, for him, it was business as usual. It would be that way for her, too, she decided.

Jo moved to stand behind the chair and look over Fletcher's shoulder at what he was reading. "Yes, I've seen that letter, but I never thought much about it. Most of the ranchers have lost head to rustlers."

"Seems like there's been a lot of rustling in these parts lately." Fletcher rose from the chair and moved to the old ledgers lying open on a corner table. "I just compared the losses Edwyn reported at year-end with the losses from previous years. I know ranching," he added, "and these numbers seem high to me."

Jo followed him and looked at Edwyn's year-end adjustments in the ledger. "It was a hard winter. We lost quite a few head to the early storms. Maybe that's why he was adjusting the accounts."

"No, no, he was a very meticulous bookkeeper. There's a year-end entry over here for winter losses, and a separate entry here for unexplained disappearances—most likely theft. It's this number that doesn't compare to other years. Look at the difference." He lifted up the ledger and pulled out the one from the year before.

Jo examined the two books. After Edwyn's death, she'd pored over the year-end statements, and thought she'd gained a thorough understanding of the bookkeeping. Why hadn't she thought to study the previous years?

She stared at the ledgers in disbelief. Had Edwyn been murdered because he knew something about the cattle rustling around Dodge? How could she have missed this?

Fletcher walked toward the breakfast tray. "Looks like we may have found something."

Jo turned. "No, *you* found it."

"Don't be too hard on yourself. I only found it because I'm used to following tracks. Hoof-prints or a paper-trail, it's all the same to me." He pulled a chair across the rug toward the table and sat down to eat.

Jo paced back and forth behind him, remembering the night Edwyn was killed and all the times she'd seen Zeb Stone, before and after. She'd never connected him with the business of ranching. Even Fletcher had called him too civilized to meddle in it.

Unable to come up with any answers herself, she sat down in the leather chair across from Fletcher and watched him eat. "How much do you know about the cattle thefts around Dodge?"

He didn't look up as he cut his eggs. "Not a whole lot. You've been my chief concern since I got here. You and Six-Shooter Hank, that is."

She tried not to let him make her feel guilty about that. "I apologize. Perhaps I can make it up to you by filling you in on some of the local crime. I do read the papers, and there's at least one herd with missing cattle reported each week. Different ranchers, small outfits and large ones, Texas-based herds driving up the trail. They start out with a certain-sized herd, then arrive in Dodge with a smaller one, and the cowboys can't explain it."

"And you think you can?"

"Just give me a chance to explain what I think. Maybe Zeb is running a cattle-rustling ring, and that's why he was so vague last night about what he hired you to do. Maybe Zeb killed Edwyn because of the letters he sent to the city council."

"How long has this cattle rustling been going on?"

"You saw the books. A few years, maybe. It seems normal to most people now."

Fletcher took a sip of coffee and nodded his head, still without looking up. "A few years, you say. If this has been going on for a few years, don't you think it's possible that you might be the teeniest bit mistaken about Zeb? After all, he's only been in these parts for two."

Feeling as if her theory had been quashed, Jo tried to prevent the inevitable loss of color to her cheeks. "Where was he before that?"

"Chicago. Meeting my sister for the first time."

Jo shifted in her chair and cleared her throat, her hopes sinking at this supposed alibi. "Are you sure?"

"Elizabeth told me she met him briefly in her first year of college—the year his family died and left him all his money. Then he courted her and proposed to her during her third and final year."

"But he could have been back and forth that first year."

"He opened his dry goods store exactly two years ago," Fletcher said, "and before that, he was burying his parents in Chicago. It was only after he inherited his money that he decided to invest it out here, in the West."

Jo twisted her wedding ring around on her finger. "Perhaps, with your resources as marshal, you could look into it. His past may very well be a fabrication."

"And my sister imagined meeting him in Chicago three years ago?"

Jo squeezed the smooth arm of the chair. She had held a loaded gun to Zeb's head and very nearly pulled the trigger. She would not have done that without the strongest of convictions about his murderous heart. "Maybe Zeb became involved with whoever started this cattle-rustling ring after he came here." Proud of herself for that little suggestion, she raised her chin.

Fletcher set down his coffee cup and wiped his hands on the linen napkin. "Your theories are all well and good, Jo, but you know I need real evidence. I'm willing to look into these cattle thefts, but I don't know how to do it without locking you up."

"But Fletcher—"

"There's no other way to keep you safe and in custody at the same time."

"But I won't be safe in jail," she argued. "I can't trust anyone, not even your deputies. Zeb might own them already, and you said yourself that if people find out why you arrested me, you won't be able to investigate."

"What do you suggest we do, then?" Fletcher rose from the chair and threw his napkin on the tray. "I can't let you off, and I can't take you with me. That would look just as suspicious. If I believe that I can't trust my deputies…"

He paced the room for a few minutes while Jo sat there, watching him.

"Unless..." he said, not looking at her, his thoughts only on his job, it seemed, and the best way to do it.

"What's your idea?" she asked.

Fletcher rested his hands on his hips. "This may sound strange, but after my altercation just now with your foreman, John—news of which will probably be all over town by midday—we could tell people we're engaged."

Despite the sleep she badly needed, Jo felt instantly wide-awake. "You're not serious."

"I know it sounds crazy, but it would just be an act to distract people. If you were my fiancée, we could be seen constantly together without raising suspicion. There'd be all sorts of gossip and no one would question what was *really* going on. I'd only be doing it to keep watch over you without raising suspicion, and to solve this case at the same time, as quickly as possible. If there's any truth to what you say about Zeb, this will rattle his cage for sure." Fletcher paced the carpet, never making eye contact. "And you'd only be doing it to help find the men who killed your husband," he added. "Maybe lighten your sentence a bit, if the judge is sympathetic."

"If it means Zeb will get what's coming to him," she replied, "I'd be willing to go along with it. Just don't expect me to play the lovesick fool. I have more important things to accomplish."

That last little bit was her pride talking, and she suspected he knew it.

It was nearly noon by the time Zeb forced himself to roll over and slide out of his luxurious mahogany bed. His bare toes touched the cold floor, and he cursed the maid for not making his house more comfortable with a fire at dawn, especially when he paid her far more than her pathetic, stubby fingers were worth.

Only then did he realize, with another irritated curse, that he'd worn his blue silk nightshirt to bed inside out.

Squeezing his hammering temples, he swallowed against the dry, detestable taste of the morning in his mouth. He was glad Elizabeth had risen early, as was her usual habit, for if she were here, just the sound of her high-pitched, chattery voice would have driven him mad.

Zeb rang for his manservant, Matthews, who assisted him in dressing and shaving, then he made his way downstairs, trying not to move too quickly. He was on his way to the library for a medicinal shot of brandy when he heard Elizabeth's heels clicking fast across the polished floor behind him, and he had to fight the urge to whip around and silence her with a slap, as he had silenced her last night.

"What is it, Elizabeth? And don't ask me how I slept."

She stopped in the center of the wide hall and cleared her throat. "I...I'm sorry to disturb you, Zeb, but Fletcher is in the drawing room. He has some news, but he wanted to wait for you before he said anything. I believe it's about Mrs. O'Malley."

Ah! Good news to wake up to for a change.

Fletcher had come, no doubt, to deliver *bad* news about a fire and a dead widow—news that would cure

Zeb's headache just as effectively as half a bottle of brandy.

He guided Elizabeth back toward the drawing room. "Nothing wrong with the woman, I hope."

"I don't know. He's been very secretive about it."

"Well, we shall find out soon enough."

Fletcher stood in his sister's drawing room at the window, his gaze following Zeb's tree-lined drive-way, his worries drifting back to Jo. He hoped she was still sitting in the church confessional where he'd left her. He felt badly about tying her to the bench leg, especially after she'd protested, but he still couldn't be sure she wouldn't try to escape, and he wanted to deliver this news on his own, without distraction.

He turned when he heard Elizabeth and Zeb enter the room. Watching them together—her slender arm looped through Zeb's, both of them richly dressed in the finest attire Dodge had to offer—Fletcher felt his heart darken with regret.

Maybe Jo was wrong about Zeb. He was Elizabeth's husband, after all. The man she had chosen above all others, the future she had embraced with her whole heart when she'd married him.

Fletcher wondered uneasily if he was prepared to kick it all out from under her.

Zeb stopped in the doorway. "Good heavens, you look exhausted. What in the world has happened?"

"I am a little tired," Fletcher confessed. "I was up most of the night."

Zeb moved fully into the room. "Busy, were you? Please sit down and tell us all about it."

Fletcher studied Zeb's eyes, hoping he would not see what he'd come here to find. "Truthfully, I wasn't busy. I was up all night, just thinking."

Zeb sat silently, staring. "About what?"

"Marriage."

Elizabeth strode toward him, her cheeks flushing, her eyes regaining some of the radiance Fletcher had not seen in her lately. "Marriage? Fletcher, what do you mean?"

"You, Liz, of all people, should know exactly what I mean. Can't you tell by looking at me?" He had to swallow the bitter realization that he'd never lied to his sister before now.

Zeb continued to stare at Fletcher, dumbfounded, and Fletcher stared right back at him, searching.

Elizabeth smiled. "Oh, do say it, Fletcher! Is it what I think?"

He would come clean soon enough, he told himself, trying to ease some of the guilt. Just as soon as all this nasty business of murder and cattle rustling was cleared up.

"You said you had bad news about Mrs. O'Malley," Zeb interrupted with a frown.

"I never said it was bad," Fletcher said, "but you can judge that for yourself." Fletcher's gut wrenched at Zeb's slipup, but he tried to hide it as the lie spilled from his lips. "Mrs. O'Malley and I are going to be married."

"Oh!" Elizabeth squealed, but Fletcher was watching Zeb, who cupped his head and winced with pain at his wife's jolly outcry. She hurried to sit beside Fletcher and threw her arms around his neck. "I'm so happy!"

"So am I," he replied, still digesting Zeb's words.

"But you've only known her a few days!" Elizabeth said with a smile. "She must be incredibly special. I thought her so when I met her. She and I will be like sisters, I know it!"

Fletcher watched Zeb, who rose to his feet and dutifully offered his hand. "I suppose congratulations are in order."

"Thank you, Zeb." Fletcher stood and shook hands with his brother-in-law.

"You've asked her, I presume."

"Of course," Fletcher replied.

"When? You must have ridden out there very early this morning," he commented, his tone brimming with curiosity and impatience.

Fletcher thought carefully about how he should answer that loaded observation. Was it best to let Zeb believe, for a little longer, that Jo might be dead, if that was in fact why he was asking?

Or was it worth the risk to see Zeb's face when he found out that she was still among the living?

"I asked her first thing this morning," Fletcher replied matter-of-factly. Then he paused to await Zeb's reaction.

The man's jaw twitched.

"She came into town to buy some things for her house," Fletcher continued, laying down more information for Zeb to take in. "There was a fire in her parlor."

"What a shame," Zeb replied, his eyes void of any sentiment.

Elizabeth covered her mouth with her hand. "Good gracious. No one was hurt, I hope."

"It was a small fire," Fletcher replied. "Clumsily started, I think."

"No doubt," Zeb said, his mood dark.

"Will you bring her for supper this evening?" Elizabeth asked. "We can all celebrate."

Fletcher glanced at his sister, so lighthearted and smiling, and he wanted to sink through the floor at the thought of capsizing her perfect new life.

Then he glanced at Zeb, saw the annoyance hovering in his eyes, and felt his instincts begin to boil. He had no definite proof of anything, but he knew something was up with Zeb, and it was his duty to find out what it was.

He supposed it was time to surrender to the one thing he'd wanted to avoid—a social evening with Zeb and Jo together.

19

*J*O STOOD INSIDE THE CITY clerk's office while Fletcher dug into his pocket for keys.

"I'm curious what the city council did about your husband's letters," he said, unlocking and opening a drawer in the large desk under the window. "Were they publicized at all?"

"Not that I know of. I never heard another word about it after he sent them."

"He didn't send them to the newspaper or anything like that?"

"Definitely not. Edwyn didn't like to bring attention to himself."

Fletcher nodded in understanding. "He took the time to make copies of the letters, so he must have been serious about the situation." Fletcher pulled a large hard-covered book out of the drawer and set it on the desk. He began to flip through the pages.

"I'm looking for the city council minutes of last July. That's when he sent the first letter."

Jo leaned forward over Fletcher's shoulder, trying to ignore the subtle scent of leather from his gun belt as she watched his sun-bronzed hands turn page after page of the ruled paper. "Here it is—council meeting on July 23. Look for your husband's name."

They both read over the minutes, but Edwyn's letters were never mentioned.

"Are you sure the first letter was dated in July?" she asked, refusing to give up hope that they would find something.

"Positive. I'll check August. Maybe he sent it late." They searched through the records, page after page, every month in the whole year.

"There's nothing," Fletcher said grimly. "No mention of either of Edwyn's letters or any cattle-theft problem." He set the book back in the drawer and leaned against the desk, the heel of his palm braced upon the top while he rubbed his forehead with the other hand.

Jo stood before him, watching the stress lines deepen around his eyes. "Zeb got rid of those letters. He must be involved in the cattle-rustling ring and that's why he came after Edwyn, and why he destroyed the police records about Edwyn's death."

"We can't be certain of that yet."

"But Zeb has the power and the access to these records."

"So do a lot of other people."

"But I know it was Zeb that night. This only confirms it. Why can't you at least say it's possible? Give me that much?"

At last, Fletcher surrendered to her on that point, and she had to fight the urge to wrap her arms around his neck and thank him properly.

"I won't say it's impossible," he replied, "but we still have to keep looking." Fletcher locked the desk and retrieved his hat from the hook by the door. "Which is exactly why I want to know more about this cattle-rustling problem." He pressed the hat onto his head.

"At least we're in agreement on *that*." Jo followed Fletcher outside into the bright sunlight and shaded her eyes with her gloved hand. He locked the door behind them and began to descend the steps ahead of her. "Let's move fast," he said, "I want to get to the stockyard before the train comes in."

Picking up her skirts in one hand, Jo hurried down the steps and followed him over the tracks toward Front Street.

A few minutes later, Fletcher and Jo approached the cattle-loading pens, packed tight with Texas longhorns shrieking and snorting and clacking their horns together, while they awaited the train that would take them east to a Chicago slaughterhouse.

Fletcher guided Jo past the station depot, and as soon as his hand touched the small of her back, he noticed a knot in his gut the size of a watermelon—which had nothing to do with stockyards, cows, or cattle-rustling. Things were getting pretty dicey around here, and he was finding it more and more difficult by the second to keep his mind on his job, when all he wanted to do was take Jo back to his room at the boardinghouse, tie her to his bed again and see where things might go from there.

God, he wanted her too much. He *cared* too much. And having her with him all the time like this, while pretending to be engaged, was turning into a cruel form of torture. But he had to remember his position. She was his prisoner and she wanted her own brand of justice with a passion that was simply too dangerous, not to mention illegal.

Hence, the colossal knot in his gut he couldn't quash...

They approached a short, stocky cowhand and Fletcher forced himself to get his mind back on business.

"Mornin'," Fletcher said to the man, who was leaning back against the gate, his face leather-brown from hours spent in the saddle under the scorching western sun. "You responsible for this herd?"

The man took one look at Fletcher's badge and stepped away from the fence. "Yes, sir. I'm the trail boss, Cory Hays." He glanced at Jo and fingered his hat. "Morning, ma'am."

"Where you from?"

"I come from Montana originally, sir."

Fletcher nodded. "This herd from Texas?"

"Yes, sir. It belongs to Mr. Addison of San Antonio. There a problem, Marshal?"

Fletcher glanced at the branding on one of the steers—the letter A in two places—on the shoulder and back hip.

Jo stepped forward and the young man smiled nervously at her. "Have you lost any head to rustlers, Mr.

Hays?" she asked directly.

Fletcher gave her a look, wishing she would remember that she was supposed to be his fiancée, not his deputy marshal.

"As a matter of fact, ma'am, yes. Or at least, that's what we think. They just seem to disappear. Mr. Addison hired extra hands this season, hoping to figure out what was happening, maybe put a stop to it. But the size of the herd keeps getting smaller and smaller as we drive 'em up the trail. It don't make a lick of sense."

"How many have you lost?" Jo asked.

"He ships about fifty thousand head a year, altogether. He probably lost close to five thousand, and he ain't too happy about it."

Fletcher squinted across the top of the pen, over the heads of cattle toward the treeless, unbroken horizon. "Do you lose them off the ranch in Texas, or just along the drive?" Fletcher asked.

"Both, sir. All year round. And it ain't just the Western Trail. I hear they go missing off the Chisholm Trail, too."

Fletcher inclined his head in a way of saying thanks. "You can tell Addison that there's a new marshal in Dodge, and I'll be looking into things for him. I'll do my best to put an end to this problem."

"Yes, sir, Marshal Collins. I'll tell him today, when I send the wire."

Fletcher placed his hand on the small of Jo's back again and directed her toward town. "I'm supposed to be asking the questions," he told her quietly. "You're just supposed to be my fiancée."

"I'm only trying to speed things up."

She said nothing more, but he felt her frustration in the way she moved—the straight set of her shoulders, the sway of her hips. He found himself wanting to explain everything better, to talk openly and reveal how completely torn he felt about all this.

"Let's go to the bakery for some bread and a pie," he suggested, hoping to untie that bothersome knot in his gut. "I hear the lady who works there has a nose for gossip, and it wouldn't hurt to get the town talking, create a diversion while we poke around a bit."

"It's the widow Harper you must be referring to," Jo said. "And she definitely loves to talk."

Fletcher offered Jo his arm and escorted her past the crowd of curious onlookers who stood in front of the Dodge House Hotel.

"I'm not sure how you'll feel about this," he said, leaning in and stealing the opportunity to breathe in the sweet scent of her perfume. "But maybe it's time you removed your wedding ring. Folks might wonder about it otherwise."

And he had to wonder, himself, why—after all his efforts to keep his mind on business—he'd noticed that she still wore the ring, and why he was pleased to have an excuse to ask her to take it off.

Jo stopped and appeared flustered. "Of course." She fumbled to pull off her gloves and fumbled even more to pull the gold band off her slender finger. "There." She popped it into her reticule and pulled the drawstring closed.

Fletcher offered his arm again, feeling far more

pleased than he should.

"I haven't told you this yet," Fletcher mentioned later, as he steered Jo's wagon across the toll bridge toward the open plains, "but we've been invited to supper tonight."

Jo held on to the spring seat as they bumped along, her sunbonnet tied tightly under her chin. "Something tells me I shouldn't ask who our dinner companions will be."

"I couldn't very well refuse the offer," he went on, apologetically. "I'm supposed to be proud about us getting engaged, and Elizabeth...well, she was just so darn happy."

"Really?" Jo replied, trying not to feel too flattered. Why should it matter that Fletcher's sister approved of her?

"They're expecting us at seven, but I don't know if it's such a good idea. I don't want you in the same room with Zeb."

"Are you worried about me, or him?"

Fletcher shook his head with what seemed surprisingly like admiration. "I've never met a woman quite like you before."

"I wasn't trying to impress you," she said, bumping shoulders with him.

"I know. That's what impresses me the most." A sexy grin passed across his lips. Jo had to force herself to look away.

Fletcher steered the wagon off the bridge and over the short grass toward a cowhand, sitting against his bedroll with one knee up while he watched his herd, his horse grazing nearby.

"Howdy," the young man greeted as he rose to stand and brush off his pants.

"Morning. I'm Fletcher Collins, the new marshal."

"I know who you are. What can I do for you?"

Fletcher held the reins loosely. "I'm looking into some missing cattle."

The cowhand removed his black sombrero and brushed the dust off it. "You'll be looking into it for a while, Marshal. Nobody seems to know where they end up."

"I take it you've lost some head yourself?"

"You take it right, but I can't help you any. It's a mystery."

Fletcher tipped his hat and they drove on, asking every cowhand they came upon if they knew anything, and the answer was always the same.

An hour later, Jo reached for the bread they'd bought at the bakery and tore off a section. "Are you hungry? It must be midday."

She handed Fletcher a thick chunk, which he ate while steering them back toward town. The cattle on either side of the road grazed quietly, stopping to raise their heads only when the wagon rolled by.

"When will Leo and Matilda be back?" Fletcher asked.

"In about a week. I wanted them to be safe. The less they know about what's going on, the better." She swallowed some bread. "Although, they'll find out soon enough, I suppose."

Fletcher didn't comment on that. He stared straight ahead and clicked his tongue at the horses. "So your house is empty?"

"What's left of it, yes. The hands sleep in the bunk-house, of course. Why do you ask?"

He answered her in a calm, indifferent tone. "I'm just thinking ahead to tonight. It might be a bit of a problem. Being engaged doesn't make it okay for me to spend the night at your house. Especially when the engagement will eventually be broken. I don't want to spoil any chances you might have for...well, for moving on."

Jo tried to suppress her hurt. Why did he feel it necessary to remind her that he was anxious to be finished with her?

She made an attempt to lighten the mood with a joke. "Well, I refuse to marry *today*, if that's what you're suggesting."

He chuckled. "It may come as a surprise to you, but there are limits to what I'm willing to do in the name of the law."

Jo playfully rolled her eyes. "Thank you! That was most flattering."

His warm gaze met hers and they shared in the moment of humor, which felt all too brief.

"It still doesn't solve our problem," he said, getting back to the more serious matter at hand. "I doubt I'll have your husband's killer behind bars by night-fall, and I'm not taking any chances with your safety. You'll need to be in hiding again."

Jo settled back in her seat, considering her options. "Your room won't do, now that everyone thinks we're engaged. That'll be the first place Zeb will look for me if I'm not at home."

She handed him another chunk of bread, and they both ate in silence for a few minutes.

"I suppose the only way around this," Jo said, swiping at the crumbs on her skirt and trying to block out all thoughts of Fletcher keeping watch over her bed, "is to prove Zeb's guilt before the sun goes down. What are the chances of that?"

He simply shook his head, which did nothing to ease her mind.

Chapter

20

STEERING JO'S WAGON ONTO FRONT Street after a fruitless search for information on the plains, Fletcher watched two local ranchers shuffle out of Zimmerman's Hardware Store. They were carrying a potbellied stove toward their wagon. One of them spotted him and yelled into the street, "Congratulations, Marshal!" In his excitement, he nearly dropped the stove.

Fletcher tipped his hat and nodded, reminding himself not to feel too proud. This was just a performance.

Jo wiggled in her seat beside him. "I hope we're doing the right thing."

"We are." Fletcher steered the wagon toward the depot again, determined to get his mind off betrothals and back where it belonged—on this alleged cattle-rustling ring. "I want to ask about the herd loading onto the rail car."

"Wait, stop." Jo touched his arm. "Deputy Anderson is waving at us. Over there by the barbershop."

Fletcher pulled the wagon to a halt. Anderson walked across the street, one hand in the air to signal them to stop, the other holding a newspaper.

"Where you been, Marshal Collins?" he asked curiously. "I been looking for you all day." He handed the newspaper up to Fletcher. "You sure have a way of making headlines. And what happened to your nose?"

"It's a long story."

Hesitantly, Fletcher unfolded the paper and read the front page. Jo leaned over his arm to look on. "Bruiser To Marry Local Widow."

"Oh, don't tell me..." Jo said, taking hold of the corner of the page to read the small print aloud.

"'Marshal Collins, the newest addition to Dodge City's band of lawmen, has decided to take a wife. The lucky lady is the reclusive widow O'Malley, who has squashed the long-held notion that she prefers to keep to herself. Other news today, Mr. Garry Owens of Walnut Street has a new overcoat.'"

Jo sat back in her seat. "Does the editor have nothing better to do?"

"Congratulations to you both," Deputy Anderson said, tipping his hat. "When's the big day?"

Fletcher glanced at Jo, who met his gaze with equal uncertainty. They were getting into this deeper and deeper by the minute. "We thought we'd wait until after the election," he replied, tapping her knee.

"Of course," Anderson said. "The family's busy enough, I reckon."

"Any goings-on this morning?" Fletcher asked, trying to change the subject.

"Nope. But folks are wondering what happened to Six-Shooter Hank and why we haven't caught him yet."

Fletcher flicked the reins. "Tell them I have a lead. We'll get him."

He felt Jo tense beside him as the wagon lurched forward and they started toward the depot, leaving Deputy Anderson to deal with a pig who had wandered into the middle of the street and stopped traffic with its squeal.

"Just wait till the newspapers get wind of what's really going on," Jo said. "You and I will be famous from here to the Panhandle."

"I'll do my best to keep this from turning into a circus."

"I doubt that'll be possible, even for you."

Her sharp tone cut through his resolve and made him wonder if any of this was worth it.

"Come with me," he said, pulling the wagon to a halt behind the depot where he could see cattle being loaded into the rail car, their hooves thumping madly over the wooden ramp, their moos and snorts muted below the hiss of steam from the train. "I don't want to leave you alone."

He climbed down and circled around the front of the team to help Jo down. She rested her hands on his shoulders while he cupped his around her tiny waist, lifting her lightly to the ground. The faint scent of orange flower water drifted on a breeze under his nose and made him all too aware of her womanly presence in his arms. Damn, but it felt good to hold her.

"I hear you two are getting married," a voice said from behind.

Startled, Fletcher dropped his hand to his gun and turned around. He found himself staring at the cowboy who had been gambling with Zeb the night before.

"What's the hurry, Marshal?" he asked. "You only just got here a few days ago. Don't you want to taste what delicacies Dodge has to offer before you settle on beef and potatoes for the rest of your days?" Glancing down at Jo, he licked his lips.

Fletcher squeezed the handle of his Peacemaker in an effort to keep control, then reached around to touch Jo's arm and sweep her behind him where this brute wouldn't be able to even look at her. He glared into the man's narrowing eyes, smelled tobacco on his stale breath and noticed a scar through his eyebrow.

"This your herd?" Fletcher demanded.

"Yeah, what's it to ya?"

"You work for George Greer?"

"As far as I'm concerned, there ain't no other outfits in Texas worth the effort."

Fletcher glanced at the large brand that covered almost the entire side of each steer.

"Any of your herd go missing on the drive?"

The trail boss smirked. "If you're talking about the rustling ring that's got everybody in a huff, you're wasting your time with me and my boys. We know how to handle a herd. Greer pays us well to make sure he gets the best. And to answer your question, Greer cattle *doesn't* go missing."

Fletcher nodded his head, still resting his hand on his gun. He could feel Jo behind him, and sensing her desire to say something, he figured he'd better move on before she found a chance to open her mouth. Taking her arm as he backed away, he helped her into the wagon, then called to the trail boss, "What's your name?"

"Why? You want to invite me to your weddin'?"

"What's your name?"

The man spit on the ground. "MacGregor. Will MacGregor."

Fletcher climbed into the wagon, in a hurry to take this new information with him to the telegraph office. He had some friends in Texas who owed him favors. With any luck, he'd get replies back before he and Jo had to clink champagne glasses with Zeb over his fancy red silk tablecloth.

Jo sat across from Fletcher in the city clerk's office above the jail, tapping her foot while they waited for the telegraph replies to come in. Fletcher had asked the operator to send them over right away, without wasting a minute, but nothing seemed to be happening. No one seemed to be at the other end of the wires.

"What time is it?" Fletcher asked, pacing the floor behind his desk.

Jo took her timepiece out of her bodice pocket. "It's almost six-thirty. I don't think we're going to hear back from anyone before seven. We'll just have to go to Zeb's house for supper."

He stopped pacing, his brows drawing together.

"You don't sound too uncomfortable with that."

"Frankly, I'm not. We've looked in the streets and on the plains and we've found nothing. I'm after proof to use against Zeb. What better place to find it than his own home?"

Fletcher raised his hand. "Wait a second. I'm not going to let you rifle through his things, and I certainly hope you don't intend to shoot him in front of my sister."

Jo's shoulders slumped with a sigh. "Of course not. And I presume he won't try to shoot me in front of her, either. That's why it's the best opportunity I can hope for."

"No."

"No?" She slid him a look. "Why not? What have you got to lose? You'll be there to watch over me, and if Zeb is as innocent as you think he is, we'll find nothing and be on our way. If he's guilty..." She stopped at that, not sure what would happen if they discovered something, what Fletcher would do.

What *she* would do.

"At least we'll get a fancy meal out of it," she said, trying to put a tidy finish on her thoughts.

Just then, footsteps thumped up the stairs on the outside of the building and the door opened. Deputy Anderson walked in with a telegraph message.

"What does it say?" Jo asked, standing.

Fletcher took it from Anderson and read it. His mouth became a hard line as he slapped the note against his thigh. "Why hasn't anyone looked into this before?"

Deputy Anderson sheepishly removed his hat. "I

guess nobody was suspecting a rancher like George Greer of stealing. He's the richest there is."

Fletcher picked his hat up off the desk and pressed it onto his head. "Rich or not, he doesn't own a square inch of land in Texas."

"Maybe he's just using the free range, like everybody else," Anderson suggested.

"This says he hasn't leased anything from the state. Where's he grazing his herds over the winter? He doesn't even own a headquarters site."

Jo stood, realizing uneasily that George Greer was casting a shadow over Zeb and his reason to kill Edwyn. "Maybe he has a ranch in Colorado or New Mexico."

"Not according to his employees and everyone who's heard of him. But we might as well know for sure." Fletcher pointed the telegraph message at Deputy Anderson. "I want you to send a couple of wires to check it out. Then find Greer's trail boss, Will MacGregor, and bring him in to see me. He was down at the depot, loading a herd not long ago."

"Sure thing," Anderson replied, going out the door.

Fletcher turned to Jo. "We'll have to cancel our dinner plans."

She swallowed hard, trying to contain her irritation. "We can't do that."

"Why not? This is the first lead we've had on your husband's murder, and I want to follow it."

"Fletcher, I'm a witness. What better lead can you ask for than that? It was Zeb who killed Edwyn, not George Greer, whoever he is."

"But if the killers were wearing hoods, you're not

an *eyewitness,* Jo, and my instincts are telling me that there's something not right about Greer."

"Why don't you ask Zeb about him?" she suggested. "He's a prestigious merchant, soon to be mayor. If anyone knows anything about Greer, surely Zeb would. Maybe he's even done business with him."

Fletcher eyed her suspiciously. "You're trying to manipulate me."

Jo sighed. "You have to admit I have a point."

He hesitated, considering it. "I suppose you do. Zeb supplies the cattlemen all the time. Not to mention that he was gambling with MacGregor last night. Maybe I should talk to him."

Trying not to show how relieved she was, Jo gathered up her gloves. "We should go, then. It's almost seven." Fletcher stood to face her. "All right, we'll go, but I don't want you asking questions about any of this. Leave it to me."

"Can I comment on the wine or is that off-limits, too?"

Fletcher offered her his arm. "Just try and control yourself. Remember the part you're playing. Your only task tonight, Josephine, is to be hopelessly in love with me."

When Zeb Stone's large front door swung open, Jo stood dumbfounded, staring at the tall butler who stood in the doorway to greet them. A sudden ripple of tension made her body go weak. Could she fool the man who had murdered her husband? Could she even face him?

Without a word, the butler invited them into the

wide front hall.

Jo walked into the magnificent house, and staring at Zeb's gilt-framed wedding portrait the size of a window, she felt instantly humbled. Elizabeth sat poised in an armchair while Zeb stood behind her resting his white-gloved hand on her bare shoulder. She looked like a princess in her sheer, lacy veil and white silk gown, the skirt trimmed with enough satin drapery to cover half the windows in this house. Zeb looked as he always did—impressive and intimidating with his dark brows, dark mustache and expensive black jacket. He was a striking figure in any context.

"Mrs. Stone is waiting for you in the drawing room," the butler announced, taking Jo's shawl and Fletcher's hat, and showing them across the shiny floor and past the ornately carved mahogany staircase.

Jo felt underdressed in her plain calico bodice and skirt, but when she glanced at Fletcher, whose spurs were chinking with each step, she thought better of it.

They walked into the drawing room, and there was Elizabeth in a pale yellow evening gown with white lace ruffles on the train, standing in front of the fireplace with her back to the door. As soon as the butler announced Jo and Fletcher, she turned gracefully from rearranging a vase of pink roses on the mantel.

"Fletcher! Mrs. O'Malley!" Elizabeth approached and took Jo's hands. "Congratulations. It seems we will be sisters." She leaned forward and kissed Jo on the cheek.

Jo glanced at Fletcher, who dropped his gaze to the floor.

"Please, call me Jo," she replied.

Elizabeth turned Jo's hands over and looked at them. "No ring yet, I see." She gave Fletcher a lighthearted wink. "I've been waiting all day for this moment."

She moved toward a round table adorned with glass figurines and vases of colorful wildflowers, and picked up a small silver-plated box.

Fletcher's lips parted with recognition. "Elizabeth, that's not necessary. I know how much that means to you."

Jo listened to Fletcher's voice, so full of guilt and anguish at having to lie to his sister this way. Seeing the sisterly love in Elizabeth's eyes as she handed the box to him made Jo realize why Fletcher was so reluctant to accept the truth about Zeb. Why she, too, now wished it was not so.

Fletcher took the small box from Elizabeth and held it in his hand. A vein pulsed at his temple. Jo saw it and touched his arm. "Are you all right?" she asked quietly.

Elizabeth gazed back and forth between the two of them, then spoke to Jo. "It's our mother's wedding ring. She wanted it to be passed down."

Jo had to swallow the guilt-ridden lump forming in the back of her throat. She glanced from Elizabeth to Fletcher, back to Elizabeth again.

"But you should have it," Jo suggested. "You were her only daughter."

Elizabeth shook her head. "No, Zeb wanted me to have something he picked out himself."

Jo glimpsed down and was not surprised at the enormous diamond on Elizabeth's finger, meant to impress even the wealthiest Dodge City patrons and voters.

"I don't know, Liz," Fletcher said, still holding the box, turning it over in his hand.

"Please," she replied, "it would break my heart if you didn't accept it. I know Mother would have wanted you to have it. She always wanted you to be happy."

Fletcher walked to the window and stood in front of the drawn velvet curtains, his back to Jo and Elizabeth. Alone, head down, he opened the box and looked at the ring.

Jo stood in the center of the room, unable to tear her gaze away from him as he heaved with a sigh. A cold knot formed in her belly. How she wanted to go to him. To tell him to call off this charade before they all got hurt.

Elizabeth strolled forward and placed her hand on her brother's shoulder. "Take the ring, Fletcher. It's been too long since you've been happy."

He turned slightly and looked at Jo. She wasn't certain if it was guilt she saw in his eyes, or something closer to what she was feeling—a sense of regret that this engagement was only a pretense, and that they were deceiving everyone.

Perhaps they could at least tell his sister the truth.

Jo stepped forward. "Elizabeth…"

Fletcher quickly crossed toward her. "Jo, please don't say another word. Elizabeth is right. Our mother would have wanted you to wear this."

Any hope for revealing the truth vanished beneath her surprise. She could barely control her breathing as Fletcher took hold of her hand, raised it to his lips, and placed a soft, warm kiss on her knuckles—a kiss so genuine, she could have sworn he'd meant what he said.

Did he mean it? And was there any way to deny that she wanted it to be real? *All* of it?

"It fits," Fletcher said rather contentedly as he slipped the ring, carved with tiny hearts, onto her finger.

"It must be fate, then," Elizabeth said, approaching. "Mother had the most beautiful, graceful hands, just like yours, Josephine."

"Oh, hardly," Jo remarked self-consciously, pulling her hand from Fletcher's and dropping it to her side. "With all the work I do at the ranch."

"That's what makes them beautiful," Elizabeth returned.

Just then, the door of the drawing room swung open and Jo turned around.

The moment immediately lost all its magic as she found herself staring heatedly into the dark eyes of Elizabeth's husband—who was also, without a doubt, her own husband's killer.

Chapter

21

"ZEB, YOU'RE BACK," ELIZABETH SAID uneasily, crossing the room to greet him. "I hadn't expected you so soon. I'd instructed Matthews to hold supper for another half hour."

Zeb stood in the wide doorway, staring into Jo's eyes. He bowed slightly at the waist. "Welcome to my home, Mrs. O'Malley."

Elizabeth gave him a smile. "They arrived only a few minutes ago."

"I see that."

He eyed Jo with interest, and despite her hellish wrath toward this man, and her desire to see him totally defeated, she felt her heart wash with fear as she whisked her hands behind her back.

"What is that you're hiding?" he asked.

He strode toward her and her stomach flared with dread. She thought she had been prepared for this, but she wasn't. Not at all. All she could think of was how he had strung a rope over the beam in her barn and ended her husband's life. The terror of that moment came rushing back at her, and her heart pummeled the inside of her ribcage.

"What are you referring to?" she asked.

"Come now, Mrs. O'Malley. You can't hide anything from me." He stood too close, attempting to lean around her to see what she hid in her hands.

Taking in the hint of whisky on his breath, Jo had to fight the urge to pound her fists on his chest and shake him senseless for an explanation as to why he was such an unfeeling monster.

Fletcher reached for her hand and laced his fingers through hers. The contact pulled her abruptly from her contentious urges and reminded her what she had come here to do.

She let her hand relax into Fletcher's, who stood next to her, appearing relaxed and composed.

"She's hiding a wedding ring she shouldn't be wearing yet," Fletcher answered good-naturedly, raising her hand to show off the gold band.

Zeb glanced at it, nodded once in an exaggerated, patronizing manner that suggested that, even if the wedding was real, she would not live to see the day.

"Sorry I'm late," he said, changing the subject and stepping back to signal the butler. "I had some important business to attend to. Get us some brandy, Matthews. No, on second thought, make it champagne. This celebration requires something bubbly."

Taking advantage of the distraction, Jo took a few deep breaths to calm herself.

The butler returned with a bottle of French champagne and four glasses on a silver tray. He filled each one and made his way around the room.

"Here's to family," Zeb toasted, raising his glass. "May we all prosper."

With that, they dutifully sipped.

Jo watched Elizabeth, curious what had drawn a woman like her to this man. She could only guess it had something to do with being alone in the world, naïve and romantic. It was the only thing that made any sense.

When Fletcher and Zeb began to discuss city matters, Elizabeth invited Jo to join her on the sofa. "I would love to see your ranch," she said, setting her glass on the marble-topped table in front of them. "I so admire you, Josephine, running it on your own. How big is your herd?"

Odd, to hear Elizabeth, adorned in silk, satin and jewels, ask about cattle. "We drive about ten thousand head up from Texas every year," Jo replied, "but we keep seven thousand breeding cows. Edwyn believed the future was in winter feeding, fencing and breeding, and I must say I agree."

"Yes, I've often thought that—"

"What's this?" Zeb interrupted as he helped himself to another glass of champagne. "Ladies discussing ranching. I believe I've heard it all." He glanced at Fletcher, expecting him to join him in laughing, but Fletcher ignored the remark and set his glass down on a table.

Jo hoped her eyes were not conveying the loathing she felt.

Elizabeth fiddled with an earring. "But Mrs. O'Malley is running her husband's—"

"She has cowhands for that, we all know. I hear your foreman, John Cook, is an ambitious man."

"He is indeed," Jo replied, hiding her hostility beneath a polite smile. "But he doesn't make decisions about land that belongs to *me.*"

Zeb strode forward and leaned his elbow on the mantel. "Maybe you should let him make some of the decisions. I hear that you're building more fences, when any wise businessman knows that cattle can be grazed for almost nothing on the free range in Texas. To dispense large amounts of capital on acres and acres of grass here, and to fence it in, is ludicrous."

"I don't believe that building something to last is ever ludicrous, Mr. Stone, especially when it can be passed down to future generations and—"

Zeb smirked and raised an eyebrow. "Why not build your bank account instead, and pass that down if you want to leave something behind. I'd wager your son would prefer a stack of cash over an obligation to break his back making hay."

Elizabeth spoke to her husband, but directed her gaze at Jo. "Perhaps Mrs. O'Malley has a point. I've heard that the open range has been overgrazed to the point of—"

"Don't be daft, Elizabeth," he replied. "The farmers are starting those rumors. Texas will never be over-grazed. There's enough acreage to feed a—"

"It's not the quantity of land that's the problem," Fletcher broke in, and everyone fell silent. "One of these days, a bad winter is going to wipe out entire herds and folks are starting to think about that. I reckon, in the future, more ranchers are going to move toward winter feeding. Like the O'Malleys." Fletcher sat in the red upholstered armchair beside Jo and crossed his legs. "But I didn't know you had an interest in ranching, Zeb."

"Doesn't everyone?" he replied haughtily. "This *is* a cow town."

Fletcher sat very still, watching Zeb until the door to the drawing room opened and the butler stepped inside. "There is someone here wishing to see Marshal Collins."

"Who is it?" Fletcher asked, still watching Zeb, who moved to sit in the wing chair in front of the fireplace.

"Yes, who is interrupting our intriguing discussion?" Zeb asked. "I hope it's important."

"It's Deputy Anderson, sir."

Fletcher turned in his chair. "Anderson is here?"

"Yes, Marshal Collins. He wishes to speak with you."

Fletcher stood. "I'll be right back. Liz, I'll trust you to make sure this lady doesn't run out on me?"

With a teasing smile, Elizabeth touched Jo's arm. "I doubt she'd want to do that."

Fletcher swept his hand lightly over Jo's cheek. "I won't be long."

She nodded. "I'll wait."

Jo anxiously watched the butler close the double doors behind Fletcher. Then she felt Zeb's dark gaze rake over her. With a subtle, sinister grin, he raised an eyebrow.

"What do you mean, he was dead?" Fletcher whispered to Anderson, as he led him across the wide hall and into the dining room, where the butler wouldn't hear them speak.

"I mean he was dead, Marshal Collins. Laid out cold behind the Long Branch saloon."

"Any bullet wounds?"

"Yep. Straight through the heart. You gonna come and see for yourself?"

As much as he wanted to, Fletcher couldn't leave Jo alone with Zeb, especially not with this new development. "Not right away. I trust you to take care of things. Seal off the area. Ask if anyone saw anything. I'll be by later to take a look."

"Yes, sir." Anderson settled his hat on his head and saluted the butler. "Don't bother yourself. I know the way out. Door's right there."

Fletcher stood in the dining room thinking, then approached Matthews. "Tell everyone I had to step out for a few minutes. I'll be back in time for supper, though. I just want to ask Anderson a few more questions and check something at the jailhouse."

"Shall I get your hat, sir?"

"Not necessary," Fletcher replied, going for the door.

He stepped outside into the twilight, hearing birds chirping in the straight row of trees Zeb had imported to line his driveway.

Fletcher looked all around the yard for witnesses. Seeing only Deputy Anderson on his horse, trotting off the property without looking back, Fletcher ducked down below the windows and circled the outside of the large stone house toward the back.

He knew the servants were busy downstairs preparing supper. Jo, Elizabeth and Zeb were still in the drawing room, and because Zeb had chosen a property on a hill on the edge of town, it was secluded enough to avoid the company and curiosity of neighbors.

Fletcher sneaked around to the back and found an open window, hoping it would take him into a closed room and not a hall or some other visible section of the house. Grabbing hold of the wooden window ledge, he pulled himself up. With one swift thrust, he was inside.

He straightened his shirt, looked around the dark room and found himself in Elizabeth's private sitting room. He went to the door and peered into the hall, then quietly walked across and tried the door on the other side. Finding it locked, he retrieved the rusty hairpin he kept on his key ring for moments like these, and gently persuaded the lock to open.

Fletcher walked in and closed the door behind him, straining to hear any sounds from the hall outside as he made his way across the room. He walked to the desk near the back wall, sat down and grabbed for whatever he could get his hands on—papers, letters, invoices, bank statements. Most letters were addressed to Zeb at Zeb Stone's Dry Goods. The invoices were for store merchandise he brought in from all parts of the country.

Reaching for the bank records, Fletcher checked over the amounts and had to swallow his surprise at the balance carried forward each month. There was enough money in there to stuff the entire county courthouse to the roof.

Fletcher searched for large deposits, but there were only standard amounts from the business, the balance having been deposited when he originally opened the account. Elizabeth's explanation about Zeb inheriting his money seemed legitimate.

Hearing silverware clinking in the dining room, Fletcher decided to get back before Jo had to sit down at Zeb's table on her own.

He left the same way he came in and, within moments, he was walking through the front door of the grand house and smelling roast beef in the down-stairs kitchen.

Matthews stood outside the drawing room with his hands clasped behind his back. "They have been waiting for you, sir," he said, opening the door to the drawing room.

Fletcher walked in, and there was Jo, sitting where he'd left her, her gaze darting up at him and her eyes shimmering with relief and happiness to see him. He took a deep breath at the sight of her sitting there, wearing his mother's wedding ring, returning his enamored gaze as if there were no one else in the room but the two of them.

Only the sound of Zeb's voice pulled Fletcher out of his stupor. "You're back, finally. What did the deputy want that couldn't wait until after dinner?"

Fletcher regarded him with an inquisitive gaze. "He came to report a death."

"Good heavens," Elizabeth said, covering her

mouth with a hand. "Who was it?"

Fletcher didn't take his eyes off Zeb, who sat calmly in the chair, revealing nothing. "No one you would know, Liz. He was a drover who'd just shipped a herd out east."

"How did he die?" Zeb asked, leaning back in the chair, his hands relaxed on the armrests.

"Looks like his heart gave out," Fletcher replied, not wanting to mention in front of Elizabeth the true circumstances, or that Zeb had played poker with the man the night before.

"What a shame. The fellow must have been working too hard," Zeb said.

"I reckon so."

"Shall we go to the table?" Zeb asked, his tone light.

Elizabeth nodded serenely and accepted her husband's hand to lead her out of the room. All Fletcher could do was meet Jo's inquisitive gaze, her pale cheeks revealing her concern.

He knew without a doubt that something was going on in this town, and Jo was a sitting duck in the middle of it.

"I'm glad you're back," she said, rising.

"Why? Did something happen? If Zeb said or did anything—"

"Nothing at all. I'm just glad to see you. I was worried about you."

"I was worried about you, too," he replied, fighting to keep the emotion from his voice, but it was no use. "I didn't like leaving you."

He offered his arm and she looped hers through it on the way out of the room.

"Then don't do it again," she said.

He wished with all his heart that he could give her that promise.

The ladies' refined presence at the diningroom table may have steered the conversation away from cattle rustling and murder, but it anchored it in far more dangerous territory.

"Perhaps we should set the date," Elizabeth suggested, sipping on red wine from a crystal glass.

Fletcher and Jo regarded each other immediately.

"We don't want to rush anything," she said, moving her food around on her plate. "With the election coming up..."

"All the more reason to plan it now. We could make it a double celebration. I would be happy to help arrange things."

"My dear," Zeb said, cutting her off, "you'll have more than enough planning to do for my victory celebration. Perhaps Fletcher and Mrs. O'Malley are wise to wait until afterward."

Elizabeth smiled politely. "Yes of course, you're right."

"But you don't plan to take up ranching, do you?" Zeb asked Fletcher. "What about your career? The sheriff's office? I hope you haven't forgotten it."

"No, I just think it's time I reevaluated certain things in life."

Was this part of the act? Jo wondered curiously.

"I think that's very wise of you, Fletcher," Elizabeth said. "Love is the most important thing."

"No, not love," Zeb disagreed. "You cannot depend

on it. Family, and the responsibility that goes with it, is what matters most."

"With any luck, I'll have a family soon enough," Fletcher said, refusing to meet Jo's gaze across the table.

Elizabeth wiggled in her chair. "I'm sure you will, Fletcher, in no time at all." Her eyes smiled at Jo, who wanted to crawl under the table and hide until this conversation was over.

"Do you want a large wedding or something more intimate?" Elizabeth asked both of them. "Either way would be lovely. We could hold the celebration here afterward. What a delightful time it would be."

Jo tried not to sound unappreciative. "Please, you don't have to go to all that trouble. We just want to keep things simple."

"It would be no trouble at all. But if you really do prefer a simple ceremony, I wouldn't dream of interfering. Your happiness is what matters most." She smiled warmly at Jo, who could not bring herself to meet Elizabeth's kindhearted gaze.

During the remainder of the meal, Jo was happy to turn the discussion toward the embroidery group that Elizabeth had begun on Tuesday evenings, then to lead the conversation into the poor selection of men's formal wear in town.

After dessert and coffee, when the table was cleared, Elizabeth gathered up her gloves and said to Jo, "Shall we retire to my private sitting room and allow the men a chance to talk business?"

"We really should be going," Fletcher said, sliding back his chair and standing.

Jo stopped him with her hand. "Please, Fletcher, sit down. There's no hurry. It's only early yet."

His eyes clouded with a warning.

Zeb signaled the footman to bring the cigars and a bottle of brandy. "Yes, do as your future bride tells you, Fletcher. You'll have to start sometime."

Jo breathed deeply to prevent herself from responding to Zeb's comment, then joined Elizabeth on her way out of the dining room. She felt Fletcher's eyes follow her, but refused to acknowledge it. She could only hope that he would do as much with his opportunity as she intended to do with hers.

Chapter 22

"*T*HIS IS SO ROMANTIC," ELIZABETH mused. "It must have been love at first sight."

Jo nodded amiably.

Elizabeth rose from the sofa and walked to the window, pulled the heavy brocade curtain aside with one finger and looked out at the darkness. "I envy you, marrying a man like my brother."

"I'm sure most women in Dodge envy you for *your* husband."

Elizabeth let the curtain fall closed. "Thank you for saying that."

"It's the truth. You must be..." Jo could barely get the bitter-tasting words past her lips. "You must be very happy."

Elizabeth sat down again. "We are fortunate in what we have—this house and the business. It's a good life, but you will be fortunate in other ways when you marry my brother. You'll be far happier than most people could ever dream."

Jo imagined that it would be true, if this engagement were not a sham. "May I ask you something, Elizabeth?"

"Of course. We're going to be sisters, remember?"

Jo knew she should focus on connecting Zeb to George Greer, but she couldn't resist the opportunity to ask a question that only Elizabeth could answer. "Do you think Fletcher truly enjoys being a lawman?"

Elizabeth touched Jo's knee. "I knew you were the right woman for him."

"Why do you say that?"

She smiled. "For someone who hasn't known him very long, you've seen right through him, past his badge."

"I suppose," Jo replied uncertainly.

"Maybe it's because you're cut from the same cloth," Elizabeth continued. "When you said earlier that you wanted to build something, I wanted to weep with joy that you and Fletcher had found each other. Fletcher always used to say the exact thing—those very words. Before he got caught up in upholding the law, of course."

"You don't approve of his career choice?"

"It's not that I don't approve. I'd approve of anything he truly wanted. I just don't believe that being a lawman makes him happy. It just keeps him from letting go of something that happened a long time ago. Something he needs to put behind him."

"Your father."

Elizabeth regarded Jo with surprise. "He told you

about that? He must trust you a great deal, because he rarely speaks of that to anyone. Maybe there is hope for him after all."

"Hope?"

"Yes—that one day he'll leave the law to someone else and follow his dreams."

"Of owning a ranch," Jo finished for her, remembering John's proposal and feeling a twinge of disappointment.

"No." Elizabeth's blue-eyed gaze intensified. "Dreams of having a family to love, people to call home. That's what he always wanted to build."

In that moment, Jo wondered how she could have thought Fletcher soulless, when all he'd ever wanted was the very thing that mattered most to her as well. A part of her wanted, more than anything, to help him find what he was searching for—to find it *with* him, the two of them, together. Perhaps it might have been possible, if things were different.

She looked down at the shiny gold ring she wore. Had Fletcher truly wished all this was real when he slipped it on her finger and told her that his mother would have wanted her to wear it? Was the love in his eyes genuine?

Drowning in confusion—and remembering that she had come here to prove Zeb's guilt, not fall in love with Fletcher—Jo removed the snug ring and handed it to Elizabeth. "It's too early for me to be wearing this."

Elizabeth accepted the tiny gold band and closed her fingers around it. "I'll take good care of it until the special day." She stood and placed it in a mother-of-pearl, heart-shaped box on the corner desk.

All Jo wanted to do now was run out of this room and go to Fletcher, wrap her arms around him, tell him that she loved him, and beg him to love her in return. But would he be ready to hear that? Or to lay aside his duty to arrest her? Jo knew Fletcher cared for her, but she also knew he would have to forgive his father and understand the man's actions before he'd ever be able to give up his obsession with the law and allow himself to be close to someone again.

Gazing uncertainly at Elizabeth, who was setting the ring box up on a shelf behind the fancy roll-top desk, Jo reminded herself that nothing with Fletcher would even come close to being resolved if she didn't find some evidence about Zeb to end this pursuit, because she knew enough about Fletcher to know that he would never let it go unsolved.

"It's a shame what happened to that man Fletcher mentioned," Jo said unsteadily. "I saw him earlier today. He looked fit as a fiddle, loading his herd onto the railcar. I believe he said he worked for George Greer."

Elizabeth returned to the sofa and sat down. "It makes you stop and think about how fragile life is, doesn't it? Makes you want to live it to the fullest."

Jo realized she'd have to be more direct. "Have you ever met George Greer?"

"No, but someone delivered something here for him once. I had to send it back, all the way to Amarillo." Jo was too startled by the comment to feign indifference. "What was it?"

"I have no idea. It was a small box from a bank and

I didn't think it proper to open it."

"Did you tell your husband about it?"

"Yes, of course. He explained to me later that it must have been a clerical error on the bank's part."

"The bank?"

"Yes. Zeb also keeps an account in Amarillo." Feeling her heart begin to pound harder, Jo cleared her throat. "Why would he keep an account there?"

"To diversify his holdings, he tells me. It's a good way to keep his inheritance safe from thieves and vagabonds and banks that fail."

"How very wise of him. Does he keep many? It must be a bookkeeping nightmare."

Elizabeth laughed. "I don't know. That was the only time I've ever spoken to him of such matters. Zeb handles those things, of course."

"Of course," Jo replied, understanding. When Edwyn was alive, he had managed their financial affairs as well. "But goodness, how very rude of me," she added. "I don't know who would be more shocked—Zeb or Fletcher—to know I'd been speaking about money with you."

They shared a smile.

"Don't worry," Elizabeth assured her. "You're my future sister-in-law, and from now on, our conversations will always be kept in the strictest confidence."

Jo smiled, and asked for more tea.

"How very clever of you, Fletcher." Zeb picked up his brandy glass and swirled the amber liquid around. "I was beginning to think you'd lost your mind." Fletcher tapped his cigar ashes into the tray.

"If folks hear I'm going to hitch my wagon to one of the Dodge City widows, they'll realize I'm here to stay, and the sheriff's office will be a snap."

"Music to my ears."

"I thought you'd like it."

"When do you plan to announce a date for the wedding? We've got to manage this in the best possible way."

Fletcher settled back in his chair, carefully contemplating his answer. "The election for sheriff isn't until November. If we move too fast, all the hoopla will be over by the time folks go to vote, and I'll be saddled with a wife. I reckon the anticipation of a big wedding—real romantic-like—will be better than the actual thing. If you get my meaning."

Zeb nodded. "I believe I do. You want to plan something marvelous, then after you're elected...a lover's quarrel, perhaps?"

Fletcher took a slow sip of brandy. "Perhaps."

Zeb studied Fletcher, as if testing him. "Mmm, no, I don't like it."

"Why not?"

Zeb ran his finger around the top of his glass, thinking. "You don't want to spend the next few months courting a woman like Josephine O'Malley. Besides, Elizabeth will be impossible to live with if she has all that time to plan your nuptials."

"It'll give her something to do."

Zeb considered that. "What will your 'widow' do in the meantime?"

"What she always does. Sit out at her ranch and let the men run things while she's waiting to marry me."

He hated saying all this, but it seemed to be working in his favor. It was exactly what Zeb wanted to hear.

He tapped his finger on the table. "And you'll be too busy upholding the law to visit her."

"Most of the time, I reckon that'll be the case."

"Most of the time. You won't become infatuated with her, will you? The effect will be lost if you decide to go through with it and push things forward."

"I told you, I'm not the marrying kind."

"But you're married to your job," Zeb commented, his eyes narrowing as he waited for Fletcher's response.

"A man's gotta believe in something."

"Yes, he does." After a pause, Zeb inclined his head. "Have you considered actually going through with it? The O'Malley land is the best around."

Fletcher raised his eyebrows. "And what exactly would I do with a ranch?"

"If we're going to own Dodge, you and I, we might as well really *own* it, don't you think?"

Fletcher lounged casually in his chair. "Interesting suggestion, but why make me marry her? Why not just buy her out?"

"That widow will never sell. I know it for a fact. And she's bequeathing the place to her son, then a whole string of Irish relations who will probably be too sentimental to ever sell."

Fletcher kept his expression deceptively cool. "Thinking about getting into the cattle business?"

"It never hurts to control things."

"But ranching, Zeb? After all that talk about not needing to own land when there's open range to be had?"

"Let's just say my interests are varied. We'll leave it at that for now while you think about all this."

Fletcher *would* think about it. Very carefully.

"So, what about that raise you promised me?" he asked, rising to his feet. "When does that start?"

Laughing, Zeb stood also. "You're a shrewd man, Fletcher. I thank you for bringing it to my attention. What did I promise you? A hundred a week? Two hundred?"

"If I recall correctly, it was an extra hundred a month."

"Gracious, that won't do at all. A hundred a week sounds better, don't you think? I wasn't exactly at my best, was I? Did I thank you for seeing me home?"

"Not yet."

"Well, I'll thank you now with your first install-ment. How does that sound?"

"Sounds mighty fine, Zeb."

"I thought it would. Use the money to buy yourself some new clothes. Take Elizabeth with you. She has excellent taste. We need to tidy up your image if we want things to go our way, and if you can get your hands on that ranch land, things will get even more interesting. I promise you that."

Fletcher spoke with restraint, hiding his suspicions for the time being. "I'll look forward to finding out what you have in mind, Zeb."

"You'll never believe what I learned from Eliza-beth," Jo said to Fletcher as their wagon rattled off Zeb's property and onto the dark, quiet street back to town.

Fletcher pulled at the brim of his hat, seeming distracted. "I'd believe anything right now. My pockets are stuffed with cash and I've committed to run for sheriff."

"You have? What did Zeb say about the wedding?"

Fletcher wouldn't look at her. "Don't worry. We're off the hook until November."

"Why November?"

"Because that's when the election will be, and no voter can resist a groom in a big romantic wedding to which they've been invited."

Jo huffed with disgust. "That must have been Zeb's idea. I'm not surprised." Fletcher said nothing. "What's the money for?"

"It's my salary from Zeb—but the job description is still pretty vague. Either way, it's shady for him to be offering cash to a lawman. I'll set it aside, write up a report about it, and see where it leads." Fletcher thought about it for another moment. "He must keep a safe somewhere hidden in the house, because I didn't see it when I snuck into his office."

"You snuck in? When?"

"After Deputy Anderson came," he replied. "That's what took me so long."

Jo turned to him. "Did you find anything on George Greer?"

"No. Just papers relating to the store."

"Well, if there was nothing in Zeb's study that mentioned Greer, he must have another hiding place, because Elizabeth told me they once received a package for Greer."

He shot her a look. "You asked her about that?"

"Don't worry. I was clever about it. We were talking about the man who died, and it came up that he worked for Greer. So *now* do you believe me about Zeb?"

Fletcher considered it. "I do believe he's up to something, and that he's not the man Elizabeth thinks she married."

Having waited so long to hear those words, Jo exhaled. She leaned in close, gave Fletcher a hug, and knocked his hat off-kilter in the process.

"What are you doing?" he asked, half laughing while he straightened his hat.

"I just wanted to thank you."

"Don't get too excited," he said, giving her a flirtatious grin with those soft, sensual lips. The glimmer in his eyes made her heart pound like a hammer. "I haven't done much yet. We still need to know more before we can be certain."

But Jo couldn't help but feel excited—although it had more to do with the handsome, rugged marshal who sat beside her, driving this rig with those manly hands, his big, muscular thigh bumping against hers. Everything about him made her feel flushed and hot with nervous energy.

What was wrong with her tonight? All she wanted to do was slide closer to him again, press her body against his, and satisfy these burning womanly urges that kept coming out of nowhere.

She sat back in her seat, working hard to control—*and hide*—her desires, but still feeling eager to make plans. "So, where do we go from here?"

He steered the wagon onto Walnut Street. "First

we'll go look at a dead body. Then we'll head home. To *your* home. And I don't care what folks say about it, Jo. I'm going with you and I'm staying to make sure that you're safe. I'm staying the whole damn night."

Jo couldn't deny, she rather liked the sound of that.

*A*FTER GOING TO SEE MACGREGOR'S body and finding him just as Deputy Anderson had described—dead from a bullet wound through the heart—Fletcher and Jo drove out to the ranch.

The horses pulled the wagon toward the barn, and as always, Jo felt a rush of anxiety at the thought of going inside, of seeing the place where Edwyn had gasped his last breath.

Not wanting Fletcher to know about this irrational fear of hers, she made some excuse and hopped down from the wagon before Fletcher drove in. She waited by the barn door, nervously tapping her foot while he unhitched the team and fed and watered the horses. When he finally walked out with his hand on his gun, she let out a breath of relief, rose up on her toes and hugged him.

"What's that for?" he asked, falling back against the

barn wall. "You're affectionate tonight, Mrs. O'Malley."

She leaned into his warm, muscular frame, gazing up at him in the moonlight. "I'm just glad you're here. You make me feel safe."

"I'm glad, too," he replied, his eyes roaming inquisitively over her face. Then his eyebrows pulled together in a frown. "Are you all right?" He touched her cheek with the pad of his thumb.

"Of course," she replied, still leaning into him.

He ran his hand up the length of her back to her nape, and she quivered with delight at all the sensations aroused by his gentle touch. "But you're trembling."

"It's cold out here," she lied.

He shook his head, his gaze still full of scrutiny. "No, that's not it. You're afraid. I can see it in your eyes. I can feel it, Jo."

She was feeling a lot of things herself.

Forcing herself to take a step back, Jo rubbed at the chill on her arms. "Well, you have to admit, this whole situation has been—"

"You don't like to go into the barn, do you?" he asked, pushing away from the barn and interrupting her.

Jo stared at him with admiration, impressed by his intincts. "What makes you think that?"

"A hunch." He moved closer. "How long has it been since you've been in there?"

She let out a sigh. "Too long."

"How do you manage to work the ranch without being able to go into the barn?"

"Leo and Matilda and the cowhands look after the chores there," she explained. "I do other things."

He shook his head, not with disapproval, but with a genuine compassion that melted her heart. Despite everything, she really *was* growing to trust him.

"I'm so sorry you saw it happen, Jo."

Tears threatened; she fought to push them away.

"But you don't have to be scared anymore. It's over."

"No, it's not," she replied. "Zeb's still out there, and I keep seeing it in my mind. Every time I think about it, I relive the panic and the terror."

He said nothing more, he only took her into his arms and held her.

"I can't go in there," she whispered.

"Yes, you can."

"Don't force me, Fletcher. I've tried many times to force myself, and it only makes it worse."

"I would never force you to do anything," he added, drawing back to look into her eyes, "but I'm here with you now. You're safe with me. Why don't you let me take you inside and show you that everything's okay?"

Her stomach began to churm with dread. "I'd rather not."

"Look, I have my gun." He pulled it out of the holster and cocked it. "Nothing will happen while I'm standing beside you."

Her heart pounded like a drum in her ears, faster and faster. "I don't know..."

"Come with me." Gently he urged her along, taking her hand and moving toward the door. "Just stay close to me."

Oh, what a way he had with his voice—that smooth Texas drawl. Even now, when she was reeling with dread, it made her whole body soften to his demands.

She took an uncertain step forward, allowing him to lead her through the door. Her breath came in short gasps and her heart felt as if it was going to burst out of her chest, until she stepped over the threshold and into the dark central bay.

The smell of moist hay and cows and manure wafted to her nose, bringing back a whole slew of memories which surprisingly were mostly about her childhood. It had been so long since she'd smelled these familiar fragrances.

Fletcher lit the lantern that hung on a post by the door, and the barn was illuminated. Jo swallowed nervously, her stomach burning as she looked up at the thick square beam overhead.

Images of Edwyn's last helpless moments—his legs kicking and his face ghostly white with terror as he wrestled with the rope around his neck—flashed like blazing embers in her mind. She was breathing hard now, staring upward, seeing things that were not there.

"It's normal to feel anxious," Fletcher said to her, dropping his gun into its holster and taking her hand. "It was a terrible ordeal, what you went through."

Frozen with fear, she could only nod.

She let the memories come, saw it all in her head, remembered huddling in the corner, waiting—God only knows how long—for Zeb and his men to leave, then longer still, to be sure they had ridden away. The rope had creaked back and forth with Edwyn's limp body, clad in his dark wool trousers and wool vest, while Jo trembled and shivered and cried until she found the courage to finally get up and cut him down, try to bring him back to life. It was no use of course.

She then saddled a horse. There had been no ranch hands around then, in the dead of winter, so she rode off into the night alone to seek help, through the snow and over crusty patches of ice. When she found the city marshal, she remembered the other dead rancher's wife, and Jo had lied about what she had seen.

She heard Fletcher's voice, speaking to her as if from a great distance away. "What can I do, Jo?" he asked. "How can I help?"

Shakily she let her gaze go to him. "Just hold me."

And suddenly, she was safe in his embrace, and the visions of Edwyn disappeared, along with her fears, as she wrapped her arms around Fletcher, rested her cheek on the firm wall of his chest and felt him stroke her hair with gentle fingers. "It's all over now," he whispered. "Everything's going to be all right."

He continued to hold her for the next few minutes, rubbing his hands over her back and kissing her cheeks until her heart slowed to a more natural rhythm and she was able to look up at the beam and not see Edwyn anymore. She glanced around at the hay and horses and saw the door to the tack room and smelled the leather. What happened to Edwyn now seemed far away, a horrible tragic nightmare that was finally part of her past.

She wiped away another tear and faced Fletcher. "Thank you for forcing me to come in here. I couldn't do it alone."

"You just needed some help," he said. "We all need it sometimes."

And you still need *me*, she thought—to help you move on from what happened to your father.

"Are you hungry?" she whispered, her muscles relaxing beneath the pleasurable sensation of his hands on her hips.

He raised an eyebrow, playfully. "Got any cookies?"

Jo chuckled, grateful for the release of tension. "That's why I keep my cookie jar full. For moments like these. Let's go inside the house."

Fletcher lowered the wick in the lantern and the barn went dark. Together, they crossed the yard, their path lit by the full moon, and slowly climbed the porch steps. Jo reached out to open the front door of the house, but Fletcher stopped her.

"Let me go first." He drew his Peacemaker and cocked it. "After that fire this morning, I'm not taking any more chances. Stay close."

They walked into the front hall, where the smell of charred fabric and wood was still heavy in the air, then checked each room for intruders who might have been lurking and waiting. They found no evidence that anyone had been there since breakfast.

Fletcher holstered his gun and turned to face Jo. They stood in the darkness of the front hall, close enough that Jo could feel his breath on her face. When their eyes met, it seemed they both realized at the same time that they were alone together in her home, and would be until morning.

"Why don't we go into the kitchen?" Jo suggested,

feeling suddenly awkward.

She led the way, while Fletcher followed. He removed his hat and sat down at the table. Jo lit a lamp and filled a plate with frosted shortbread cookies from the jar beside the window.

"Would you like some coffee?" she asked as she set the plate down on the table.

"I reckon I'm going to need it tonight."

She knew he planned to stay and guard her safety, but where did he plan to do it? From downstairs—or closer to her bed?

The idea of him nearby while she slept made her tremble with excitement and nervous anticipation. Would she even be able to stay out of his arms? How would it be possible, when she was so completely infatuated with him, in every possible way?

Warily, she filled the stove with kindling and lit it, then prepared the coffeepot and set it to boil. She sat down at the table across from Fletcher and reached for a cookie. "Do you think anything will happen tonight? Zeb's already tried once."

"Killer or not, Zeb has good reason to keep you healthy for the next few months. He wants a wedding to ensure my election to the sheriff's office."

"Did he actually say that?"

"Yes, after I convinced him of it."

Jo swallowed the sweet shortbread. "Clever of you, Marshal, but I still can't trust him. If he thinks I might expose him, our wedding will hardly seem important, even if it does stand to get you elected."

"Well, there's more to it than that," Fletcher said.

He gazed at her uncertainly and her stomach

lurched. "I'm not sure I want to know."

Fletcher ran his fingers through his hair. "Tonight I learned that Zeb wants your land," he said finally. "He knows you won't sell, and he wants me to get my hands on it by marrying you."

The walls seemed to close in around Jo. Now she was beginning to understand. "Is that why he killed Edwyn? For our land?"

"I don't know. Maybe."

A chill grew inside her. "How could he do that? Take a man's life—Edwyn was a father!—just for a piece of land! What kind of monster is he?"

"Jo—"

"If Zeb thinks he can get away with this..." Her thoughts began to race dangerously as she considered the implications of Zeb's intent. "The land is to go to Leo after I'm gone. If anything happens to—"

Fletcher covered her hand with his. "I won't let anything happen. You're safe with me, and Leo is safe with his uncle, and all of this will be cleared up before we let him come home. Trust me."

She stood up. "Maybe I should just sell to Zeb. Get out of here while we still can. The land isn't as important as our lives."

"No, Jo. I know what it is to give up your home and everything you've worked for because something didn't go according to plan. It can change your life forever. I won't let that happen, and if he's guilty for what you believe he is, he'll soon find himself in front of a judge and jury."

"But Fletcher..."

"I'll keep you and Leo safe, I promise." Fletcher's

eyes burned with intensity as he gazed up at her.

Jo struggled with the anger and fear boiling within her. She dropped her forehead into her hand to suppress the throbbing in her head.

"Believe me," Fletcher continued, "the thought of losing you makes me want to destroy him, too."

Jo's anger cooled at the sound of those words on Fletcher's lips, and the touch of his fingers, lacing through hers. Slowly, she sat back down. "So you *do* believe that he's capable of murder?"

"Yes."

"What changed your mind?"

"Will MacGregor's murder tonight, for starters. Besides that, everything I've learned about you in the past couple of days, and what I've seen from Zeb. You've won me over, Jo. Lock, stock and barrel."

But in what way? Was he just talking about the facts of the case? Or did he mean something else?

Fletcher glanced down at their joined hands. "I see that you took off my mother's ring."

Jo could barely speak. She was still so shaken by what he'd just said, and what he might mean by it. "I gave it back to Elizabeth. I didn't think it was appropriate for me to be wearing it."

"Because we're not married yet," Fletcher said matter-of-factly.

Yet?

Jo nodded, fighting to keep from leaping across the table, settling herself on his lap, and kissing him senseless.

"It looked perfect on you."

Heaven help her, every word that came out of his

mouth tonight was filling her with hope and feverish longing. She wanted him with every breath in her body, and it was becoming impossible to imagine resisting him all night long, when he would be here, within reach, perhaps even in the privacy of her bedroom.

Fletcher stroked her knuckles with the pad of his thumb and she felt another sizzling surge of desire in her core. "When I told you my mother would have wanted you to wear it, I meant it."

Jo felt her chest heaving, as if she'd just run a great distance. "Fletcher, I don't know what I would have done these past few days without you."

He kissed each of her fingertips, and the heat of his lips sent her senses whirring. "I'm glad I found you," he said softly. "Not because of what's been happening...just because."

A sense of urgency filled her as he touched her cheek. Her eyes fell closed and she turned her face into his palm.

"I need to kiss you," he whispered, rising to his feet and moving toward her.

Thank God... "I think I'll collapse in a heap if you don't."

Her last words were smothered on her lips as he pulled her to her feet and claimed her mouth with his. The kiss was velvety and tasted like the sugar cookies. Jo reached up to his shoulders for support, deepening the kiss until her entire body melted gloriously into his. She trembled from the overwhelming desire flooding her body, and her complete and undying trust in this man.

As the coffeepot hissed and steamed and filled the air with its heady aroma, Jo held Fletcher tighter than she'd ever held anyone.

"Let me stay with you tonight," he whispered in her ear, his hot breath sending gooseflesh down her arms and legs.

"I thought we'd already decided that," she managed to say.

"No, I mean let me stay *with* you—in your bed."

Her senses spun madly for the thing she had wanted so desperately, but dared not suggest.

Giving herself over to the intensity of her feelings, she nodded, then felt him sweep her off her feet and into his capable arms. As he carried her up the stairs to her bedroom, she wanted to give him everything, no matter what the future held in store for them.

Once inside, he kicked the door shut with his boot, carried her to the bed and eased her down onto her back. She inched toward the pillows, watching him in the moonlight from the window as he ripped off his vest, tossed it onto the wing chair in the corner of the large room, then quickly unbuttoned his shirt. She nearly lost her breath at the sight of his smooth, muscular chest and broad shoulders. He was so much of a man...so strong and brawny....

He crawled onto the bed beside her. His nearness, and the heat of his hard, naked flesh under her fingertips as she ran her hands over his shoulders and back, aroused her to the point of trembling.

He held her in his arms, kissing her lips and cheeks and neck, causing a fever in her blood that couldn't be doused. "Jo, I know this is where you and Edwyn—"

She drew back, realizing that he was still uncertain about this. "Fletcher, there's something you should know about Edwyn and me." She leaned up on her elbows. "He was a good man and I miss him, but we never loved each other, not the way a man and a woman ought to."

"But he was your husband," Fletcher replied in a low voice, still laced with desire. "And all the times I saw you staring at his portrait, and how determined you've been to avenge his death…"

"He was my husband only on paper," she explained. "But his heart always belonged to another—someone he loved before he ever met me. It was before he came to America. They were engaged, but she broke it off to marry another man. That's why Edwyn left his home country. I was nothing but a mail-order bride, because he needed a wife to help him on this ranch, and to help him forget about her."

"He told you this?" Fletcher said with a frown.

"Yes. That sea chest in the den, it's filled with the woman's letters and Edwyn's, too. I was never angry about it, because he was honest with me from the start. So you see, we were just friends."

Fletcher touched his forehead to hers. "I didn't know."

"It doesn't matter. Edwyn's gone now, but you're here, and I want you in ways I've never wanted any man. I never imagined it could feel like this." She wiggled her hips on the bed, pressing her body closer and tighter to his rock hard pelvis. She felt his erection between her legs and nearly lost her mind with anticipation.

"Take this off," he whispered in a husky voice, reaching for the buttons on her bodice and unfastening each one. Within seconds, she was sitting up and shrugging out of it, while he kicked off his boots. It was all hurried, desperate and passionate. She couldn't wait to be naked in his arms and feel his body pressed hotly to hers beneath the sheets.

She lay back on the pillows while he straddled her to unhook her corset in the front. As it came loose and he pulled it out from under her, she took a deep breath, welcoming her body's freedom.

"Now this," he whispered, pulling her skirt and petticoats down over her ankles. He rolled down her stockings and began to untie her boot laces. "These, too."

Wearing only her chemise and cotton drawers, she sat up and pushed him onto his back. She felt his Peacemaker against her knee. "This will be the first to go," she said in a low, mischievous voice, then unbuckled his leather belt and pulled it away.

He raised his hips in compliance, but reached for the gun before she tossed the belt onto the floor. "I'll keep *that.*" His large bicep tightened as he slid the weapon beneath his pillow. Then she pulled his trousers off of him.

Now, completely naked, he rose up and eased her onto her back again. Her body tingled with unleashed desire as he pulled off her chemise and flicked his tongue over her breasts. Meanwhile, the explosive sensation of his hips thrusting between her legs made her ache for more.

"I need you inside me," she whispered breathlessly.

She gasped as he slowly, teasingly entered her, his forehead resting on hers, their bodies moving together in perfect unison. Shivers of lust shook her as her passions grew to a peak. Within moments, she was soaring to a new height, pulling him deeper inside and holding him there as her body throbbed and quaked with rapture around him and he groaned and spilled fiercely into her.

Many moments later, when they were lying side by side, finally catching their breath, he turned his head on the pillow to look at her. His green eyes were warm with affection, but something had changed.

"I've never felt like this, Jo. It makes it so difficult, because—"

She blinked back a tear. "Please, Fletcher, I want to pretend for just one minute that nothing exists outside of this room."

"Okay." He pulled her in to rest her cheek on his shoulder. The clock ticked steadily on the bedside table, and the crickets chirped outside the window.

Fletcher waited a long moment before he finally spoke again. "We can't just ignore it. I think you're right. Zeb wants your land, and he might want you dead as well, to cover up what happened to Edwyn. He's definitely up to something with George Greer, something to do with the cattle rustling, but I have no proof yet, and I don't know how to get it. It's making me crazy."

"Maybe the wires you sent will help us," she said, lifting her cheek to look at him.

"Maybe." But Fletcher's dark tone revealed his doubts. He sat up, leaned against the oak headboard and raised a knee under the light sheet. "Maybe you *should* leave Dodge."

Jo tucked a lock of hair behind her ear and sat up, too. "What are you saying?"

"I'm saying that you could pack a bag and go. Go to Leo and take him someplace safe—someplace no one knows about."

"But you'd have to set me free," she said, reminding him that she was still his prisoner and a suspect for attempted murder.

All he did was stroke her shoulder, back and forth, lightly with the tip of his forefinger. "I'm aware of that."

She leaned up on her elbow. "But you've never let anyone go free in your life. You don't bend the rules, remember?"

He stroked her hair. "Maybe things have changed. Maybe *I've* changed."

Stricken, Jo leaned forward and hugged him. "I can't let you do it. The law is your life. Besides that, I don't want to leave you."

"I don't want you to leave, either,' he replied, "but I think it would be best. And you wouldn't be a fugitive. Only you and I know what really happened. I've never filed a report."

"You haven't?"

"No."

She shook her head as if to clear it. "But still, I can't let you do that. I wouldn't want you to always think of me as the criminal you let escape from justice. And I understand if you don't want to marry me. It wouldn't help your reputation any, once I'm arrested.

It certainly wouldn't buy you any votes as sheriff, but at least you'd know that I tried to do what was right. And maybe, under the circumstances, it might be considered self-defense. He fired first, remember?"

Fletcher regarded her with disbelief. "I don't want to be *sheriff*, Jo. All I want is *you*."

It was the most bizarre thing. She laughed and sobbed at the same time. "Well then. We'll just have to prove that Zeb killed Edwyn and that he's guilty of cattle theft. The truth has to come out, and then I'll be safe to live my life here on the ranch, where I belong. I just feel sorry for Elizabeth."

Fletcher wet his lips. "I know my sister. If she's married to a killer, she'll want to know. And she's a survivor. She'll recover."

Jo hugged him again, and then snuggled down under the sheet to hold him close, and enjoy what time they had left together, through the rest of the dark night.

Chapter

24

"**I**F I'M GOING TO FIND anything to use against Zeb," Fletcher said the next morning, tossing the sheet aside and sitting up on the edge of the bed, "I'm going to need some time. I definitely want you to go and stay with Leo in Newton."

"I still don't want to go," she said. "I don't want to be away from you." Staring at his bare, muscular back in the pale light of the rainy dawn, Jo waited anxiously for his response.

"I'm not giving you a choice. I can't protect you and investigate Zeb at the same time."

"I can take care of myself," she assured him. "I know how to use those weapons you took from me."

Fletcher picked his trousers up off the floor and shook them before pulling them on. "I don't doubt that, but whether you can protect yourself or not isn't the point."

"Then what *is* the point?"

"The point is I'd be thinking about you. I'd be worrying when I wasn't with you and distracted when I was. Not a good mix for a man in my line of work." He pulled on his trousers.

"What if Zeb catches on to what you're doing?" Jo asked. "I don't think I could bear..."

Shirt half-open to reveal his muscular chest and rippled stomach, he crawled onto the bed, on all fours above her, and cupped her face in his hands. Her body burned with another heated wave of desire that simply would not recede.

"Zeb is beginning to trust me," he said. "And I promise I'll be careful."

Jo ran her open palms down his chest, then rubbed her thumbs across his soft, moist mouth. "Do you have to get dressed right now? The men won't be expecting breakfast yet. They're always slow when it rains." She pulled him in for another more demanding kiss.

Fletcher gently pushed her down onto her back and smiled. "I'll stay on one condition."

"What's that?" She hurried to unbutton his trousers again.

"You promise to leave town."

"But I don't want to go," she insisted.

"I told you, I'm not giving you a choice."

As he pressed his open mouth to hers and settled himself snugly between her quivering, welcoming thighs, Jo was incapable of arguing.

It had just stopped raining when Leo hopped out of his uncle's buggy, splashed into the mud and hurried into the Newton post office. Inside, he removed his hat to discover the brim was holding enough rainwater to fill a bucket. He accidentally spilled it onto the floor. He tried to spread the puddle around with his boot so no one would slip, then made his way to the counter. "Anything for Cecil O'Malley?" he asked the postmaster.

The gray-haired, craggy-faced man turned and retrieved a pile of envelopes from the box behind him and, without a word, slapped them onto the unpainted counter. Leo gathered them up and thanked the man, but he'd already turned away to finish sorting the mail.

Once outside, Leo replaced the rain-drenched hat on his head and flipped through the letters. His eyes widened at the sight of the return address on the last one—*Edwyn O'Malley, Dodge City, Kansas.*

Leo spun around and hurried back into the post office. "Where did this letter come from?" he asked the postmaster.

The man faced him and peered over his spectacles at the envelope. "Return address says Dodge City. Maybe it's time you learned to read."

"I *can* read. But this letter's old. Look!"

The postmaster glared at him, then snapped the envelope into his hand and held his spectacles between two fingers to examine it. "Postmarked January 10. You're right. It must have gotten lost for a time. Now if you'll excuse me."

Leo turned and walked out of the building, staring in stunned silence at his father's penmanship on the outside of the dirty, tattered envelope. Leo heard the post office door fall closed behind him. He stood beside his uncle's buggy, the letter in his hand making his heart ache with grief. He looked at the familiar writing again and, before he could think, ripped open the flimsy envelope and read what was inside.

After preparing breakfast for the men and seeing them off to work, Jo grudgingly packed a bag. She left a note for John on the bunkhouse door, asking him to see to the animals for the next few days and ensure the men were fed from the cookhouse. She didn't explain where she was going, only that she would be gone a while.

She *was not* happy about it.

The rain fell mercilessly from the ashen sky as she crossed the muddy yard toward the wagon. Holding her umbrella over her head, she climbed onto the wet seat beside Fletcher, who wore his long brown slicker and his hat pulled forward on his head, the brim dripping with rain. She curled her gloved hand around his arm.

"We have one last hour together," she said, trying to keep her mood light when all she wanted to do was beg him to let her stay. The wagon swished through a deep puddle and she thought about how to convince him. "I think you need me for this."

He was quiet for a moment, then he shook his head. "I can't take that chance, not with your life. You should be with Leo. Take him somewhere safe, in case things get dicey."

Jo couldn't very well argue with that. When it came to her son, she would do anything to keep him safe, and Fletcher knew it.

He squeezed her hand with reassurance, and she felt a love in her heart swell far beyond what she had ever believed possible.

If only it was not such a painful love. If only there was no fear—because if anything happened to Fletcher, she would blame herself for how things turned out, for getting him involved in this. "Please, be careful," she said.

"Nothing will happen," he promised. "I'll find the evidence we need, and I won't quit until I uncover the whole truth."

They drove through the rain and over the low, sodden hills, crossing mile after mile of weather-beaten landscape, but Jo couldn't herself relax. She had a bad feeling.

By the time they reached the railway station, the train was there and waiting with hissing bursts of steam. Jo's clothing was soaked straight through to her petticoats. She was shivering, and her heart was aching at the thought of saying goodbye to Fletcher. What if she left Dodge and something terrible happened to this man she had given all of her heart, body and soul to?

While she waited in the wagon, Fletcher ran into the station to purchase her ticket, and returned a few minutes later. "I bought a ticket all the way to Topeka, just in case anyone sees you get on and asks where you're going. Change seats along the way—cars if you can—and try to get off without too many folks noticing. Don't tell anyone you're getting off at Newton, and when you get there, take Leo somewhere else. Go north and contact me later."

Jo nodded as he helped her out of the seat and retrieved her valise from under the canvas in the wagon bed. He led the way to the platform and stepped up onto the train, turning around to take her hand and pull her up.

Carrying her folded, dripping umbrella, Jo entered the train and followed Fletcher down the narrow aisle until he found her a seat to herself at the back of the car. He set down her bag.

"I guess this is goodbye," Jo said shakily, facing him.

The lady in the seat behind her coughed.

"Will you be all right?" he asked.

"I'll be fine." But Jo had to fight the crushing urge to throw her arms around his neck and beg that he come with her and leave all this behind them. "Will *you* be all right?"

"Of course. I know what I'm doing."

Yet, she did not feel reassured. All she felt was a sense of gloom—that this was not going to end well—and heartache at the idea of losing him forever, when they'd only just found each other.

The conductor blew a whistle outside.

Suddenly, Fletcher grabbed Jo's hand and pulled her out the back door. It slammed behind them and they paused on the small outdoor space at the back of the train.

His mouth came down upon hers. The kiss was urgent and desperate, and Jo wrapped her arms around his broad shoulders, tears spilling from her eyes; she felt his steel badge pressing against her heaving breast.

"I don't want to go," she said, breathlessly.

"You have to."

The train began to puff and shudder. He cupped her face in his hands and kissed her again. "Remember what I told you. Keep to yourself."

"I will."

He moved down the steps, hopped off the tracks, and looked up at her as the train began to chug. It pulled away from the station and he waved good-bye, then he returned to the wagon and sped off.

In that moment, when she lost sight of him, Jo felt as if her heart had been ripped from her body and would never, ever, be returned.

After visiting the telegraph office only to learn there were no reply wires from Texas, Fletcher checked in at the jailhouse and found Deputy Anderson busy with paperwork from the night before.

He walked in and shook the rain from his hat at the door, trying also to shake all the doubts and uncertainties from his mind.

He'd done the right thing, he told himself, sending Jo away like that. It was the best thing for both of them—even though he'd sacrificed his professional integrity in the process. Unfortunately, it was eating away at him now, because it was exactly what his father had done, and what Fletcher had never been able to forgive him for. Maybe the time had come to rethink all of that.

But now wasn't the time. He had to keep his mind focused on this case.

"Any problems last night?" he asked the deputy as he hung his hat on the hook by the door.

"Nope. Only the usual sluggers after midnight at the keno table. Folks were asking about you though. Wondering where you were and if you were still looking for Six-Shooter Hank."

Fletcher crossed to the desk where Anderson was sitting. He flipped through the pile of affidavits the deputy had written out, reviewing them for anything out of the ordinary. "You can tell people I have a hunch we won't be seeing him again." He shuddered inwardly at the thought. "Any wires delivered here for me?"

"Nope. And I asked around about George Greer like you told me to, real casual-like. No one I talked to ever met him. I'm beginning to think the man's a ghost. Hey, you're dripping on my papers."

Fletcher stepped back. "If I was rustling cattle, I'd keep a low profile, too. Let me know if anything comes in today. When you're finished there, go get yourself something to eat. I'll take over as soon as I get back."

"Where are you going?"

Fletcher retrieved his hat from the hook and settled it onto his head. He opened the door and looked out at the curtain of rainwater dripping from the roof. "To talk to someone who knows something."

Fletcher walked past Zeb's store, peered through the window to see him talking to one of the town councilors, and kept right on going. He walked all the way up Railroad Avenue in the pouring rain until he reached Zeb's house, then rapped hard on the door.

Matthews finally came and met him with an unimpressed glare. "Marshal Collins. Do you not own an umbrella?"

Fletcher kicked his muddy boots against the door-step. "My Stetson does the trick and keeps my hands free. Sorry about the mud."

"I'm sure you are. But I'm afraid Mr. Stone is not at home this morning."

"What about Elizabeth?"

"Mrs. Stone is in the drawing room."

Fletcher stepped inside and handed his dripping coat and hat to Matthews, who carried them away at arm's length. A moment later, the butler returned. "Mrs. Stone will see you now."

"Thanks a bunch." Fletcher followed him.

Elizabeth rose from the sofa, her hands held out. "Fletcher! What are you doing here?"

"I came to talk to you."

"Would you like some tea?"

"I'd prefer coffee, if you have it."

She smiled wickedly. "I do, but Zeb insists I always offer tea first." She gestured to Matthews, who backed out of the room and closed the double doors behind him.

Elizabeth led Fletcher to the sofa. "You're dripping wet. It must be important, whatever you came to talk to me about."

"It is," he replied, "but I don't know how you're going to react."

Elizabeth's smile faded. "You haven't broken off your engagement, have you?"

"No, nothing like that. It's..." He hesitated. "It has to do with Zeb."

She frowned. "Is he in trouble?"

Fletcher stared into his sister's concerned eyes. "Why would you think that?"

Rising from the sofa and turning her back to him, Elizabeth began to rearrange some flowers in a tall vase. "No reason. You just seemed uneasy."

Fletcher watched her slender arms flit around the tall vase, moving a geranium here, replacing another there.

He rose to move around the table, where he could see her face. "Elizabeth. I need to know if I can trust you."

"Of course you can," she replied. "I'm surprised you even have to ask."

"Well, this is different. I need you to keep something from Zeb."

While the rain beat hard against the windowpanes, Elizabeth slid the vase to one side, so that it was no longer between them. "You know I'll do anything for you, Fletcher."

He took her by the hand. "Then come over here and sit with me."

They returned to the sofa. Fletcher kept his voice low. "There's been a cattle-rustling problem in Dodge lately. The herds that arrive are significantly smaller than they were when they started out."

"I've read about it in the papers."

Just then, the drawing room doors opened and Elizabeth jumped. Matthews walked in with a tray. "Set it here, please, Matthews. Then you may go."

"Yes, Mrs. Stone." He set the coffee tray down, peered suspiciously at Fletcher, then left the room.

Elizabeth poured two cups. "Go on."

"I think I may know who's responsible for the thefts," Fletcher said, accepting the cup of coffee from his sister.

"Who?"

"A man named George Greer. Ever hear of him?"

Elizabeth nodded. "His name came up last night when Jo and I were talking."

"I know. She told me. That's why I'm here."

"Well, I don't know anything else besides what I told her," she said nervously. "We received a package that was meant for Greer. That was all."

"And Zeb told you he and Greer had accounts at the same bank in Amarillo?"

"Yes."

"Have you ever heard Greer's name mentioned besides that one time?"

"Never. But Zeb doesn't discuss business matters with me. Do you think he knows Greer?"

Fletcher sipped his coffee. "Zeb knew Greer's trail boss. The man who died last night."

"I see." Her face went pale. "Have you spoken to Zeb about any of this?"

"No, and I don't intend to just yet. This is difficult to say, Elizabeth, but I think Zeb might be involved somehow."

"Do you have any proof?"

Fletcher felt suddenly ill equipped to be having this conversation. He lowered his gaze. "No."

"Something tells me you want my help."

His eyes lifted. "Yes."

Elizabeth sat back. "He's my husband, Fletcher.

You're asking me to go behind his back." The wind and rain continued to rattle the window, obscuring the view outside. Elizabeth stared blankly at it.

"What do you need?" she asked finally, meeting his gaze.

"I need to get into his study for another look around."

"*Another* look? Fletcher, don't tell me..."

"Sorry, sis. I was pressed for time."

She shook her head at him. "All right. I'll send Matthews on an errand. I'll ask him to...oh, I'll get him to book the church for your wedding. That should keep him busy. Reverend O'Grady loves to talk."

They both stood. "Thank you, Liz. And is there anywhere else you know of where Zeb keeps papers or correspondence?"

"The store, perhaps. I've only been in the office once, and he shooed me out."

"Then that sounds like a good place to try next."

Late in the afternoon, just as the dark clouds began to separate in the sky over Newton, Jo drove toward her brother-in-law's homestead in a buggy she'd hired from the station. She sat next to the quiet driver, her eyes burning from the long train trip across the stormy plains. It had been exhausting, to say the least.

Not to mention heart-wrenching. She had sat uncomfortably in her hard seat with her forehead resting against the cool windowpane, watching lightning split the sky in the distance, but thinking only of Fletcher and the danger they were all in.

She also wanted to tell him that he needed something more than a drifter's empty existence, moving from town to town in the name of the law. Everything she'd learned about Fletcher since she first met him told her that what he really wanted was a real home and a family. That's how he was raised, and until his father's tragic death, it had been what he wanted out of life.

But Jo supposed that such thoughts of the future was putting the cart before the horse. First, she and Leo had to survive, and Zeb Stone had to finally get what was coming to him—because he couldn't continue to profit from the pain and losses of others. There simply had to be some justice in the world.

Knowing it was time to see Leo at last, and not wanting him to know about the details of the situation, she forced a smile and climbed down from the leather buggy seat. She wondered what he would say when she appeared unexpectedly at the door. He would probably think she had come to check up on him. Somehow she would have to convince him that was not the case.

Wishing there had been time to let someone know she was coming, she accepted her valise from the driver, lifted her skirts, which were trimmed with mud at the bottom, and walked across the dirt yard to the house. Three chickens clucked and scurried out of her path.

Before she reached the steps, the front door swung open and Matilda walked onto the covered porch. Her cheeks were flushed with concern. "Josephine! What are you doing here?"

"Hello, Matilda. I needed some time away, myself,

and thought I would join you. Where's Leo?"

Cecil, Edwyn's brother, appeared behind Matilda. "Good heavens, Jo, what are you doing here? Didn't you get the wire?"

"What wire?"

"The wire we sent a few hours ago—no, obviously you didn't get it."

Icy dread began to coil through her veins. "Where's Leo?"

Matilda came down the steps and took hold of Jo's bag. "Maybe you'd better come inside."

"No, I won't come inside until you tell me what's going on. Where's Leo?"

Cecil came down a step. "He went back to Dodge City."

"What!" Jo hollered. "You let him go?"

"He went on his own without telling us. He left a note and took the morning train."

"Let me see the note."

Cecil darted into the house and reappeared with a sheet of paper, handing it down to Jo.

"It says he knows who killed Edwyn," Jo read in a panic, "and he's going to take care of things. *Take care of things!* What does he mean by that?"

Matilda shook her head. "I don't know, Josephine, but he's probably arriving in Dodge right about now." Jo stuffed the note into her bodice pocket. "When's the next train out of here?"

"The last one for the day will leave in about an hour."

Jo darted toward Cecil's barn, leaving her bag with Matilda for safekeeping. "I'll need a horse to get me to the station."

"I'll go with you," Cecil said, following. "Don't worry, Josephine. We'll find him."

"Just get me to the station, and then send a wire to Marshal Collins. He needs to know what's happening."

With a hiss of steam and a coughing sputter of smoke from the smokestack, the train from Newton puffed wearily into Dodge City. Leo made his way down the aisle, holding on to the backs of the seats to keep his balance as the train shuddered to a slow stop. Local folk gathered on the platform, but none were there to greet him, he knew. For once, he was on his own, able to complete his business in town before going home to surprise his ma with the good news.

He patted his coat pocket one more time to check for his father's letter, then started off toward Zeb Stone's Dry Goods to see that it was delivered to the most powerful man in Dodge. If there was one person who could make use of such a letter, it was his good friend, Mr. Zeb Stone.

Chapter

25

CW/HEN THE DOOR TO THE jailhouse opened,
Fletcher leaned forward at his desk, expecting a complaint about a drunken brawl or a stolen
horse. He stood quickly when he recognized his sister.
"Liz, what are you doing here?"

Elizabeth walked in wearing a dark blue afternoon
dress and a matching velvet hat with ribbons and a
face veil. She clutched her reticule in her tiny gloved
hands, peering uneasily toward the jail cells. "May I
speak to you in private?"

"Of course. We'll go outside." Fletcher moved
around the desk and escorted her out the door and
around the side of the building. "What is it?"

She glanced over her shoulder. "Did you see Zeb
today?"

"Yes, but I didn't talk to him. I waited for him to
leave the store, then I checked out his office."

"Did anyone see you?" she asked anxiously.

"Don't worry. I have a knack for that kind of thing."

"I certainly hope so."

Fletcher leaned against the wall. "What brings you here, Liz? You seem nervous."

"Well, I just don't want to get into trouble with Zeb. Ever since we went through his den this morning, I've been worrying. What if he notices something out of place?"

"He won't. I put everything back exactly where I found it." Fletcher stepped away from the wall. "You don't seem convinced."

"I'm just...well, the real reason I came here is because I have something more to tell you, and I fear I may be going too far."

"You can trust me, sis. I'll take care of everything."

Her chin began to quiver and she lowered her face and pressed her finger under her nose. "I'm not sure you can."

"Why not? What's wrong?"

She took a moment to regain her composure. "Zeb is my *husband.*"

"I know that, Liz," he said gently. "But if he's guilty of something, I can't let it go because he's married to you. Do you understand that?"

Her gaze darted upward. "Of course I do. That's not what I mean to say." She paused, biting her lip. "If he is in some kind of trouble with the law, as his wife I will have to support him. But what if...what if I don't wish to?"

Fletcher relaxed against the wall, coming to understand her predicament. "Then you won't. I'll be here for you, no matter what."

She wiped under her eye and sniffed. "Then I came here to tell you that Zeb came home this afternoon, and went into his study for quite some time. After he left, I looked in and noticed the rug had been moved slightly." Leaning closer to Fletcher, she quietly added, "It was not in the same place it was when we were in there this morning."

Fletcher's pulse quickened. "What are you telling me?"

"That I believe he keeps papers under the desk. In the floor."

"Did you see them?"

"I pulled the rug aside and lifted the floorboard, saw what was there, but I was afraid to touch anything. Matthews was hovering around in the front hall and, if he caught me, he would most certainly inform Zeb."

"You did the right thing. Where is Zeb now?"

"He said he was going back to the store, but I followed to come here. I just saw him go to the Long Branch."

"He likes his brandy, that's for certain." Fletcher took Elizabeth by the arm. "Let's go back to your house. I want to see what's under that desk."

"Are you sure, Fletcher? Maybe this is too dangerous."

"Danger, my dear sister, is what I'm here for."

Zeb pulled his gold timepiece from his coat pocket and squinted to read the time. "I suppose I should saunter down to the store," he said casually to the bartender. "I don't trust anyone but myself to count my cash."

The bartender snickered and gathered the empty glass and brandy bottle from Zeb's place at the bar.

"I'll settle up with you next week," Zeb said, turning unsteadily to leave the saloon. "And that brandy is putrid. Don't serve it to me again."

He staggered once, then gained his footing and pushed through the swinging doors into the dusky evening light.

A few minutes later, Zeb reached the mercantile, walked in and shut the door behind him. He flipped the sign over to read CLOSED.

"Did we make a bundle today, Gerald? I certainly hope so. My tab at the Long Branch is getting out of hand."

Gerald laughed dutifully, then reached under the counter. "The O'Malley kid delivered this for you this afternoon."

"O'Malley, you say?"

"Yes, sir," Gerald replied, holding the sealed envelope out. "It's addressed to you, sir, as mayor of Dodge City."

Zeb slowly moved forward and grasped the letter. "A bit premature, perhaps, but I do like the sound of it. You can count the cash tonight, Gerald, but if you leave with one cent of my money, you'll regret it."

Zeb walked toward the back of the store and went into his office. He sat down at the oak desk, leaned back and crossed his legs. "This should be amusing," he said aloud to himself.

He ripped open the envelope and held up the first

page to read:

> *Dear Mayor Stone,*
> *I thought you should be the one to see this.*
> *Sincerely,*
> *Leo O'Malley*

Zeb flipped to the next page to discover a letter written some time ago by the boy's father.

> *Dear Cecil,*
> *I have a most disturbing matter to discuss with you regarding the cattle-rustling enterprise that I mentioned in my last letter. It seems the guilty party is a man named George Greer. I've finally come to suspect him after spotting one of his men branding cattle on my land. He drove them to town through a section of fence he removed and repaired afterward. I did not risk a confrontation, but I plan to inform the county sheriff and the town council anonymously. What will occur after that I can only hope will not involve me greatly. I have not told Josephine about this matter. You know how independent she can be. I trust you will keep it to yourself until I've had a chance to contact the right people.*
> *Your brother, Edwyn*

Zeb stared silently at Leo's brief note for another minute, feeling his head begin to throb as he considered the boy's obvious meaning. Then, with an angry thrust, Zeb shoved back his chair and stood. The boy was ambitious to deliver this note the week before the election, Zeb thought with mounting fury. What the devil did he hope to gain from it?

This would have to be taken care of immediately.

Quite some time after dark, Jo and Cecil leaped off the evening train and onto the wooden platform in Dodge City. Jo raised her skirts to hurry toward the jailhouse—her boots pounding over the damp ground as she went—all the while praying that Fletcher would be there. She reached the calaboose and pulled open the door, but found the jailhouse and cells empty.

"Come on, he might be upstairs in the clerk's office," she said to Cecil, who was faithfully following behind her.

She dashed up the stairs on the outside of the building, but found the door locked. She clutched at the knob, shaking it in frustration.

"Where else would he be?" Cecil asked as they descended the steps.

"He might be patrolling the streets, but I can't spend all night searching for him. I have to find Leo."

Cecil glanced toward the saloons and theaters on the south side of the tracks. "That ain't no place for a lady. I'll look for Marshal Collins and explain things. You go home. That's the only place Leo would have gone."

"I hope so."

Jo hesitated, trying to think if there was another, better alternative. "I wish I had my gun," she said under her breath, frustrated at the feeling of helplessness, then she wished Cecil luck and ran toward the boardinghouse where Fletcher had promised to leave her wagon.

Jo had no idea what time it was when she finally drove into her own yard, back aching and eyes burning from fatigue. She'd worked the horses hard to get there, fearing the worst, wanting nothing more than to find Leo safe in the house, munching on sugar cookies, but when she saw the dark windows and dark bunkhouse, her hopes sank.

Still clinging to the possibility that he might be in his own bedroom upstairs at the back of the house, she hopped down from the wagon and went to the door. She ran up the stairs.

"Leo? Are you here?"

The absence of a reply sent her bursting through every door, her hopes shrinking with the discovery of each silent, empty room. She gathered herskirts in her fists and ran down the stairs. "Leo!"

The kitchen, too, was empty. Where was her son?

Struggling to think clearly, Jo went into Edwyn's study and lit a lamp, took a rifle from the display on the wall and loaded it. She carried it through the dark hall to the front door and walked out of the house and into the cold night.

For a few seconds, she stood on the porch looking all around. She could make out the rolling pasture where crickets chirped and a cow called out from somewhere in the distance. There was no wind, not even a whisper of a breeze.

She looked toward the barn and noticed light through a crack in the vertical plank wall. Her insides jolted with new hope. All she wanted now was to take Leo into her arms and know that he was safe, to hold him for a few minutes. After that, she would think of nothing but protecting him.

She ran down the porch steps and across the yard. She heard a horse nicker, a pig snort. Her feet tapped lightly over the damp dirt.

As she drew closer to the barn door, her heart began to pound against her rib cage.

Jo stopped just outside and leaned a hand against the wall. Last night, Fletcher had helped her to face her fear and go inside. Now, she was alone.

Struggling for breath, she tried to smother the anxiety rising up inside her. She could not let it keep her from finding Leo. She straightened and forced a deep breath into her lungs, reached for the door latch and pulled it open. The barn was quiet.

She stood in the open doorway peering in, her blood pulsing through her body at an alarming speed. She wanted to call out for Leo, but could push nothing from her fear-constricted throat. Again, she tried to get a breath.

Suddenly, a hand squeezed around her arm and yanked her into the barn. Her rifle was plucked from her grasp.

Disoriented, she stumbled forward onto the hay-strewn floor. Something struck her in the back of the head, and she lost consciousness.

Feeling numb, not quite understanding where she was or what was happening to her, Jo tried to make sense of her thoughts. A dull ache throbbed at the back of her skull. She fought to open her eyes, but her injured body just wouldn't cooperate with her brain.

"What's happening?" she managed to mumble, but to whom she had no idea. She felt herself being lifted and placed on the back of a horse. She knew she was straddling it, leaning forward with eyes closed, her cheek resting on its coarse mane. Her wrists were bound together behind her. Thoughts began to form.

Her eyes flew open just as a rope came down over her head and tightened around her neck.

Shock flooded through her. She bolted upright.

The horse took a startled step sideways. Nearly losing her balance and falling off, Jo realized with surprising clarity that the mare was the only thing keeping her from hanging.

"Whoa, girl," she said, trying to calm the horse, who had taken a few steps forward. The rope was stretched and pulling against Jo's jaw. "Move to the left, girl."

"I doubt she knows her left from her right."

The sound of Zeb's deep, surly voice sent a wave of nausea through Jo. She looked down and saw him standing by the tack room door, aiming a rifle at her.

"Where's Leo?" she demanded, but her voice was raspy under the tightening of the prickly rope.

"I was hoping you'd tell *me.*"

Thank goodness, she thought, Zeb hadn't found him. At least not yet.

If she was going to keep breathing, Jo needed slack in the rope. She pressed her knees together to get the horse to move.

"There's no point in trying," Zeb said, lowering the

rifle to lean on it.

"You're going to slap her on the rump anyway, right?"

Zeb smiled sardonically. "I thought I'd just shoot her, but then it wouldn't look like a suicide, would it? Your idea is better."

Jo glared down at him, sickened by the self-satisfied glint in his eyes. "I should have killed you when I had the chance," she said.

"Yes, you probably should have. I guess Six-Shooter Hank wasn't as scary as the paper made him out to be. You're a coward, Mrs. O'Malley. You let your husband hang in front of your eyes and you couldn't even kill me for doing it."

"You won't get away with this, Zeb. Fletcher will know it was you. He already knows Will MacGregor worked for you, and somehow he'll prove you killed him last night."

"So what if I did? If Fletcher has a problem with it, I'll take care of him, too. But I'm tired of talking. I'm thirsty and I want to get back to Dodge to find that boy of yours, before he blabbers all over town what he knows."

The mere mention of Leo shook Jo to the core. She felt a rage inside herself like she'd never felt before, and yet she knew she was at Zeb's mercy. She had to stay calm. "Please, Zeb, leave Leo alone. He's just a boy."

"I told you I didn't want to talk anymore." He raised the rifle and pointed it at the peaked roof.

There was no way out of this! He was going to spook the horse and she could do nothing but watch!

Just like the last time!

He pulled the trigger and the bullet ripped through the roof, booming in Jo's ears like a thunderclap.

The horse reared up. Jo held on with her legs as the noose tightened around her neck and chafed against her skin. She was barely on the mare's back anymore. Most of her weight was hanging in the rope. She couldn't breathe!

The mare's front hooves slammed onto the ground. Choking, feeling her heart burn, Jo shut her eyes and thought of Fletcher. She prayed he would save Leo.

Just then, the mare moved back, and Jo's weight lightened in the rope. She coughed and struggled for breath. Confused and trembling uncontrollably, she leaned forward onto the horse's mane again.

Somewhere in the whirlwind of her consciousness, she heard Zeb laughing. "Looks like I might just have to shoot her after all. To hell with a suicide."

"Zeb, no..."

He raised the rifle and aimed it at the horse's head. Jo squeezed her eyes shut, feeling tears spill out as Zeb pulled the trigger again.

The gun clicked.

"Oh, for pity's sake," Zeb said, staring at the weapon.

Jo began to sit up, but fear flared through her anew when Zeb dropped the gun and walked toward her. "What are you doing?" she asked, sobbing now.

He didn't answer. He just slapped the horse on the rump.

The mare darted forward. Jo's body lurched with the horse, then whipped back and she fell off. All air was cut off. She was hanging from the neck, swinging and kicking, praying it would be over soon, and that Fletcher would save Leo....

Fletcher didn't even have a chance to think. He walked into the barn and focused everything on shooting that rope in two. He aimed his rifle through the dim light, shut one eye and fired. The noise frightened the barn animals to shrieking and Jo dropped to the ground in a heap of skirts and petticoats.

Fletcher held his rifle in steady hands and fixed his aim on Zeb's black heart.

"Where the hell did you come from?" Zeb asked, his tone dripping with irritation. "I thought you were taking care of the saloon district tonight."

"It doesn't matter much. The only thing that matters is where you're going. And that's straight to hell."

Zeb raised his hands in the air. "You won't shoot me. You've never shot anyone in your life."

"I haven't wanted to—until now."

Zeb glanced down at Jo, who had wrestled her hands free and was tugging at the rope around her neck. "So...you *did* become infatuated with her."

"Shut up, Zeb. I'm taking you in."

Zeb spoke in a businesslike tone. "Why don't we talk about this? I'm sure we can come to a profitable arrangement, for both of us."

"I said shut up," Fletcher said, "and I meant it. Unless you want to leave here with your brains in a bucket."

Zeb considered it. "No, I don't suppose I do." He took a step forward and held out his wrists. "Go ahead, then. Take me in. You'll have a hell of a time convicting me, though. I have a lot of powerful friends."

Fletcher lowered the rifle to his side and pulled his cuffs out of the back of his belt. "It shouldn't be a problem."

"You sound full of confidence."

"I am, *Mr. Greer.*"

Zeb froze. "I beg your pardon?"

"I found your signature as Greer all over the papers under your desk. You're going to jail for a long time, Zeb."

But just as Fletcher flicked the handcuffs open, Zeb pulled a small revolver out of his pocket.

"Fletcher, look out!" Jo shouted, scrambling to her feet with the rope still tied around her neck.

Zeb fired. Pain coursed through Fletcher's side and he stumbled back into a pile of hay.

"No!" Jo called out.

Zeb leaped onto Fletcher and went for his throat. Choking, Fletcher tried to push him off.

"No one's taking me in," Zeb said, growling between clenched teeth. He squeezed Fletcher's neck. "I've come too far."

Fletcher gasped for air, kicking and pulling against Zeb's hands. His gut throbbed with pain. Blood soaked his shirt.

Without warning, a garden shovel made an arc through the air and smashed against Zeb's head. He jolted under the blow and dropped like a sack of corn flour onto Fletcher's chest.

"Are you all right?" Jo asked, pulling Zeb off. "You're shot!"

"You don't say." Fletcher tried to sit up, but Jo

pushed him back down. "Lie still. I'll get the wagon."

Fletcher's stomach churned. "I don't feel so good."

"Hang on!" she yelled over her shoulder, darting toward the barn door and pulling the double doors open.

He stared up at the gambrel-roofed trusses high above him and waited for Jo to come back. Damn, but his side hurt. And his heart was pounding like a hammer. He shut his eyes tight against the pain, wishing it hadn't come to this. He'd done none of the things he'd wanted to do with his life. He'd been wasting so much time.

Jo, where are you?

Soon he began to feel cold, and though there was still so much he wanted to do in this life, he just couldn't hold on anymore. He slipped into unconsciousness.

Jo raced toward the wagon, leaped onto the seat and slapped the reins hard against the horses' backs. "*Yah! Yah!*"

Startled into action, the team trotted into the barn. Jo jumped down. "Fletcher! Wake up!" She knelt beside him and tried to shake him, but he was completely out. Panic swept through her. She put her ear to his chest. "Where's your heartbeat?"

The soft thumping relieved her fears, but she still had to get him to the doctor. The horses were tired, but there was no time to unhitch and change them.

She pulled Fletcher up by the arm and felt an excruciating stab of pain in her shoulder as she lifted him and tried to stand. "Hold on. Don't give up now," she said, wobbling under his weight.

As gently as she could manage, she lowered him onto the back of the wagon. Her heart ached at the sight of his unconscious form and the blood soaking his shirt.

Feeling the effects of her own wound—hoping she'd not opened it up to bleed under the strain of what she'd just done—she hurried to climb into the wagon seat, barely even aware of the noose still around her neck. She was about to flick the reins when she looked down and saw Zeb, sprawled in a heap beside a saddle horse.

Jo stared down at him. Was he still breathing, she wondered frantically, or had she killed him with the shovel? She had to know.

Quickly hopping down, she rolled him over onto his back. She placed her fingers under his nose and felt the heat and moisture of his breath.

Operating only on instinct, she dragged him by the arm across the barn floor toward the wagon, pulling with all her might, feeling another excruciating pain in her shoulder. *Oh, God!* It was too much. She couldn't take it anymore. She let him drop for a moment while she searched around the dimly lit floor for Fletcher's handcuffs. After spotting them a few feet away, she strained to roll Zeb over again onto his stomach, then fastened the cuffs onto his wrists behind his back. "That ought to hold you."

Struggling with his heavy, limp body, she groaned and staggered as she lifted him onto the wagon to lie beside Fletcher, then she climbed back onto the seat. "Let's go," she said to the horses.

They drove out the opposite door, and Jo slapped the reins to urge them into a gallop, praying with all her heart that she would make it to Dodge in time to save both the lives she was trying to save.

Chapter

26

*J*O SAT BY THE FRONT window in Dr. Green's office, tapping her foot on the floor, waiting impatiently while he operated on Fletcher in the back room. She thought of how she'd suffered earlier in the day when she'd said good-bye to Fletcher on the train, and how she'd not thought the pain of their separation could be any worse. Yet, here it was—*much worse.* The misery on the train had been compounded by fear when she learned about Leo's disappearance, and now it had swelled, yet again, to a breed of torture she'd not thought possible.

She dropped her forehead into her hands and shuddered with dread and trepidation, fearing she would be sick if the doctor came out and told her that Fletcher was dead. *Please, let him live. Even if we can't be together, just let him live.*

Voices rose in the street and Jo sat up. The front

door of the doctor's office swung open.

"Ma!" Leo called out, rushing to her and wrapping his arms around her waist.

She stood and cupped his head in her hand, bending forward to kiss his cheeks. "Oh, Leo! I'm so glad to see you." Tears welled up in her eyes and she exhaled with relief.

Cecil walked in behind Leo.

"You found him," Jo said, her heart overflowing with gratitude.

"Sure did. Just a short time after I sent Marshal Collins after you."

"Where were you?" she asked Leo, stroking his hair and lifting his chin so she could see his face.

"I was sitting on the steps at Jensen's Boardinghouse with John, waiting for Marshal Collins."

"Whatever for?"

"To tell him about the letter I found, and that I gave it to Mr. Stone."

Jo took his face in both her hands. "You did a very foolish thing, Leo. You should have come to me first."

"I know, Ma. I'm real sorry. I only wanted to make you proud of me, but I won't ever go against what you say again. Uncle Cecil told me everything."

She stroked the hair off his forehead. *Ah*, to see her son's face and hold him close in her arms...her dear, sweet boy. She was so very grateful to have been spared the loss of him, which would have been unbearable.

"And from this day forward," she said, "I won't keep things from you either, Leo. I'll try to give you more freedoms. I'll agree to that because you're getting older. But remember, you're still my son, and there will still be rules, until you are older."

"Yes, Ma," he groaned good-naturedly.

Jo held him close and he allowed it for a moment, then stepped back and straightened his shirt. "So, is it true?" Leo asked pointedly.

"Is what true?"

"What John told me about you and the marshal— that you two are in love?"

Caught off guard, Jo stepped back. "John told you that?"

"Yes, Ma, while we were talking at the boarding-house. He went there to have a word with the marshal about it. That's how we met up with each other."

"What exactly did John plan to say to the marshal?" Jo asked uneasily.

Leo looped a thumb through his belt. "He was going to tell Marshal Collins that if he didn't treat you right, he'd be sorry for it, because you deserve to be happy."

"I see," Jo replied, putting it in her mind to thank John one of these days, then worrying about how she was going to tell Leo that what he'd heard wasn't true, that it was only a charade. At least, she thought it was.

Wasn't it? Could she dare to hope?

"Will there be a wedding like folks have been saying?" Leo asked.

Jo shuddered inwardly. "Well, I'm not sure, Leo. Things are very complicated with the marshal and me." Not wanting to go into any more detail than that, she stated the obvious. "Do you know what happened to him?" Her stomach turned over with dread.

Leo peered up at her somberly. "Yes, Ma, and I

hope he's all right, 'cause I like him a lot. I think Pa would have liked him, too."

An hour later, Jo sat next to the bed waiting, holding Fletcher's hand. "Please wake up," she whispered softly in his ear. "Don't die on me."

Touching him, so still and lifeless, made the pain in her heart resonate through her entire body.

She sat back and watched him. Teardrops fell from her eyes onto his bare forearm. "Please be all right. I don't know what would have become of me if you hadn't walked into my life when you did. You saved me, Fletcher."

Just then, his finger twitched under hers and her skin prickled everywhere. "Fletcher, it's me. I'm here. Try to open your eyes." He shook his head slowly back and forth, enough to spark a tiny fragment of hope. "You're going to be fine. The doctor said the bullet went straight through and didn't hit any major organs."

Fletcher opened his eyes and stared up at her for a long moment. She wasn't even sure if he recognized her. Her heart was beating like a drum.

"You saved me, too," he said at last, groggily. "And I don't just mean from Zeb."

Jo stared at him in disbelief, her emotions flooding her senses until she felt as if she might collapse from the weight of them. She leaned down to hug and kiss him. "Oh, Fletcher, thank goodness you're all right."

He pulled her in for a kiss and held her as their lips joined tenderly. "What happened to Zeb?" he asked, rubbing his temple.

"Deputy Anderson came and arrested him, took him to the county jail after the doctor made sure he was all right. He just has a bump on his head that'll be sore for a while."

Laughing quietly, then wincing from the pain it caused, Fletcher squeezed Jo's hand. "Now they can call *you* The Bruiser. It's time I retired the title anyway."

"Retired it," she repeated, not quite understanding his meaning.

A knock sounded at the door and Deputy Anderson walked in. "Marshal Collins, glad to see you're awake."

"Thanks," Fletcher replied. "What's up?"

Anderson removed his hat and turned it over in his hands a few times. "That's what I came here to find out. Mrs. O'Malley sent for me."

Fletcher gazed up at Jo, his eyes filling with concern. She squeezed his hand one more time, then stood up from the chair, feeling nervous butterflies invade her belly. "I called Deputy Anderson here so that I could confess my crime."

Fletcher tried to lean up on his elbows. "Jo, you don't have to—"

"Yes, I do. I need to tell him this, or I won't be able to live with myself. It's the right thing to do."

Fully prepared to be handcuffed and dragged off to jail, Jo turned to face Deputy Anderson.

Fletcher tried to protest one more time. "Jo, please, don't—"

"I'm Six-Shooter Hank," she said quickly. "I was the one who broke into Zeb's store that night. Only

I wasn't there to rob him. I was there to shoot him."

Anderson gaped at Fletcher, as if he were searching for directions about what to say. Fletcher shook his head back and forth on the pillow. "Jo, you shouldn't have done that."

"Yes, I should have. I can't let you keep my secret. You'll hate yourself for it, and I care about you too much to let you live with that."

Fletcher blinked a few times, a hint of a smile grazing his colorless lips. "I haven't told her yet," he said to Anderson.

Jo whirled around. "Told me what?"

His sleepy eyes glimmered in the lantern light. "While you were on the train to Newton, I got a wire from a lawman friend of mine in Chicago. Zeb's real name is Jack Curtis. Stone and Greer were only two of the names he's used. We're looking into the rest." Fletcher wet his lips and paused for a break. His voice was raspy with fatigue. He had to speak slowly.

"Zeb's been wanted in Illinois and in three other states for murder and theft among other things, and with the evidence I found in his house, he'll be convicted for a lot more than that. There was a one thousand-dollar reward out for his capture."

"A reward? Are you telling me that—"

"Yes, ma'am," Anderson interrupted. "He was wanted dead or alive, so you won't be going to jail, even if you had shot him that night. The way things stand now, you'll be collecting a thousand dollars, seeing as it was you who cuffed him and dragged him all the way back to town. And that couldn't have been easy. He ain't no lightweight."

Jo collapsed onto the chair, too shocked to believe it. "I had no idea."

Anderson replaced his hat on his head. "Is that all you wanted me for, ma'am? To tell me about what you did that night?"

"Yes, and to thank you, of course."

Anderson smiled and tipped his hat. "My pleasure, ma'am. Take care, now." He turned and left the room.

Overwhelmed, Jo held Fletcher's hand. "What will Elizabeth do?"

"My sister's a tough lady," he replied. "She'll start over. We both will."

Jo struggled with a painful yearning that was squeezing around her heart, a yearning that would stay with her and plague her forever, she was certain. She loved this man so much, she would have given her life for him tonight. How would she survive if he decided to pack up and leave Dodge?

"Will you take Elizabeth away from here?" she asked.

Fletcher tried to move but winced with pain. His face had no color. His eyes were underlined with dark circles. Jo felt suddenly guilty for being so selfish right now, for wanting to know what he planned to do with his future, and whether or not that future would involve her and Leo.

"Can I do anything for you?" she offered, rearranging his pillow under his head.

He touched her cheek. "You already have. You've helped me. I...I feel like I understand things better now."

"What things?" she asked.

He wet his dry lips. "I'm not a lawman, Jo. It's just something I've been doing to make up for what my father did, to prove I'm not the same as him. But I *am* like him. I know that now. I'm his son and I'm darn proud of it, because he was a good man. It's time I acknowledged that. I'm not saying that what he did was right—there were probably other ways he could have handled it, and the outcome might have been different. But at least he was honest about everything. And he let those men go free because he loved us so much, he was afraid of something bad happening to us. I understand it now, because it's just like how I feel about *you.*"

Jo squeezed Fletcher's hand. "Can you forgive him?"

"I already have. I did a lot of thinking after you left, and now...I just miss him. I wish he was here. I wish he could have met you."

Hearing him speak those perfect words only made her love Fletcher more, but that didn't make this any easier, not if he still planned to take his sister away, and leave Dodge City for good.

"Since you're handing out forgiveness today," Jo said, "do you think you could forgive *me,* too? I know I went against everything you believed in and I even asked you to break the law to set me free, but I'm sorry for that. I just want you to know that."

He pulled her closer to cup her cheek in his hand. "God, Jo, how can you even ask that? You thought you wanted to kill Zeb, but you didn't, and I know you never would have been able to. You even dragged him back here to save his wretched life. You were willing to confess everything just now, to go to prison because you felt it was the right thing to do. I don't know anyone with more integrity than that. There's nothing to forgive."

She laid her cheek on his chest and closed her eyes with gratitude. Everything she had feared so deeply—that she was a killer...that Fletcher would never be able to forgive her—it was all gone now. There was only the warmth of the man holding her in his arms, and a feeling in her heart that was so sweet, so complete, it was almost painful.

Perhaps now, she could live with letting him go.

"Still, I'm sorry that all this had to happen," she said, wiping a tear from her cheek. "I'm sorry that you were shot, and that you had to arrest your brother-in-law, and that things didn't work out for Elizabeth."

"I'm not sorry," Fletcher replied. "Zeb was cruel to her. Now she has an excuse to be rid of him. And as for you and me..." He raised her chin with a finger. "I don't think I ever told you that I loved you."

She stared blankly at him, numb with shock, until a cry of joy broke from her lips. "You do?"

He nodded. "Oh, yes."

"I love you, too," she whispered with laughter. "More than I ever thought I could love any man. I didn't even know feelings like this were possible."

Fletcher raised her hand to his lips and kissed it. "When I saw you in that noose, Jo, I thought I'd lost you forever. Then, I thought I was dying, and all I could think about was how I'd been wasting my life doing something that just wasn't me, and how you're everything that I want, and you make me see everything I want to be. I don't want to lose you, Jo."

Jo sat back, almost afraid to believe this could be happening, that he could be saying these things to her. "I don't want to lose you either."

"Is that a promise?"

"Yes." She kissed his hand, again and again.

"But there's only one thing that still bothers me about all this," Fletcher said, frowning. "Actually, about you."

At his words, Jo's heart flinched a little, but she forced herself to speak. "What is that?"

He stared at her for a moment, looking reluctant to tell her. "Well...if you really want to know...it's your name."

"Josephine? You don't like it?"

"Oh, I like Josephine fine. It's the Mrs. O'Malley part that I'm gonna have a problem with. You see, I was kind of hoping you'd change it—to Mrs. Collins."

Jo's heart swelled with happiness as Fletcher grasped her hand in his and brought it to his lips.

"Will you?" he asked. "Will you marry me, Josephine? For *real*?"

Laughing and crying at the same time, Jo flung herself at Fletcher and planted her mouth on his.

"Ow! My side!" he groaned, peeling her off him and laughing. "Have pity on an injured man. I take it that's a yes?"

"Yes," Jo sputtered, still wiping at the tears that flowed freely down her cheeks as Fletcher reached up to kiss her.

"I can't wait to tell Leo" she said. "He'll be so pleased, because you know he thinks the world of you, Fletcher. As do I."

Their lips met, and her mind spun with joy.

"Hey," Fletcher said softly, gazing into her eyes with a love she never imagined she would ever know. Not in this lifetime. "I guess that old saying is true after all."

"About what?"

He tilted his head and smiled. "A rose by any other name does smell as sweet."

Jo grinned and leaned closer to touch her lips to his. "Everything smells sweeter with you in my life."

And with that, he drew her into his arms, and the future, like the wide-open prairie, felt absolutely dazzling and full of promise.

Author's Note

Dear Reader,

I hope you enjoyed book two in my Dodge City Brides Series. If you haven't read book one yet, please continue on for more information about PRAIRIE BRIDE. You'll also find an excerpt for the third book in the trilogy, A TIME FOR LOVE, which provides an interesting twist on the Dodge City setting, because we see it through the eyes of a modern twentieth-century woman who inadvertently stumbles across a portal through time. It's quite an adventure. (It's a newly reissued edition of a novel that was originally published in 2011 under the title TAKEN BY THE COWBOY.)

If you enjoyed this romance novel, I'd love for you to check out my Highland romances as well, which feature rugged alpha male heroes in a Scottish setting. For more information about those books, please visit my website at www.juliannemaclean.com, and while you're there, don't forget to sign up for my email newsletter to be notified about future new releases. I also have a monthly autographed book giveaway, which is available for my newsletter subscribers.

And if you would like to know when an ebook edition from my backlist goes on sale for 99 cents (or is occasionally offered for free), please go to my author profile on Bookbub and click the blue "follow" button. You'll be sent an email whenever there's a flash sale.

Thanks again for reading one of my books, and as always, happy reading!

Julianne

DODGE CITY BRIDES
THE SERIES

USA Today bestselling author Julianne MacLean delivers three breathtaking and passionate full-length novels featuring rugged alpha-male heroes of the West, all sworn to protect the women they love…

PRAIRIE BRIDE
Dodge City Brides Series – Book 1

A loveless marriage of convenience on the Kansas prairie turns out to be far more than she bargained for...

HE'S PART OF THE WEST
Briggs Brigman has been burned once before, and the last thing he needs is a beautiful wife who will spend hours in front of the mirror, primping herself. He knows how hard the prairie can be on a woman, and all he wants is a stalwart bride who won't complain about hauling water from the creek....

SHE'S A CITY GIRL WITH NO IDEA WHAT SHE'S IN FOR...
All Sarah MacFarland wants is to escape her fearful life in Boston and start fresh with a new identity. Answering an advertisement for a mail order bride seems like the perfect solution, until she meets her soon-to-be husband—a ruggedly handsome, strapping farmer who leaves her breathless on their wedding night. But is it possible that two tormented souls can find happiness, when all they know is betrayal, and when trust is the only way out of a tumultuous past that simply won't stay buried?

"You can always count on Julianne MacLean to deliver ravishing romance that will keep you turning pages until the wee hours of the morning."
—Teresa Medeiros

A TIME FOR LOVE
Dodge City Brides Series – Book 3

HERO AND PROTECTOR
Former bounty hunter, expert gunslinger, and the toughest sheriff Dodge City has ever known, Truman Wade is a real man from the tip of his black Stetson right down to his spurs and leather boots. He's never met his match in a gunfight, but he's never met a gorgeous, gutsy woman from the twenty-first century either…

TORN BETWEEN TWO WORLDS
Newly single after a rocky breakup with her self-absorbed fiancé, newspaper columnist Jessica Delaney crashes her car in a lightning storm and soon finds herself dodging bullets in the Wild West. Before the night is out, she's tossed in jail for a murder she didn't commit, and if things don't seem complicated enough, the impossibly handsome sheriff in charge of her arrest has danger written all over him. Jessica knows she needs to get home, but when Sheriff Wade's enticing touch sets her heart on fire, she begins to wonder if fate has other plans for her, and soon she must choose between the life she longs for in the future… and the greatest love she's ever known.

Read on for an excerpt from

A TIME FOR LOVE

Dodge City Brides Series – Book 3
Copyright © 2020 Julianne MacLean Publishing Inc.

rologue

Dodge City, Kansas
Present day

JESSICA **D**ELANEY SAT IN THE waiting room outside the Operating Room, barely able to move,
much less comprehend what had just happened to her
brother. "How much longer?" she said to her parents.
"He's been in there for two hours."

Jessica's mother blew her nose, while her father sat
in silence, squeezing his wife's hand. "I'm sure they're
doing their best," he said. "We'll hear something
soon."

Jessica rose from her chair and walked to the edge
of the waiting room to peer down the long hall at the
surgery doors to the O.R. She thought of Gregory
lying on the table under the lights, a team of masked
surgeons working over him. What were his chances?
Did anyone ever survive a bullet wound to the chest?

Feeling nauseous all of a sudden, she returned to her
chair and sat down. She stared at a framed painting

on the wall and wished this day had been different. Gregory didn't deserve to be lying on that table. He was too young, and such a good person.

At least the gunman was behind bars. The convenience store clerk had noticed the out-of-state license plate just before he called 911.

An orderly in a white uniform walked by pushing a cart stacked with folded blue hospital gowns. Jessica watched him while he steered the cart onto the elevator. When the doors slid shut behind him, she thought of Liam, her fiancée.

Should she call him and tell him they were still waiting for news?

Jessica chewed on a thumbnail and recalled their conversation hours ago, when she'd called him at work....

"Liam, something terrible just happened. Can you come with me to Dodge?"

"When? Now? I'm in a meeting. I can't just skip out."

She fought to keep her voice steady. "Gregory's been shot. He's on his way to the hospital. I need to go right now, and I'd really like you to come with me."

He was silent for a moment. "God, Jessica...is he going to be okay?"

"I don't know. That's why I need to go now—to be with Mom and Dad."

"Of course. You should go."

"Can't you come?"

She heard him sigh heavily on the other end of the line. "It's a really bad time, Jess. We've got clients coming in tonight. It could be a million-dollar deal. If I'm not there, it might cost me my job—and you don't know what kind of day it's been for me." He began to tell her about the mountain of emails and texts he still had to get through.

Jessica covered her forehead with her hand. She didn't want to hear the details. Not now.

She interrupted him. "Look, don't worry about it. I'll go alone."

"Let me know how he's doing. Call me later."

"Sure." She hung up without saying goodbye and drove from Topeka to Dodge alone....

The squeak of the surgery doors swinging open pulled Jessica from her thoughts. She stood up to look down the hall again and saw a doctor in O.R. greens walking toward them. His shirt was drenched in sweat. "Mom, Dad...someone's coming."

Her parents stood up.

The doctor, who looked to be in his mid-thirties, kept his eyes on Jessica as he walked the length of the hall. A terrible rush of anxiety exploded in her belly as he came to stand before them.

"Mr. and Mrs. Delaney," he said, "I'm Doctor Jake Spencer."

He shook her father's hand, while Jessica put her arm around her mother.

"I'm sorry to tell you this," the doctor said. "We did everything we could for Gregory, but I'm afraid he didn't make it."

Jessica stared blankly at the doctor, who kept his gaze fixed on hers. His eyes filled with empathy, while hers filled with tears.

Her parents said nothing for a moment, then her mother let out a sob. "Please, no."

The doctor put his hand on her shoulder. "I'm so sorry, Mrs. Delaney. The wound was deep. The bullet entered his chest and punctured a lung. It lodged in the wall of his aorta. We tried to stop the bleeding and put a graft in place, but it bled too heavily, and we couldn't stop it. We did all we could do. I massaged his heart to pump it manually, but...I'm very sorry."

Jessica's mother leaned into her husband and buried her sobs in his chest. All Jessica could do was stare at the doctor while she listened to her mother's weeping and the sound of her own blood rushing through her veins. She still couldn't believe what the doctor was saying.

"Will you be all right?" he asked. His voice was caring. Almost shaky. His green eyes were compassionate and sincere. He reached out and touched her shoulder.

Jessica managed to nod.

"If you need anything or have any questions," he continued, "you can contact me at any time." He handed her his card.

"Thank you," she replied.

He made a move to leave but turned back. He shook his head in frustration. "I'm sorry, Jessica. I did everything in my power to save him. I wish I could have done something to prevent it from happening."

His expression was tight with strain, as he bowed his head and walked away.

Her grief swelled as she stared after the doctor, until the doors to surgery swung closed behind him. She choked back a sob and turned to embrace her parents.

It wasn't until many hours later, after they left the hospital and went home to call their friends and relatives, that Jessica wondered how the doctor had known her name.

Chapter

1

One year later

JESSICA SHIFTED NERVOUSLY IN THE driver's seat, her fingers like vice grips around the steering wheel. She'd driven for two hours, slicing through a rain-battered dusk, wishing that she lived closer to Dodge and her parents. If she did, she wouldn't have to spend so many hours traveling from one city to the other.

Maybe it was time to move home, she thought, for the tenth time that month. There wasn't much keeping her in Topeka anymore—not since she broke off her engagement to Liam.

She was self-employed and could write her fitness column from wherever she pleased. All she needed was a good pair of sneakers for running, her laptop, and wireless Internet at a nearby Starbucks. Her apartment was a sublet. She could give a month's notice and be out of there in a heartbeat. The change would do her good.

Not that she wasn't happy in her work. She loved what she did. There were no problems in that department, but everything else seemed so uncertain and unpredictable.

Her brother had gone out to buy ice cream after supper one night, and he never saw another sunrise again.

Jessica had imagined she'd be married by now with a kid on the way, but the man she chose for a husband turned out to be a self-absorbed child, and she was suddenly single again, paying off debt from a honeymoon she had no choice but take alone.

Yet, she was ever hopeful, waiting for a sign from above, a clue to suggest what she was meant to do with her life. There had to be some greater purpose.

Should she stay in Topeka, or move home to Dodge to be closer to her parents?

They weren't getting any younger and wouldn't be around forever. If she'd learned anything over the past year, it was to make the most of each and every day, because you never knew when it could all end—just like that—with no warning whatsoever.

Come on, destiny. Which is it? Topeka or Dodge?

A flash of lightning and an instantaneous thunderclap caused her to jump in her seat. Rolling her neck to ease the tension in her shoulders, she flexed her fingers on the steering wheel and repositioned her slick palms. The windshield wipers snapped noisily back and forth.

Another crash of thunder overlapped the last.

Counting the seconds to keep her mind occupied, Jessica raked stiff fingers through her hair. She'd just finished a cup of bitter service-station coffee, and now her brain, whirling with caffeine, couldn't match the lightning with the correct thunderclap.

Maybe the radio would take her mind off things. She tuned into a fiddling festival, then tapped her thumbs on the steering wheel to "Oh! Susanna." Other vehicles passed her at dangerous speeds, their tires hissing through puddles on the slick pavement. She glanced impatiently at her watch, wondering how much longer she'd have to fight this storm.

Ahead of her, a white freight truck lumbered slowly up the incline. Knowing she'd have to pass, she glanced over her shoulder and signaled to cross into the passing lane.

She barely managed to gain any distance when her car suddenly hydroplaned and began to fishtail. Instinctively, she slammed her red stiletto pump onto the brake, realizing too late what she had done. Her heart pummeled her ribcage as she tried to regain control, but it was no use. The steering wheel was useless as the vehicle spun around in a dizzying circle.

Oh! Susanna, don't you cry for me....

The car whipped around and flipped over, bouncing across the pavement like a child's toy. The world spun in chaotic circles. Jessica's head hit the side window. Glass smashed, and steel collapsed like tin all around her.

Frozen with fear, she felt all her muscles constrict. *Please, stop! Get me out of here!*

Lightning split the ashen sky. The car lit up and sizzled with one electrifying pulse after another.

The light...it was too bright. She couldn't see. She squeezed her eyes shut.

All at once, the world became silent except for the echoed thumping of her heart in her ears. There was no pain, only blackness. She felt as if she were floating, detached from everything but the extraordinary quiet, the complete absence of all cares and misgivings. She felt no fear now. Was this death? Maybe she would see her brother....

Something wet trickled down her forehead and onto her eyelashes.

The distinct visceral sensation sucked her out of the tranquil beyond, and when her eyes fluttered open, she found herself lying on her back, gazing up at the dusky sky, watching silvery clouds roll and twist and turn in the most fantastic way.

Then real, conscious thoughts began to form in her brain.

She'd been in a car accident. She was lying in the grass. Her hair was wet. Was it blood?

Blinking in panic, she touched her throbbing temples but discovered the wetness was only rain. Relieved, she sat up and realized she was sitting in a puddle of mud. A damp chill rippled up her spine.

Had she been thrown from the car? She couldn't remember anything that violent. Of course, she had shut her eyes and blacked out. Or at least she thought that's what happened.

With trembling hands, she rose up on her knees and rubbed the side of her neck where the seatbelt had chafed her. Next, she touched her scalp, feeling a gritty, sandy residue. Shattered glass, she realized, as she studied the pads of her fingers. And her head—*Good Lord.* A bump was already sprouting at her temple.

Wondering if she had a concussion, she carefully tried to stand. She pressed her hand into the gooey muck to keep her balance and rose to her feet. Her stiletto pumps sank deeper into the puddle, right up to the ankles of her skinny jeans. She noticed that her favorite black belted jacket was ruined. A button was torn off, and the pocket was ripped.

She glanced around, searching for her car.

Where was it? And why couldn't she hear traffic from the road?

Bewildered, she scanned the rolling prairie for the vehicle. Surely it was somewhere.

She rested her hand on her stomach that churned with nausea. It was a normal reaction, she knew, after what she'd just been through. In fact, it was a miracle she was even able to stand.

But where was her car?

The only explanation she could come up with was that she must have been wandering around in shock for the last little while and had left it behind—along with her purse and cell phone. And the strange floating sensation.... That must have been some kind of dream state.

So where was she, exactly? To her left were miles of flat, green prairie. To her right, a small hill. She decided to climb it to see what was on the other side.

When she reached the top, she stepped onto a country road pocked with puddles and wet stones.

She pushed her damp hair away from her face to look around, and her heart sunk.

More miles of prairie. In every direction.

How had she gotten this far? And which way should she go?

She stared transfixed at a distant flicker of lightning far off, just above the misty horizon. A quiet breeze fanned the odor of cow manure into her face, and nervous dread swelled inside her.

Something didn't feel right. She couldn't possibly have walked much of a distance. Could she?

Well, she thought, taking a deep, steadying breath and resolving to stay rational. There was no point standing around doing nothing. That road had to lead somewhere.

Off she went.

After walking a few miles on the dirt road through the pouring rain, Jessica wished miserably that she had worn her running shoes instead of her stupid "sexy-girl" shoes, but there wasn't much she could do about it now. All she could do was try to ignore the excruciating sting of the blisters—which felt like hot coals burning the balls of her feet—and walk with an awkward limp.

A short while later, she sighed with relief when the setting sun finally peeked through the thick blanket of clouds. Raindrops glistened like tiny diamonds as they fell, weightless and softer now. Lifting her wrist to check the time, she realized she'd lost her watch. *Damn. It was brand new.*

Reaching a fork in the road, she stopped to look at

a dilapidated wooden sign that read: DODGE CITY. The sign pointed left, so with little choice, she limped in that direction.

By the time she spotted a town up ahead—unfortunately it didn't look like Dodge City-—the rain had stopped, and darkness had folded over the terrain. Though she felt like a drowned rat, she was relieved to have found some signs of civilization.

She couldn't wait to find a phone and call her parents. They were probably worried sick.

As she limped across an old plank bridge that led into the town, she heard the faint music of a brass band, and each time its cymbals crashed together, it was once too often for the pounding sensation in her head.

Then a horse-drawn wagon rumbled by.

She stopped abruptly and stared at it—*what the heck?*—then stepped off the bridge and walked up the wide main street. She glanced around for a phone booth, but found herself distracted by the buggies, the cowboy costumes on the men, and the music from inside a place that looked like an old saloon. A piano man played "Oh! Susanna," and a banjo plucked along with it.

That song again.

She stood shivering at the corner of two unpaved streets, looking left and right. Wide boarded sidewalks and hitching rails fronted the buildings; saddled horses and mules were lined up, side by side.

Good God, there had to be at least six inches of slop underfoot and it smelled like horse poo.

What kind of place was this? Had she stumbled

onto the set of one of those reality shows where they throw people into a historical time-period and watch how crazy they go?

When a couple of ragged looking cowboys staggered by, waving whisky bottles and revolvers in the air, Jessica decided to walk a little faster. She hadn't seen any women yet, only men, and she suspected this wasn't the safest place to be standing around, taking in the sights, because it all looked pretty sketchy.

Stepping up onto the boardwalk, she paused outside a bar called the Long Branch Saloon, which made no sense because the Long Branch was part of the Dodge City Museum—a re-creation of historic Front Street, mostly visited by tourists. But this didn't look anything like that. It seemed far more real. Almost too authentic.

She backed into a post to let a group of men in tattered cowboy costumes pass by, then glanced at the swinging doors. From where she stood, she could hear glasses clinking and dice rolling. There was a click and clatter of poker chips and billiard balls while a man hollered above the music, "Twenty-five-to-one!"

Her stomach churned again. She really needed to find a phone.

She decided to try the saloon but shrank back when she glanced at the window. June bugs. She hated June bugs. When she was seven years old, her best friend's little brother had planted some in her bed during a camping trip and they'd given her the heebie-jeebies ever since.

Trying not to think about that anymore, Jessica

shivered with disgust, pushed through the doors, and collided with a thick wall of cigar smoke. Her nose crinkled. Stifling a cough, she gazed uneasily over the crowd.

Most of the men wore hats and looked as if they'd just walked out of an old movie.

Focusing on what she had come in for, she approached the bar. "Excuse me. I've been in a car accident and I need to get to a phone. Do you have one that I could use?"

The bartender, who wore a white shirt with the sleeves rolled up, topped by a brown vest, stared at her while he polished a shot glass.

"Sir?" she asked again. "Can you at least tell me how I can get to Dodge City? The *real* Dodge City?"

"This is it, darlin'. You're exactly where you want to be."

Now this was getting ridiculous. "No, you don't understand. I've been in an accident and I need a phone."

"Don't have no phone, but I've heard about 'em."

Jessica stared at the man for an agonizing second, then turned on her heels and walked to the window. A snake handler wandered by carrying a lantern. Following closely behind him was a squealing pig.

She rubbed her throbbing temples and squeezed her eyes shut. Maybe she did have a head injury and this was all a hallucination, or maybe she was unconscious and dreaming.

She returned to the bar. "Is there a telephone *any-where* in this town?"

"Not that I know of." He turned around and placed

the polished shot glass on a shelf.

Enough was enough. Jessica pushed a damp lock of her hair behind her ear and took a deep breath to calm herself.

"Are you fixin' to buy a drink, ma'am," he asked, "or are you just gonna stand there and stare at me all night?"

Jessica glanced around the saloon at the rough and tough looking clientele and held up a hand. "No thanks. I'll find help elsewhere." Struggling to keep it together, she walked out.

Squinting through the darkness, she searched for a friendly face or a shop with some lights on, but all she saw were those same two drunken cowboys flinging bottles, laughing uproariously and spitting tobacco.

Suddenly a shot rang out in the street. Panic exploded in her belly, and she ran back into the saloon. "Is there a police station nearby?" she said to the bartender. "I really need some help."

"You'd be looking for Sheriff Wade," he casually replied. "He's just over that way in the city clerk's office, not far from the depot and the water tank." He pointed a bottle of whisky toward the window.

"Is it far? I have to walk there by myself."

"Not far, but a young woman ain't safe roaming these streets alone during cattle season. These cowboys have been on the trail a while and have a hankering for more than just the chuck wagon, if you understand my meaning." He leaned over the bar and glanced down at her skinny jeans and muddy red pumps. "They'll be takin' a shinin' to you, even dressed the way you are in those britches."

"I'll be fine." She turned and walked out the door.

She hopped off the boardwalk and down onto the street with a splash, groaning when she sank ankle-deep into the mud. No matter. She'd be at the sheriff's office soon enough, and this whole thing would be straightened out.

She stopped, however, when something tickled and buzzed behind her ear. She scratched and tousled her hair, then realized with a terrible surge of panic that a June bug was stuck in her hair!

Jessica shrieked. She tried to brush it away, but it was tangled in her long, wet locks. She tossed her head around, flailed her arms in all directions, and jumped through the puddles to try and escape.

Boom! Another gunshot ripped through the night. Her heart exploded with fear, and she tripped backwards over a plank in the street. Down she went, splashing into a puddle on her backside. No sooner than her butt began to throb, she looked up to see a man falling out of a second story window!

He dropped onto the over-hanging roof and rolled straight toward her. Jessica scrambled to her feet and slipped through the slick muck, barely escaping the plummeting man's path. Just as she slid out of the way, he landed heavily in front of her, splashing muddy water onto her cheeks. A second later, a metal object dropped into a puddle beside her.

"Sir!" she hollered, dropping to her hands and knees to help him. "Are you all right?"

He was face down in the mud, and Jessica was just about to roll him over when the saloon doors swung open, smacking against the outside wall. Men and women poured out and gathered on the boardwalk to stare at her in shocked silence.

"What in God's name happened?" someone asked.

"This man fell out of a window," Jessica replied. "He needs help."

The stranger ran toward her and together, they rolled the injured man onto his back. Jessica stared in horror at his face. A clean bullet hole gaped between his eyes, and blood trickled down his nose.

"Dear Lord," the stranger said. He stood up and quickly backed away.

"Somebody call 911!" Jessica shouted. She pressed her ear to the man's chest to listen for a heartbeat. When she heard nothing, she knew there was no hope, but she still wanted an ambulance. A cop car, too.

If there was such a thing in this backward place.

"Will somebody call an ambulance?" she shouted in frustration.

"Now...just be calm, miss," the stranger said. "We don't want any trouble."

"What are you talking about?" she replied. "I don't want to cause trouble. I'm trying to help him. Doesn't anyone have a cell phone?"

That particular request was met with blank stares.

"I saw her wavin' a gun around like some kind of lunatic!" someone offered.

"I wasn't waving a gun," she explained. "I was trying to kill a June bug."

There was a series of 'oohs' and 'ahs' from the crowd as everyone backed away in unison.

Realizing she was quickly becoming a primary suspect in this man's murder, Jessica raised both hands in the air and stood. "Look, everyone needs to stay calm. It wasn't me. I was just trying to help him."

"Do you know who this is?" the stranger asked.

Jessica shook her head. "No."

"That's Left Hand Lou!" someone called out from the crowd.

Before Jessica had a chance to comprehend what this meant, people rushed over to get a look at the corpse.

"He's wanted in three states!" someone hollered. "You just killed the fastest draw this side of the Mississippi!"

What did they think she had done? She hadn't shot him! And what did they mean—*the fastest draw this side of the Mississippi*? This wasn't *Gunsmoke*, for pity's sake.

"Wait a minute," she said. "Seriously. There's been a mistake."

Just then, a deep voice cut through the commotion. "Can I ask what's going on in this little gathering of yours?"

Unable to discern from where the voice had come, she looked all around through the darkness.

"Ma'am? I asked you a question." The crowd parted, clearing a wide path for the inquiring man to approach. Jessica was finally able to get a glimpse at him, although the brim of his black hat shadowed his face from the dim lantern light spilling out of the saloon.

He moved slowly toward her, and she was taken aback by how handsome he was, with dark hair, blue eyes, and a fit, muscular build.

Closing the distance between them, he pushed his

open black coat to the side. His purpose was clear as he rested his large hand on an ivory-handled revolver holstered to his leather gun belt.

His trousers—also black—were snug and worn at the knees, and his boots were spurred. Jessica hadn't actually looked at his feet, but as he walked, the sound of the spurs jingling alerted her senses to everything about him.

Someone moved aside, and a gentle stream of light reflected off the shiny star pinned to the man's lapel.

It read: Sheriff.

Thank God.

He angled his head and spoke in low voice—sort of like Clint Eastwood, but not exactly. "Ma'am, you look a little distressed. Can I be of some assistance?"

His observation, which couldn't have been closer to the truth, melted all her cool bravado in an instant, and she was so relieved, she could have grabbed hold of his shirt collar, pulled him toward her, and kissed him square on the lips.

"Yes, you can," she replied. "I'm so glad you're here. Thank you for coming so quickly."

He chuckled softly, but the smile in his eyes was cold and calculating.

"I wouldn't thank me just yet," he drawled, as he wrapped his big hand around her arm and tugged her closer. "Because by the look of things here, missy, you're gonna be spending the night in my jailhouse."

The crowd murmured approval, while Jessica glanced up at his ruggedly handsome features, bronzed by wind and sun, then cautiously lowered her eyes to the gun at his hip.

He shook his head at her, as if she'd been a very naughty girl, and said, "Tsk tsk tsk," while she paused to think carefully about the best way to handle this.

Follow Julianne on Bookbub to be notified whenever one of her ebooks goes on sale for 99¢ or is offered for free.

Books by
Julianne MacLean

HISTORICAL ROMANCE

The American Heiress Trilogy:
To Marry the Duke
Falling for the Marquess
In Love with the Viscount

Can This Be Love Trilogy
(American Heiress Spinoff):
Love According to Lily
To Annabelle, With Love
Where Love Begins

Love at Pembroke Palace Series:
In My Wildest Fantasies
The Mistress Diaries
When a Stranger Loves Me
Married By Midnight
A Kiss Before the Wedding–
A Pembroke Palace Short Story
Seduced at Sunset

The Highlander Series:
Captured by the Highlander
Claimed by the Highlander
Seduced by the Highlander
The Rebel – A Highland Short Story
Return of the Highlander
Taken by the Highlander

The Royal Trilogy:
Be My Prince
Princess in Love
The Prince's Bride

Western/Americana Historical Romances
Prairie Bride
Tempting the Marshal
Adam's Promise

Time Travel Romance:
A Time for Love

CONTEMPORARY FICTION
A Curve in the Road
A Fire Sparkling

The Color of Heaven Series:
The Color of Heaven
The Color of Destiny
The Color of Hope
The Color of a Dream
The Color of a Memory
The Color of Love
The Color of the Season
The Color of Time
The Color of Forever
The Color of a Promise
The Color of a Christmas Miracle
The Color of a Silver Lining

ABOUT THE AUTHOR

Julianne MacLean is a *USA Today* bestselling author of more than thirty novels, including the contemporary women's fiction *Color of Heaven Series*. Readers have described her books as "breathtaking," "soulful" and "uplifting." MacLean is a four-time Romance Writers of America RITA® finalist and has won numerous awards, including the *Booksellers' Best Award* and a *Reviewers' Choice Award* from *Romantic Times*. Her novels have sold millions of copies worldwide and have been published in over a dozen languages.

MacLean has a degree in English literature from the University of King's College in Halifax, Nova Scotia, and a degree in business administration from Acadia University in Wolfville, Nova Scotia. She loves to travel and has lived in New Zealand, Canada, and England. MacLean currently resides on the east coast of Canada in a lakeside home with her husband, daughter, and mother. She invites readers to visit her website for more information about her books and writing life, and to subscribe to her mailing list for all the latest news: www.JulianneMacLean.com

Made in the USA
Monee, IL
07 March 2021

62179758R00198